Threesome
and Other
Tales of Sex
in the Real World

John Boase

Order this book online at www.trafford.com
or email orders@trafford.com

Most Trafford titles are also available at major online book retailers.

Printed in the United States of America.

ISBN: 978-1-4907-0733-4 (sc)
ISBN: 978-1-4907-0732-7 (e)

Trafford rev. 08/08/2013

www.trafford.com

North America & international
toll-free: 1 888 232 4444 (USA & Canada)
fax: 812 355 4082

These stories arose primarily out of many personal chats and extensive email correspondence over several years. I thank all of those correspondents, almost all of them women, who willingly shared with me their thoughts about sex and their experiences of sex. One of the virtues of the Internet is the ease of correspondence that it enables. It is also clear that the Net facilitates an incredible range of sexual opportunities including sharing. I've corresponded with folks along the whole spectrum of sexual practices, excluding of course the no-go areas for serious writers of literotica: under age, incest, bestiality and non-consensual.

I have had a lifelong fascination with human sexuality. I personally believe that we are as we are according to how we come to terms with our sex drive. I hope I do justice to the joys and wonders of sex in my stories and poems.

All of the episodes in these stories are authentic. In some cases I have amalgamated incidents from different sources where it has suited my purposes.

Why write about sex? Well, why not? It is central to the lives of most people. It gives people joy, it excites their fantasies, it gives purpose to relationships and . . . it can also tempt people and get them into trouble. It has everything for this writer to engage with and I hope my readers share that view!

Not all pieces here involve sharing but it is a major theme. Sharing is a practice more common than one might think. Men wanting to watch their women having sex with another man is a common fantasy. I have also had women tell me how much it turns them on to watch their husbands having sex with another woman or to make a loving display for their partner by having sex with another man or woman.

Sharing is not all-consuming for everyone. I had correspondence with six couples who meet once a year for three days, at a discreet location. One of the women confessed to me that she had spent day three knitting!

In my book of 1200 erotic sonnets ('Erotic Muse—Sonnets about Sex' www.trafford.com/robots/01-0477.html) I put this one at the beginning:

Writers of Erotica
We write erotic poetry and prose
From fascination with the human state;
Some think us warped, debauched, turn up their nose,
Our works the prudes and moralists berate.
Our subjects are deliciously diverse,
G-spots and wet spots, few things are taboo;
Outsiders might consider us perverse,
An ill-considered, superficial view.
We're normal people, ordinary folk,
We work, have kids and mortgages, commute;
In spite of censure critics may invoke
We ply our craft with purpose resolute:
To celebrate with creativity
The joys of human sexuality.

A comment about female sexual fantasy.

I invited women on www.erotica-readers.com, a classy site for female erotica, to submit their most cherished fantasies to me so that I could write them each an individualized sonnet. Six women chose to share with me. I gave them the options: accept the draft sonnet, reject it or ask to have it modified. Five accepted the draft, loving the idea of having their fantasies enshrined in published verse. For all of them the devil lay in the detail. The sixth one asked me to modify a line to make it clear that she 'was kneeling **on** the fur coat' when she did the deed in question. I did that and she was over the moon.

The key word for me is 'celebrate' human sexuality: not titillate but celebrate. That's what I try to do in my writing.

I hope you can share my fascination with and my enjoyment of this important element of the human condition.

John Boase
Victoria
Australia
2013

Contents

Threesome   1

A Young Woman's Account of Sharing Herself   11

Hello Sailor(s)   15

Voyeur   28

Dinner Party   43

University Days   51

A Tale of Sharing from an Old Friend   56

A Weekend   59

Believe These or Not   61

Margaret in San Francisco   64

Eric the Artist   87

Skinny Dipping and Sharing . . .   99

An Affair to Remember   102

Episodes of Sex in Public Places   113

Asian Lady   117

A Week of Sharing   122

My One and Only Time with Another Woman   130

A Passionate Relationship   138

Working Woman   144

Hubby's Friends   152

Fulfilling a Fantasy   172

A Night I Cheated   185

Four Women: a Tale of Self-indulgence   192

Carnevale   200

Chateau   209

Threesome

I had long encouraged my wife Charlotte to explore and express her sexuality with another man, preferably in my presence as I had long harboured a wish to watch her have sex with another man. She is not a young woman but has a body that many women half her age would dream of. She is also strikingly beautiful and is highly intelligent, having retired from twenty years in senior management. She reads, paints, gardens, keeps fit, loves going to horse races, loves good food and good wine, goes to movies and theatre and has travelled widely. In short, she is a thoroughly interesting woman. She has turned heads all her life and continues to do so.

In retirement her libido has taken off. Retirement provides the essential luxury of time to discover the subtleties of one's sexual responsiveness while not abandoning the occasional episode of frenzied coupling. Time has allowed us to really discover the essence of our sexuality: to explore, express and enjoy our sexuality.

We had discussed inviting a second man into our sex lives but had never done anything about it. Then, out of left field one day, we resolved to make it happen. The decision was mutual.

We put our profile on a web site, seeking the right man to enter and enjoy our world of erotic adventure and erotic tranquility. We got the usual number of boring Net losers whose idea of sexual attraction was a photo of their erect cock but we were patient and eventually a man of potential got in touch with us. We began corresponding by email, over some weeks until we were satisfied with his bona fides. If he was going to put his cock into Charlotte's body he had to be the right man!

We then exchanged phone calls. He proved to be well-spoken and well-educated, considerate and courteous.

We laughed at his answer on his profile to the question: 'Does size matter?'

'If it does I'm in trouble'.

Eventually I set up a meeting with him to check him out in person. He and I met at a city bar, for about an hour. Our discussion began with current affairs and politics but progressed to what we were really there for. He passed his first test very well. I insisted that we agree on a mutual commitment to make pleasuring Charlotte our priority. He agreed readily.

It was opportune for him then to meet Charlotte in person. I arranged a picnic at a lovely gallery in the countryside where I knew we would enjoy privacy as well as a beautiful environment. We took along a picnic hamper, he the wine. I drove to the venue, about a forty-five minute trip, allowing Charlotte and our friend to take the train and to have time to themselves.

They got so carried away with conversation that they nearly missed getting off at the station. When I saw them cross the street smiling animatedly I knew that things had gone well. I did the chauffeur act, opening the doors for them and putting them in the back seat.

Charlotte and I had been to this bush gallery before and we knew it well. It was the first visit for our friend and he loved the place. I took our rugs and hamper to the spot we had chosen while Charlotte took our friend through the gallery. On their walk to the gallery they stayed apart. On their return from the gallery they were holding hands.

We went for a walk through the bush on an established track, admiring the mountain scenery. I walked ahead of them to give them an opportunity to chat. I suspect that they enjoyed a kiss or two as well but I had resolved not to spy on them.

We had a magnificent lunch. Charlotte did herself proud with the cuisine. Our friend had chosen good wines and we drank well. We had all dressed smart casual style for the occasion. The atmosphere was friendly, cordial, auspicious.

When it came time to leave I suggested to Charlotte that she remove her bra to make the return trip more interesting. I put our friend and her in the back seat again. I had hoped to be able to see them in the rear vision mirror but it proved to be impossible. I had to rely on Charlotte's account when we arrived back at our apartment.

Our friend had not been assertive during the drive, indeed he was the perfect gentleman. With a couple of glasses of good wine aboard, Charlotte eventually took the initiative and kissed him, at the same time taking his hand and putting it on her breast which she had bared by undoing buttons on her silk blouse. He kept his hand there until discretion dictated otherwise. Charlotte has superb tits and our friend remained enthusiastic to keep his hand on them, to state the obvious. He did put his hand on her knee but did not attempt to reach under her skirt.

We dropped him at a railway station and drove home, pausing only to buy two bottles of good wine which we proceeded to drink between episodes of fucking. The occasion had turned both of us on, big time. Our friend had passed his second test. We were confident that we were getting things right, preparing the way for a successful threesome.

We agreed to meet a month later, at a five star city hotel taking a room at the day rate, 10 am to 4 pm. We shared the cost.

Again Charlotte prepared one of her wonderful hampers and our friend brought along the wine. We had agreed to dress for the occasion and it was coats and ties for us men and a very stylish black pants suit for Charlotte. She looked gorgeous and very, very sexy.

We began by having pastries and a delicious sauvignon blanc. The conversation was animated and interesting. Our friend's activities included being a director of a theatre company so he could tell many a good tale of life on the boards.

After perhaps thirty minutes I winked at Charlotte and nodded my head. She smiled and took herself off to the bathroom. Our friend and I remained dressed. I handed him our share of the tariff in an envelope.

Charlotte reappeared in a black silk shirt of mine. We were soon to discover that she also wore a stylish pair of black panties bought specially for the occasion.

She sat between us on a sofa and we lost no time in taking a breast each, ministering to her with hands and lips. She undid the only button on the shirt that she had fastened, then discarded the shirt to reveal her womanly magnificence.

She stood in front of us in only her black panties, firstly the back view, then the front view. They were cut high on her hips, providing provocative glimpses of the lines of her bum cheeks.

The tease continued when she again turned her back to us and told us to take off her panties.

'Let's take a leg each', I suggested to our friend.

We drew them down, exposing her glorious bum, a shadow down her crack. I began to kiss one cheek and to rub my face on it. Our friend took my lead and did the same on the other cheek. Charlotte's skin is satiny, her bum without imperfection.

We took turns in rubbing her panties on our faces, in putting them to our noses. Charlotte's arousal scent and her wetness were evident in the fine fabric.

We took turns in running our tongues up her bum crack, feeling her response when our tongue tips touched her bum hole.

As the final phase of her tease she turned back towards us, revealing a perfectly waxed cunt. She later told me she'd had it done a couple of days before. There was no sign of redness, just a beautifully hairless slit. Our friend and I were both becoming more and more uncomfortable in our trousers.

She ran her fingers through her slit, anointing our eyelids with her juice. Is there any more erotic gesture that a woman can offer?

She took the shirts of each of us, then took herself off to the king sized bed while we undressed. She lay down the middle of the bed to give us room either side of her wonderfully shapely nakedness. Our friend and I were both erect. His profile response about size had been honestly stated but he was up and hard, as I was. I was bigger than he but Charlotte later said that she enjoyed the different sensations from our varying sizes though I couldn't perform in front of him as will be revealed below.

I had discussed with her a way to begin, so as to avoid embarrassment or hesitancy. She had agreed and I had told our friend in advance. He was happy with the suggestions.

We began by taking a breast each, stroking and suckling. I left the kissing to him. Our hands strayed elsewhere over her body. Charlotte was later to say that having two mouths and four hands on her body was blissful.

When she was ready to proceed further Charlotte tapped me on the head in a prearranged signal and I went down on her, scissors style. I began at her perineum and worked slowly up her slit while our friend continued to kiss her and caress her breasts, belly and hips. She reached down and took his cock into her hand. It was an amazing experience for me to be using my mouth on her cunt a few inches away from her hand on another man's erect cock. His balls were on the smallish side but they were tensed up. He was later to prove that he could produce a respectable volume of semen.

I had wondered whether Charlotte would hold back when she came. I need not have wondered. I felt all the tell-tale signs and she just let go, revelling in her femaleness and her responsiveness. She has very long orgasms and our friend was later to confide in me:

'She cums forever'.

There was a very funny moment at this point. I had briefed our friend by email that Charlotte was partial to having a fingertip inserted in her bum hole occasionally; before, during or after a cum.

Having brought her off with my mouth I sought to insert a fingertip there, only to find that he had beaten me to it! I had to work hard to suppress a laugh. Charlotte and I still laugh about that though she has no memory of it.

Interestingly, in a gesture that Charlotte was later to describe as perhaps the most erotic of the day, our friend stroked her hair and kissed her eyelids in the aftermath of her orgasm.

That was the end of our prearrangements. I then left the bed and took a seat nearby, allowing our friend to have my lady all to himself. He rolled on a condom and positioned himself between Charlotte's legs, lifting them to the vertical in a technique that we rarely use because my cock can give her discomfort that way.

This was our first threesome and I had wondered what my responses would be, as any man would. Charlotte had made me promise not to become jealous, knowing that had been a predisposition of mine in earlier years.

In fact I found myself fascinated, overawed, excited, aroused . . . and a hundred other such things. Charlotte helped by looking at me from time to time and smiling. She knew that she was exploring and expressing her sexuality with another man but she also knew that she was bringing me pleasure. It was evidence of her generosity of spirit as well as her sense of personal adventure.

I drew my chair up behind our friend. He was not a tall man but his body was pretty trim for a man of fifty nine. He had a lot of body hair but it was very fine, not the usual coarse kind. My body hair is light but I had also shaved my lower belly for the occasion to give Charlotte an experience of a smooth man and a hairy man.

So there I was, sitting behind the hairy bum of a man whose cock was going into my wife's cunt, whose balls were swinging with the movement, whose bum and thigh muscles were contracting with the effort of his thrusting. What an experience! My cock had never been harder as I watched them and stroked it.

After a while he withdrew and turned her on her side, facing away from him. That didn't surprise me as his eyes had been like saucers when he was looking at her bum: contoured, satiny smooth, without blemish. He entered her again from behind, held her by the hips and maintained his thrusting while never taking his eyes off her bum cheeks. It got too much for him as I knew it would. He moaned, threw back his head, pulled out his cock, ripped off the condom and shot off onto her thigh and her bum cheek.

It was the first time in my life that I had ever seen another man cum. I had moved in close to the bed when I knew that he was getting close so I had a good view of what his cock and balls did during ejaculation. He produced three spurts and a few drops which Charlotte proceeded to rub into her skin.

Our friend had stipulated no photography, a view which I wish in retrospect that I had not respected, having a 'Museum' setting on the camera. I also believe that he would have appreciated a photographic record, albeit without faces which is what I think he was worried about. There were lots of memorable moments I would have liked to have caught for the record. I'll mention two.

After his first cum our friend continued to lie behind Charlotte, both of them half-asleep, with two fingers part-inserted in her cunt. It was as erotic an image as I can recall. The other shot came after lunch, again after a cum. He was lying exhausted, his semen-filled condom drooping off the end of his flaccid cock. I can still laugh about that image.

After our friend had cum and dozed and cuddled Charlotte he yielded the bed to me. I started well with a good hard shaft sticking out in front of me but I found to my amazement that performing in front of another man was not my scene and I lost my hardness. I used my mouth again and Charlotte did not complain. I knew she had faked an orgasm for our friend and I whispered to her that I knew, forcing her to suppress a giggle, but there was nothing fake about the series of orgasms she had from my mouth. When our friend visited the bathroom I regained my erection and filled her with it. I nearly lost consciousness with the force of my ejaculation. My instinct was to put it in her as deeply as I could.

By then it was time for lunch. Charlotte put my black silk shirt again and our friend and I put on hotel gowns. At one point I told a joke and Charlotte rocked back with laughter, exposing her hairless slit. Both sets of male eyes went straight to the centre of the universe.

I had wondered how things would resume after lunch and I had given my lady a code word to use if she wanted me to initiate proceedings. I needn't have worried. At the appropriate time she simply stood up, discarded the black shirt, paraded her nakedness across to the bed, lay on her belly, looked at us with a bold glance and asked 'Who's going first?'

Such a comment can come only from a sexually confident woman. Charlotte is nothing if not that.

Our friend looked at me and I nodded for him to have his turn. His cock was up and ready to go. He rolled on the necessary then mounted her from behind, again gazing constantly at her bum cheeks. He stretched her bum hole then put a fingertip into it while he thrust into her cunt. She reached under herself to stroke her clit, provoking a lovely loud orgasm that nearly bucked him off her body.

I sat to the side of the bed, watching and stroking. I had no difficulty in gaining or maintaining an erection while watching but I couldn't keep it up while performing in front of him. That caused me no embarrassment, I might add. I accepted my response for what it was. It might seem incongruous for someone who has known the blessing and the curse that is satyriasis (an obsession with sex) since the age of fourteen could lose his erection while making love to a beautiful woman but that is what happened to me on the day.

He turned Charlotte over and they lay quietly for a while, stroking and kissing and cuddling, moving sufficiently for him to stay hard inside her.

Then something very funny happened. There was a knock at the door and a maid entered. Her eyes and face registered something between shock and surprise as she saw a naked man in a chair stroking his cock and a coupling couple on the bed.

She froze on the spot, wondering what to do. Our friend withdrew and walked towards her, I think to shield Charlotte from her gaze, his condom rapidly losing its grip on his quickly receding maleness. She gave a yelp and ran out the door. We three burst into laughter. What else could we do?

Touching and cuddling resumed and brought renewed erections. Our friend donned a fresh condom and mounted Charlotte again, with renewed energy.

She met his thrusts with her own and they were soon fucking with noisy vigour.

The visuals started to get to me and I felt familiar stirrings in all the right places. I dashed across the to bed and drew Charlotte's hand towards me then promptly shot off onto her palm. Our friend held still while he watched this then, obviously himself turned on by what he had seen, took a few more thrusts before he released. Thus Charlotte ate the semen of one of her men while the other man shot his semen into her body. The recollection of that still gets both of us aroused.

I went to the shower, leaving them dozing in each other's arms, peacefully. I was a gentleman and picked up his discarded condoms and disposed of them.

He showered next, then chatted to me while Charlotte took her turn. We spoke about a range of things to do with the day, all six hours of it. He raved about Charlotte's facial beauty and her wonderful body. We paid compliments to each other on the volumes of semen we had produced, two lots each, perhaps a silly male thing to mention. I thanked him for the way he had adjusted to the situation. His reply was interesting. He said:

'There was a lot of love in here today'.

I knew what he meant.

We parted on amicable terms, still trying to come to terms with the sexual beauty we had created and experienced.

When Charlotte and I arrived back at our apartment we fell into bed and fucked our brains out, then fucked again in the bath tub shortly after while drinking a good white wine. In the bath I requested the joys of her bottom so we found a position, a touch awkward admittedly, that allowed the tip of my cock to enter her little opening successfully under the water. She had enough energy left to give my cockhead a few mischievous nips with her bum ring.

I have read that couples who enjoy a successful threesome often return home to fuck themselves silly.

Would we do it again? Yes, with the right man at the right time. I sometimes role play the presence of a second man. My brief acting experience in undergraduate days comes in handy.

I am also encouraging Charlotte to make love to another woman, something she has never done. It would be my suggestion that the two women go away for a weekend, perhaps take in some art and theatre as part of their liaison. On the other hand if they prefer to use our home, I would be prepared to volunteer my services as a naked waiter, without sexual intent. I don't wish to watch them.

We have had an offer to join five other couples who meet at a suburban home for shared sex but we have declined the invitation. Another man in the room is quite enough for us!

A Young Woman's Account
of Sharing Herself

I think my husband (now ex) and I both knew when we married that our relationship would be volatile at times. I think he also realised that there would be occasions when he might not be able to satisfy my sexual needs which at times could be overpowering. I did ensure, however, that I looked after his sexual needs and I did everything he wanted. But there was a tacit understanding that I might occasionally look for something more than he could offer. He accepted that.

Not that a queue formed at my door! But one man did attract my attention, a young single man who had a beautiful body and a package that his Speedos barely concealed. My husband was an engineer, working on a major project in a rural area. I was teaching at a local school. The man I found attractive was a tradesman who was doing seasonal work in town.

I saw him frequently at the beach, at weekends. My husband would be poring over drawings and technical papers at home and I would take myself to the surf beach in a very tiny bikini. The tradie didn't notice me so I took matters into my own hands one Sunday and followed him into the surf. Incidental conversation turned into flirting. I suppose my manner was forward but that was (and still is) me, the way I am.

Even when we left the water the front of his Speedos was impressive. He had a run of fine hair up to his navel and into the bum part of his swimsuit and light hair across his chest. I liked that. I'm not into really hairy men.

For all his rugged handsomeness he was unsure of himself in the company of an intelligent woman who was blatantly offering herself to him. I had to take the initiative, hoping not to frighten him off with my forwardness. Looking back I felt almost like a mother reassuring her son that everything would be all right, that the bogeywoman didn't represent a threat to him.

Let me digress for a moment. At age 18 I had had my first fuck. I was very fortunate in that my lover, who was an older man, was sensitive, responsive, attentive but also passionate when it mattered, the ideal man to induct a young woman into the best that sex has to offer. And he had a very big cock, soft and hard, so my introduction to sex had an added element of surprise and delight. I used to love soaping his cock in the shower. I loved the way it flopped around in my hand. He taught me to rejoice in my sexuality and to be proud of what I could offer a man.

The tradie and I set up a dinner date. In those days the only 'restaurant' food one could buy in little country towns was in the local club, in this case a golf club. I knew my food then and I have long since developed into an accomplished cook. That's not a boast, it's what came of long, long hours of practice and experiment when other people were off doing something else.

'Club grub' was universally awful. I learned that the club trick was to order two appetisers. The appetisers, although typically prawns slurped with some sauce or other, were preferable to the gluggy pasta or the 'Steak Diane' swamped with what tasted like packet sauce and deluged with fries; or baked potatoes and other vegetables that had been cooked and heated beyond reasonable limit.

Country towns are also hotbeds of intrigue and gossip so we were careful to avoid holding hands, kissing, the more overt signs of sexual attraction. Our conversation, however, was animated and I could feel the sexual tension building.

We kissed with great passion in the car park, shielding ourselves from the occasional patron leaving the club. Most of them were pissed anyway, having found yet again their refuge from reality in booze and poker machines. There was no breath testing then. One had to be driving erratically to attract the attention of the police.

'We need to go somewhere', I said. 'I know just the place'.

We drove separately, he following me to a secluded little car track that led to the beach. Where to do it? The answer was simple. He had a mattress in the back of his station wagon, saving money by sleeping in his vehicle during the weeks of his job.

He stayed hard after he lost his load, something that remains unique in my experience. He then turned me over and took me from behind. He didn't seem to have any idea that I had a clitoris so I took care of myself in that department. When I came he went off a second time.

Afterward we ran naked by moonlight through the shallow edge of the surf, kicking up the water, splashing each other, laughing at our antics.

When I got back to our rented home I found my husband asleep at his drawing board. I left him that way and went to bed.

Knowing that my occasional lover would be leaving town shortly I put it to my husband that we might organise a threesome. He agreed without hesitation which surprised me.

We invited the tradie to a barbecue at our place. He got on well with my husband, alleviating my worry that they might not hit it off. Thank god, I thought, no friction! You never know what might happen the first time around, even if your husband has agreed to it happening.

I wore only a white shirt, nothing underneath. When I grew tired of them discussing football I simply took off my shirt and presented my nakedness to them.

'Get your clothes off. I want some action', I said with intent.

Both men sported hard cocks.

The tradie took me first, bent over the outside table. He held me firmly by the hips and thrust himelf to a big, noisy cum. My husband followed, again from behind. Both men lost their loads within minutes. The situation got to them.

We then went into the bedroom.

Tradie went first. I decided that I wanted something more fulfilling so I took his cockhead in my hand and stroked my clit with it. I got off twice this way before he lost the plot and filled me a second time. My husband, having witnessed the action, turned me onto my belly and took me vigorously with tradie lying adjacent on the bed and stroking my shoulder blades.

Our visitor then left, leaving my husband and I to contemplate what had happened. I mopped up their accumulated semen but sat naked on a towel on the sofa in case of further leakage, sipping a glass of white wine with hubby.

I tried not to be too analytical about events but there were many things that came to mind. A hard cock in each hand, different kissing styles, different mouth pressures on my nipples, the constant slapping of balls on my flesh, the signs of impending male ejaculation, the flow of warm semen into me, my pride in my nakedness, the uninhibited way I came, the strong sense of female fulfilment I felt at having taken two men.

We revisited the memory of that episode occasionally until our divorce twenty years later.

Hello Sailor(s)

I was in a bathroom in the Intercontinental Hotel, Sydney. I'd had a pee and was standing with my long black skirt in my hand, still with top, stockings and lacy black panties on. I was about to fuck a man I'd met only about an hour earlier.

My heart was beating hard. What on earth was I doing here? What had possessed me to come up to his room?

And yet I was excited, aroused at what I was doing! This adventurous, perhaps risky behaviour was new territory for me.

'Calm down', I told myself. 'You can't let him get the impression that you're naive and breathless. You must appear as a woman of the world. Just settle down, go out there and do what comes naturally'.

I took several deep breaths, then opened the bathroom door and stepped out.

'Here goes!' I thought.

But I get ahead of myself!

I was 37, a mother of three, the eldest of them twelve. I had rejoined the work force and aspired in the longer term to a position in senior management.

My hubby of fifteen years had been indifferent of late, noticeably so. He'd been working hard and I was conscious of the stress that his work put him under. I'd also say that he'd returned from a three-day residential conference with semen stains on his underpants.

'Careless of him', I thought as I tossed them into the washing machine.

I didn't say anything, just shrugged my shoulders in resignation at men and their dicks. I hoped he'd used a condom.

One Saturday soon after I resolved to get dolled up and go into the city for some time on my own. I'd take in a new exhibition at the art gallery. I love art and can lose myself in a gallery. This day would allow me to indulge myself, to clear my head of cobwebs, to refresh body and soul. A day all to myself! How wonderful!

I got hubby to drop me at the railway station. He needed the car for sporting transport duties for our kids.

I looked and felt like a million bucks, if I do say so myself! I brushed up pretty well. My body was good, with only a hint of a 'mummy tummy', nothing that sucking it in couldn't hide. I was good-looking, or so I'd been told over the years. All things considered, I boarded the train in high spirits.

I window shopped for an hour or so, enjoying the displays. I had lunch by the harbour: oysters and a glass of white wine. The water was sparkling. I took an outside table to soak up the sunlight. Life was good!

I got to the gallery around 12.30. The exhibition was brilliant, just what I needed for personal stimulation. I went slowly from painting to painting.

Towards the last of the paintings I became aware of the presence of someone.

'Which painting have you liked the most?' a voice behind me asked. He had an American accent.

'Mmm . . . probably the two big landscapes . . .' I replied.

'I was thinking the same', he said.

I turned to find a trim, straight-backed, good-looking man of about 50 with cropped grey hair. He was slightly taller than I. He had warm eyes and a ready smile. He wore grey slacks with a white shirt and highly polished black shoes.

'What part of America are you from?' I asked, out of interest rather than seeking to prolong the conversation.

'Boston', he answered. 'Beantown, we call it'.

'What brings you Down Under?' I inquired.

'US Navy', he replied. 'My ship is berthed at Garden Island'.

'*Your* ship?' I said.

'I'm the captain', he replied with a smile. 'I've taken a couple of days shore leave. I'm at the Intercontinental Hotel. Why don't we go there for a drink?'

'Why not?' I thought to myself.

'Sure', I said.

The hotel was only a short walk from the gallery. We chatted as we walked but he made no advances on me.

We sat in the atrium area and had a glass of excellent white wine. He was gentlemanly, for sure, but there was an unmistakable sense of a developing sexual atmosphere. When we'd finished our wine he touched me on the hand, looked closely into my eyes and said simply:

'Shall we go up to my room? I find you very, very attractive'.

'Why not?' I said.

We were kissing as soon as the door of the room closed. He was beautifully smooth-shaven which I like. Our tongues were soon working. He put a hand on my bum and drew me to him. I could feel his hard-on.

'I need to visit the bathroom', I said when we broke off kissing.

Which brings me to when I sallied forth with my black skirt in my hand. I'd thought about removing my wedding ring but The Captain had seen it and taking it off could have seemed silly so on it stayed.

The Captain was at the window, his back to me. He was naked. He turned to reveal a stiff, businesslike cock. His chest and belly hair were going grey. He was in very good shape for his age, not an ounce of flab on him.

He took a seat and watched me undress.

'What beautiful breasts!' he exclaimed when I tossed aside my bra. I smiled my approval of his compliment. My 36Ds are good. I enjoy the look on a man's face when he gets a look at them.

Off with the lacy black panties and—voila!—there I was, naked in the presence of a stranger! I'd overcome my earlier nervousness and was now bent on having a good time and giving him a good time. I did a slow pirouette to show him everything. His eyes were wide and staring.

He beckoned me to him. For a while he just pressed his face against my belly, both his hands on my bum cheeks. He then put his nose to my slit and took several deep breaths. I'd have had an arousal scent.

I'd had a trim so the visuals of my slit would have been clear for him.

I dropped to my knees and took his cock in my mouth, cupping his balls as well. He had a lot of hair in his groin and on his sac. It tickled when I went right down on him.

'Dear god that feels amazing!' he murmured, eyes closed, as I brought my oral skills to bear. I can work a cock with the best of them.

'I should do something nice for you now', he said after a while.

He led me to the big bed, turned down the bedclothes and drew me on with him. He then slithered down between my legs and put his mouth on my cunt. I thought I'd hit the ceiling at the first touch of his tongue on my clit. The Captain sure knew how to pleasure a girl with his mouth. He took me to places far, far away, into realms of pure bliss. He got the pressure just right.

I tried to hold back awhile, revelling in the sensations his tongue was creating, but in the end I had to surrender to my impulses. I had an all-consuming cum, one that surprised me with its force and its duration. He left his tongue resting on my clit for a short time, then resumed his ministrations to bring me to another cum.

'Put it in', I whispered with fervour in my voice. I spread my legs for him. He went in slowly but easily. I was so, so receptive!

He told me how beautiful my cunt felt, how gorgeous my breasts were, how he loved my long legs wrapped around him. I told him how wonderful his cock felt inside me. I meant it!

He picked up his rhythm with my encouragement and we were soon fucking vigorously. He bore down on me over and over again. His taut bum muscles were flexing in my hands. His balls were slapping on me.

'Aaaahhhhhh!!!' he cried suddenly and held his cock at full length as he came, his body tensed, his face contorted with the effort. His big thrusts gave way to little ones to let him finish. He'd done himself proud with his load.

He lay panting on top of me, unable to move. His cock took ages to soften. I felt a trickle of cum down my bum crack when he pulled out.

We cuddled and kissed. He used his fingers to bring me off a couple more times.

We held hands, lying on our backs with our eyes closed, saying little. We may have dozed.

In time he rolled on his side, facing me, and put my hand on his cock. It got hard again as I held it.

He turned me onto my belly and straddled me. His fingers parted my cunt lips and I felt him insert the head of his cock. He held it there, making very complimentary remarks about my bum, hips, back and neck. Hey, I like being told I've got a good neck!

He soon stopped the gentle treatment and quickened the pace of his thrusting. I put a hand between my legs to stroke my clit. I came twice before The Captain announced that he too was going to cum. His cock dropped out when he started and I scored a spurt up my bum crack before he got it back in again. He sure put a lot of energy into his cums.

He lay on me afterward, as he had done earlier. Again he softened slowly.

I headed off to the bathroom for a shower. I couldn't stick around any longer. I had to get home.

The Captain was still naked on the bed when I emerged from the bathroom. I gave him a peck on the cheek and a pat on the cock, thanked him for the company and made to leave.

'Can we meet up again?' he asked. 'We sail on Saturday. I can make it here on Thursday. Is there any chance you could make it?'

I thought quickly. I hadn't had a day off work in ages and the prospect of another session of raw sex was very appealing.

I gave him my cell phone number and told him to ring me during my lunch hour on the Tuesday.

'Are you ok with the idea?' he asked.

'Sounds fine to me', I replied. 'I just need to confirm a couple of things'.

'Oh, just one other thing', he said. He had a funny look on his face. I wondered what was coming.

'Would it be all right with you if I brought along a friend from the ship?'

'Male or female friend?'

'Male, 45, one of my officers. He's a terrific guy. I'll guarantee that you'll like him'.

'Do you two share all your women?' I asked.

'We've shared once, only once', he said.

'Did your wife find out?' I inquired.

'My ex, you mean? I hope she knew. She was the woman we shared', he replied with a smile.

'Why are you asking me this?' I went on, mindful of my train times.

'I thought about it on the spur of the moment', he said, moving to open the door for me. 'You seem an adventurous type'.

'I'll let you know when we chat on Tuesday', I said. I wanted time think about his proposal. A touch of suspense would keep his interest.

With that I left.

The Captain rang at 1.15 on Tuesday, right on cue. I was eating lunch at my desk.

'Thursday will be fine', I said, sparing him having to broach the subject. 'And you can bring along your friend'.

'Sounds good to me', he said, 'I'll get a day rate room, same hotel. Say, 10.30? I'll meet you in the foyer.'

'10.30 it is', I said. 'I should make it by then but don't worry until after 11'. I'm sure he picked up the mischief in my voice. I felt cheeky.

I had an appointment for a full wax that afternoon. I decided that I had to live up to my reputation for being adventurous!

Bloody hell! What had I let myself into? Fucking a stranger on Saturday and taking on two men a few days later! This was crazy, I thought, but I resolved to go ahead with the arrangement. We go through this life but once . . .

I rang a close friend and confided in her. She confessed to me that she had taken on three men at the one time in her wild youth.

'How was it?' I asked.

'It was different, that's for sure . . . Two of them had me twice. It got messy!' she replied with a laugh.

'Would you do it again?' I inquired.

'How about including me on Thursday?' she said.

I did all the usual things first thing on Thursday, kids' lunches etc. Hubby had no reason to think that I was taking the day off work. He and I rarely rang each other at work so there was little chance of his finding out about my 'sick day'. I rang the office. I'd rescheduled the only two appointments that mattered on the day. Everything seemed set, ready to go.

My friend volunteered to drive me into town so that I wouldn't have to take the train in my finery.

'I want you to arrive looking your best', she said. 'The least I can do is drive you in . . . and pick you up, if you like'.

The Captain was in the lobby at precisely 10.30. He gave a big smile and hugged me.

'So good to see you again!' he said with genuine enthusiasm. He took my hand on the way to the elevator.

'Is your friend here?' I asked as we ascended to floor 21.

'He's in the room', he replied.

His friend was an African-American whom I mentally christened 'AA'. He was a massive man. He had to be well over six feet. Even fully clothed he obviously had a superb body. He had a handsome face and a shaved head.

'Hi, I'm Clive', he said then kissed me on the cheek. 'I'm pleased to meet you'.

Holy fuck! He had huge hands and huge feet. I wondered if his penis would be of similar dimension! Years before I'd seen a porn movie featuring a massively hung black man. I'd never encountered a really big one. I wondered how I'd cope if AA were to have a donkey dick.

We sat around, enjoying a glass of white wine and chatting. Both men were polite and courteous but I could feel their eyes appraising my body. Frankly, I enjoyed it!

'Well, I guess I might start things off', declared The Captain, and proceeded to undress. His cock was not yet erect.

'You next', I said to AA.

There wasn't a hair on his body!!! He was smooth all over!!! He had a gorgeous physique: broad chest, tapered waist, sculpted legs and a magnificent bum. Michelangelo would have loved him as a model!

His penis was no monster (thank goodness!) but it was thick and the head of it was very big and bulbous with a pronounced ridge. When his cock hardened as I undressed the end of it swelled almost to disproportion.

'That cockhead would make a girl's jaw ache and would stretch her cunt', I mused to myself.

I marked down in my memory that I would drag my tits across AA's bum cheeks before our day had ended. God, any red-blooded woman would want to feel her tits on that beautiful butt! It was a genuine clit stirrer!

I did a slow strip for them, making sure they had time to savour every part of me. I took my panties off last, with my back to them. They made appreciative comments about my bum. Then I turned to reveal my hairless cunt. Their eyes were on stalks. AA's hand went instantly to his cock, pulling on its engorged end.

I lay between them on the bed, shut my eyes and enjoyed hands and mouths all over me. Fingers would find their way into me, only to be replaced by other fingers. One of them put his mouth on my bum hole and tongue-fucked it, I haven't a clue which fellow. I had a series of overwhelming cums. I held nothing back.

I'd wondered beforehand how I would respond to two men. I knew for sure by this time. I felt in control, holding them captive with my sexuality. I was the boss!

The Captain went first into me. Was he pulling rank, I wondered idly as he mounted? AA concentrated on my nipples as his commanding officer got fair about the business of fucking me, hard cock up my cunt, a grunting man on top, no frills sex!

The Captain eventually unloaded and AA took his place, again on top. I felt that big cockhead go all the way up! He lifted my legs up and went in deep, over and over and over again, no frills in his technique either. AA was a heavy cummer and his spurts were warm and copious.

We rested. I needed to! I snuggled in against AA's back and pressed my tits on him. The Captain in turn cuddled into my back and put a hand on my hip.

We lay this way, at peace with the world, for 20-30 minutes. Then The Captain ordered sandwiches and white wine from room service.

We sat naked while lunching. I sat on a towel. Both men looked constantly at my body. I ogled AA when he went off to the bathroom. What a back! What a bum! What legs!

When our lunch settled my sense of mischief got the better of me.

I simply HAD to rub my tits on AA's muscled bum cheeks. I put him on the bed, turned him onto his belly and knelt across him. Fucking hell, a woman's fantasy bum!

My position put my bits and pieces well on display. I soon felt The Captain's tongue, finger then cock tip probing at my bum hole.

'Can I take you in the ass?' he asked.

'You can but you'll need some lubrication', I replied. I was no stranger to bum sex. Hubby and I did it occasionally.

'I don't have any. Do you?' he asked.

'No, but there's a pharmacy downstairs in the arcade', I advised.

The Captain dressed and departed to the pharmacy. AA and I kept up our play. I dragged my tits up his back, then turned him over and stroked them across his face. When I checked with my hand I found him hard again but The Captain was to be next man in. I turned AA over again and went back to putting my tits on his bum cheeks: stroking, dragging, flopping them on his glorious buns.

On impulse I resolved to put a hundred kisses on his bum, all across its smooth surface and all the way down his crack. I counted to myself, for fun. At about kiss number 50 The Captain returned and undressed. He got hard quickly when he ogled my 'tits and ass'. A couple of strokes on his shaft and he was ready.

The Captain lubed me well with a finger then positioned himself and poked his cock at my bum hole. He was gentle with his entry and gentle with his thrusting. When he rested I gave him a few squeezes, eliciting gasps from him. I was still leaning over AA, resting my arms on his bum. I reached for my clit which was very, very responsive. A look at AA's lovely legs was enough to get me going.

The Captain asked if it was ok if he could pick up the pace of his thrusting. The lube had made me comfortable and I told him to do what he had to do to cum.

I came an instant before The Captain did. My cum might have taken him beyond the point of no return. Hubby always comments on what it feels like to have me cum with his cock in my bum. Tell me about it! Ask a woman how it feels to cum on a cock in her bum!

AA was going to be disappointed, however, if he sought to fuck me in the bum. That big end could put a girl into the emergency room with embarrassing symptoms!

The Captain withdrew from my semen-filled passage and retired to a chair with a glass of wine. AA tried to get into my bum and, though dubious, I was prepared to let him try. The Captain's load and the lubricant, I thought, might just do the trick for that big cockhead. I lay on my side, reached back and positioned the tip of his cock at my opening.

'Go slowly and gently', I told him. 'I don't know if this is going to work'.

He pushed and got his tip past my bum ring. He held it there for a while, then pushed in a bit further.

Discomfort!

'Uh oh', I thought. 'This *isn't* going to work!'

His next push hurt, so much so that I reached behind and redirected him into my cunt.

'You're too big for my little hole', I told him, frankly but nicely. 'Fuck me in the cunt'.

I was on my side, facing away from him. He had a firm grip on my hips and began thrusting strongly and relentlessly, really giving it to me. I joined in the spirit of the moment, feeling myself fly with rampant lust.

That big end of his made me feel every thrust. I'd feel 'opened' when he pulled back then pushed in again.

'When it's thick it does the trick', my mum told me once. How right she was!

AA turned me onto my front and got in again. This time he was deadly serious about getting his jollies.

It is an incredible feeling to be fucked senseless by a very tall, muscled, athletic man who 'covers' you in the real sense of the word. God, did I know I was being fucked!

When he started making his cum noises I told him I wanted it on my skin. After a final, desperate thrust into my cunt he pulled out and shot his load on my bum cheeks and up my bum crack. There was cum everywhere. Those big balls of his lived up to their visual promise, even second time around. I wormed my way down the bed and licked our juices off his cock. He kept twitching, especially when I put my mouth on the sensitive end of his cock. Even when soft the end of it was a mouth filler.

It came 2.30 and AA had to return to the ship.

'Someone's got to do the work', he remarked as he dressed. He gave me a farewell hug and kiss. Nice fellow, I decided. He'd given me a good time and I'd given him a good time.

I rang my friend who had volunteered for transport duties. I called from the bathroom so The Captain couldn't hear me.

'I'm in town now', she said. 'The car's in the parking station near the hotel. What time will I see you?'

'Come up now to room 217', I told her. 'The room is booked until 4 o'clock'.

The Captain had showered after his anal excursion and was sipping on a glass of wine. A knock came at the door.

'Who could that be?', he asked.

'Go into the bathroom and don't come out until I knock', I said.

I let my friend into the room.

'What the fuck is this all about?' she inquired.

'This!' I replied, knocking on the bathroom door. A naked Captain emerged.

'Oh my god!' exclaimed my friend.

'Er . . . Hello . . .' stammered The Captain.

'We have the room for just over another hour', I stated. 'Can you get it up again?'

I was conscious of the impertinent nature of the question!

'Well, I can try . . .' ventured our man friend.

I gestured to my friend to get undressed. She has a slender body, smallish tits, a well-shaped bum and a big bush. She told me later that she would have trimmed it had she known but of course she wasn't to know that an opportunity might arise for her to fuck as well.

The Captain stayed soft when we took turns to kiss him and play with his man bits so my friend and I looked after ourselves while he watched. I started on top, for a cum each, then I switched to being underneath, for another one. By that time The Captain was hard again.

I nodded towards my friend.

'She's yours', I said, and headed for the shower.

When I came out of the bathroom, all fresh and sweet-smelling, I found my friend on top of The Captain, giving him the ride of his life. She bore down on him one last time when his man-cum noises began. She told me on the drive home that she'd put her fingers into her cunt but hadn't found much cum. That didn't surprise me. He'd unloaded into my cunt and bum, after all.

At precisely 5 minutes to 4 we vacated the room.

As an afterthought I stuffed a wad of tissues into my panties as a precaution against possible leaks on the drive home. I didn't want to leave any evidence in the washing basket. It proved to be a wise move!

'Can we stay in touch?' said The Captain as he kissed me goodbye, on the cheek.

'Let's just leave things where they are', I replied. 'Thanks for a lovely time. And say thanks to Clive for me. I think we should leave it there'.

And we did, with a parting wave. We honked as we drove past him. He gave us a wide grin.

The Captain and AA had had a good time, I concluded. I had, too. One day I'd share myself again, I thought. My confidence was sky high. I hadn't lost my touch!

And I'd paid back hubby for his indiscretion. I didn't plan to tell him about my sailors. The memories of those two meetings were for me and me alone.

Voyeur

*I*t is said that there is something of a voyeur in us all.

Let me admit at the outset that I am an obsessive voyeur, not merely an occasional opportunist. I have been since a young age. It started for me at high school. Girls used to sit in groups on the grass during breaks. Though girls and boys areas were segregated there was a popular sitting spot on the demarcation line of the areas. Boys could stand close enough for conversation with girls, only a matter of a couple of yards away. That spot was close enough for sharp-eyed boys to catch glimpses of the girls' panties when they flipped their tunics to sit or when they parted their knees while sitting, their tunics riding up. Some girls could be relied upon to give a flash. They had to be doing it deliberately, as a tease. They probably noticed my frequent presence and possibly accommodated my interest. I used to chat to a mate, making sure that he had his back to the girls so that I was looking in their direction.

That's where I did my apprenticeship in voyeurism. White cottons were universal. Tiny panties were almost unheard of even for mature women in those days, I later found out.

The girl next door was my age. Unfortunately her bedroom was on the other side of the house but the bathroom was directly opposite my bedroom window. The bathroom window was frosted of course and I had to be content with a pink shape and only from her tits up. Only once did she undress before realising that she'd forgotten to close the window. I saw her tits, an image that provided me with stimulation for many sessions of masturbation.

I didn't rely entirely on voyeuristic pursuits. I had girlfriends and went through the usual processes of exploring their bodies. We had a scale of 1-10 for how far we got with girls. 1 was 'felt her tits on the outside' and 10 was 'got it in'. I can recall plenty of claims by friends of 1 through 9 but no one ever claimed a 10.

University enlarged my scope for voyeurism. There was rising ground around a sports field where female students would lie in the sun at lunch time. Jeans were uncommon in those days and most of the girls wore skirts. They'd hike their skirts up to get sun on their legs. They also put on a good show when they sat down or stood up. Occasionally one would lie with her knees up, providing the best viewing of all.

My most vivid memory of undergraduate days was a girl who was in an amateur drama production with me. We became friends though not in the romantic sense. She'd come to my room in college for a chat. She would assume some unladylike poses, seemingly unaware and innocent of what she was putting on show. I'm not talking about glimpses, I'm talking about extended episodes of looking straight up her skirt at her panties. She varied the colours, to my delight. She also wore the very first g-string that I ever saw. I freaked at that, I can tell you!

There was a telescope on the college roof to allow residents to spy on the windows of the neighbouring college for women. There was no booking system and I couldn't be bothered queuing. I did once see a girl in transparent orange pyjamas doing exercises to flatten her tummy (she kept turning sideways to look at it in a mirror, as though hoping she might trim down in minutes). Eventually it came out that the girls also had a telescope trained on our building. The hide of them!

A student of my vintage had a telescope trained on a nurses' residential building some distance away. He had a chart on the wall, squares matching the windows, each square marked with likely times for viewing. I looked a couple of times through his scope. The nurses would come off duty, undress and shower. We couldn't see the communal shower, of course, and in fact all we saw was the girls from the waist up. I scored fleeting glimpses of a few sets of tits but that was all. It was enough to keep me interested.

A friend of mine shared a house not far from campus. I visited him a few times. Directly opposite was a seedy hotel frequented by working girls. I struck it lucky twice from his room.

One the first occasion I witnessed an Asian man taking on an Asian woman he had hired. I couldn't see everything but I witnessed him thrusting for a short time, with her legs extended upward, then her on top going hell for leather.

It was all over quickly. She dismounted, in a matter of fact manner, wiped herself and got dressed. She departed without acknowledging his presence, no doubt to prepare for her next client. I guess he had paid in advance.

The other occasion was funny. There were three men of Middle Eastern appearance, fully dressed, sitting around a table, passing around a long pipe to smoke. They were oblivious to the presence of two naked women, no doubt hired. The women decided to amuse themselves. They went into the bedroom and bounced around on the bed. Both women had big tits so the bouncing was worth watching! I'd hoped they might go down on each other but no such luck. When their energy ran out they just sat on the bed and talked. The men went out soon afterward, leaving the women to entertain themselves.

Working in the CBD provided wonderful opportunities to walk through the park at lunch time. The visual pickings were excellent. By then I was married but my voyeuristic instincts had daily stimulation. On a good viewing day I'd see several pairs of panties.

Over ensuing years our marriage declined. We hadn't been able to conceive a baby and my professional life made overwhelming demands on my time and energy. Moreover, my wife found God through a friend of hers who introduced her to an evangelical church, the kind where people close their eyes, raise their arms, smile blissfully and proclaim fervently 'Praise the Lord!' This outfit took over her life. She was a nurse and when the opportunity came along to mix nursing with missionary work in Africa, she took it. She and her friend went together. We hadn't had sex in months and we both knew that our marriage was over. The paperwork to formalise divorce was routine. I think that she and her missionary friend were lovers.

I remained living in our house. I was 'off the scene' for a year, relying on self-help for sexual gratification.

Then along came Sue, a new neighbour, a recent divorcee with no kids in tow. I invited her in for a welcome drink and found her friendly and gregarious. I'd be remiss if I didn't mention her wonderfully curved body and . . . well . . . her big tits. She'd looked after herself, that's for sure. She wasn't a bad looker, either, very attractive indeed.

I discovered her habit of nude sunbathing quite by accident. I was gardening over by her fence when I heard a noise. I peered through a small hole in the fence and saw her setting up a sun lounge. She was stark naked. Those big breasts looked good enough to feast on. Her bush was trimmed back neatly. I found myself quickly erect.

Sadly, my inside vantage point did not allow me to see her chosen resting spot, nor did my house have an upstairs room which would have given me a clear sight of her. Bugger! To a voyeur this was extremely frustrating. So much on offer and unable to be seen!

There was only one solution. I rang a builder mate and got a quote for an attic room at the back. I told him what I wanted and why I wanted it. He laughed and promised to deliver the goods. We climbed onto the roof to ensure that he got the angles of sight right.

My neighbour commented on the attic but would not have guessed the reason for its construction.

A month later the attic was finished. The view into her yard was perfect. And there was another bonus which I hadn't considered, why I don't know because in retrospect it should have been obvious. I now had an unobstructed view of her bedroom window as well as her back yard! The attic gave me a visual angle over the small trees that had hitherto blocked her bedroom window.

I set the attic up carefully: an easy chair for comfort during the long viewings that voyeurs are accustomed to; a telescope on a tripod; binoculars; and a digital camera with a long lens, also on a tripod and remote shutter control for steadiness. A true voyeur can become very excited when watching successfully and a shaking hand does not produce good photographs.

I liken voyeurism to hunting, in fact it is hunting is its own way. The thrill is of course in viewing but there is also a sense of adventurous pursuit in watching.

I felt sexually attracted by the woman but my hopes were put on hold when a black sedan started to park outside her place. I saw him alight from his car. He was a fellow of maybe 45, tall and slim, clean-shaven, pleasant looking rather than handsome.

Several days of bad weather ruined my hopes of an early sighting. It is depressing for a voyeur to be deprived of opportunities. I tried for a couple of nights to look into her bedroom but heavy rain on my window and hers made that impossible.

It took ten days to get lucky. I saw her arrive home around 7 pm and I figured she would head for the shower straight away. I trained the 'scope on her bedroom. She had not drawn the curtains. I watched her get undressed, then put on her night shirt after her shower. My elevated vantage point allowed me to see her from the knees up. I masturbated as I kept my eye glued to the eyepiece. The attic had begun to pay for itself!

Earlier I described genuine voyeurism as an obsession. It is just that. Time doesn't matter to a voyeur. Patience is everything. A mere glimpse can be overwhelmingly exciting and is sufficient to ensure there is a next time.

The following weekend I scored my first success at viewing her sunbathing naked. I alternated between the 'scope and the camera, taking perhaps 200 shots of her. When she walked back into the house I kept the button pressed down for a series of continuous shots.

I spent several hours looking at my shots and working on the good ones—and there were plenty of good ones! The lens on my Canon camera is top class.

It was important to maintain the security of my attic when friends visited and asked to see it. I had to pack my voyeur equipment away for the time.

I found myself devoting more and more of my time at home to watching. My neighbour, thinking herself protected by the trees, rarely drew her bedroom curtains. I became accustomed to seeing her undress and dress. My dream, however, was to see her have sex with her man of the moment.

I got highly excited one night when the bedroom light went on around 11. My heart started pounding when I saw them kissing. His hands were all over her body. When they were both naked to the waist, however, she turned off the light, leaving me with only my imagination. Voyeurs have to accept such disappointments. Frustration is part of the life of a watcher. One shrugs one's shoulders and thinks of the promise of next time.

Ensuing weeks saw me achieve mixed success. Cooling weather denied me nude viewings in the back yard. The bedroom window, however, became promising.

I'd just about given up watching one night when—bingo!—I got lucky in a way that surprised me. My neighbour had brought home a woman friend! She had a bi-side, I reasoned. They were larking it up in the bedroom, still clothed. They were drinking something. My camera lens told me it was vodka.

My own drinking made a bathroom visit inevitable and I dashed off, annoyed at the interruption to my viewing. When I returned her visitor was down to her panties and was playing around with exaggerated body movements, her hands over her head. I took a bunch of shots of her but when I looked at them next day almost all of them were blurred. My hand must have had 'voyeur's shake'!

My neighbour was down to her panties soon afterward and joined in the dance. They were in high spirits, pausing only to swig on their drinks. I guessed that they were fairly intoxicated. When they fell into bed they both went to sleep! The light remained on but there was no action. I remained at my watch for some time, fruitlessly as it turned out. Even a veteran voyeur can take only so much of seeing two women curled up asleep in their panties.

The clock said 2 am when last I noticed the time before falling asleep in my chair. When I woke at 7 am my neighbour's bed was made up and there was no sign of the women.

I never saw that woman again. A one-night stand, I supposed.

My neighbour took a vacation thereafter and I thought 'that's that' for a couple of weeks. 'Voyeur's vacation' as well!

Then luck came my way. I answered a knock on my door, to find a woman who announced herself as my neighbour's sister, come to house sit for two weeks. She was vivacious and very pleasant to talk to. Her tits were smaller than her sister's but still worth a look! Her ankles were beautifully tapered.

I immediately invited her to dinner and she accepted. We related well to each other but when I suggested that we get to know each other better she declined the offer though with style. I wasn't going to get my end wet that night!

She did, however, leave the light on in the bedroom while she undressed. When nude she turned towards my place and stood for ages, smiling. Then, with a 'thumbs up', she extinguished the light. She was onto me!

Next day she came over again.

'You watch my sister, don't you?' she asked.

'I'm only human', I replied. 'Will you tell her?'

'She's already told me', her sister replied.

'Fuck!' I thought. 'Where is this going?'

'Should I stop? I don't want to get into trouble with the law'.

'She enjoys you watching', she said with smile.

On her return home my neighbour came over. I would have blushed crimson when I opened the door to her.

'You know why I'm here, don't you?' she said as she entered. 'You've been watching me'.

'I'm sorry if I've caused you embarrassment', I said, my voice faltering. 'I just haven't been able to resist looking. You're very attractive'.

'I'll get to the point', she said with a smile. 'Now I know why you put on the attic. I quite like being looked at in the way you've been doing it. I'm happy for you to continue. In fact, I might take it one step further for you. How does that sound?'

'Tell me more', I said, barely able to speak.

'Would you like to watch me and Charlie?'

'Who's Charlie?' I asked, still tentative, still trying to assess the situation.

'He's my friend with benefits', she replied. 'He owns the black car you'll have seen out the front'.

'Would he know that I'm watching?' I asked.

'He'll do what I tell him to do', she responded. 'He'll be ok with being watched'.

'Jees, I don't know what to say', I said.

'You could start by asking me what I'd like to drink', she said, taking a chair in the living room.

I felt awkward in not being able to offer her chilled white wine. I improvised by putting a block of ice into a glass at room temperature. She was happy with that.

'So, are you getting your money's worth with the view?' she asked with mischief in her manner.

'I think you have a divine body', I said sincerely. 'I never tire of looking at it'.

'Would you like to look at it now?' she asked.

'Are you serious?' I inquired, not knowing what to think.

'Is this serious?' she asked as she took off her clothes to stand naked before me.

'Holy fuck!' I said spontaneously. 'How good is that?'

'Pretty good, I'd say but then I'd be biased', she replied. 'Would you like to touch me?'

'That would be special', I blurted out.

She moved over to me. I reached out and put my arms around her, my face against her firm belly.

'Are you hard?' she asked.

'Yes', I replied.

'Take it out and show me', she instructed.

She inspected my cock with intensive interest, then put a tiny kiss on the end of it.

'He's cute. Would you like to fuck me?' she asked.

'I'd love to', I said.

'Well you're not going to now,' she said as she put on her clothes. 'Today you're only going to see'.

'Some other time, perhaps?'

'Maybe, if you're a good boy. By the way, Charlie will be over tonight. I'll leave the curtains open. Start watching around 9 o'clock'.

With that she left, giving a wave of her hand.

My heart was thumping. I was somewhere between disbelief and shock. I'd been sprung, however careful I thought I had been, but had been fortunate to find a woman who was not about to rush off to the police to report me. She was an out and out exhibitionist who got off on being watched. I felt an overwhelming sense of relief. She was a kindred spirit!

I set up at 8.45, giving myself time to pour a glass of wine and to put the bottle into an ice bucket. I sat naked. Just after the appointed hour the bedroom light came on and my neighbour and her man entered the room. He was fully clothed, she was bare from the waist up. They kissed and stumbled their way to the bed.

He lay on top of her and gave a series of dry thrusts, his cock still in his pants. She still had her skirt on, hiked up around her waist. Their kissing grew more passionate. His mouth was on her tits, one then the other.

They then separated, stood and undressed. Her final garment was a white thong. She turned her back to him to remove it, at the same time giving me a thumbs up.

Charlie's cock emerged, ready for action. He had a shaved patch at his groin.

They treated me to a display of incredibly visual sex, doing it all ways with energy and enthusiasm. It was a voyeur's delight. I got off twice, getting a renewed erection in a very short time. I was surprised at the volume of semen that I produced both times. I was so engrossed that I forgot about taking photos.

Charlie appeared to cum twice, the first time into her cunt, the second time onto her belly.

They lay alongside each other for a while then my neighbour left the bedroom, giving a secretive wave to me. Charlie yawned and followed soon after.

It was some time before Sue returned to the bedroom, alone. Shortly afterward I saw the black car drive off. She gave me another wave then turned out the light.

I went to bed but couldn't sleep. My mind kept going over and over the things I'd seen. I'd never before seen a couple fucking. I hoped, fervently, that it would not be the last time I witnessed anything so arousing.

Two evenings later a knock came at my door. It was Sue.

'I've brought the wine this time', she said light heartedly. 'And I've made sure it's chilled. You can do the honours', she remarked as she handed me the bottle.

We sat on the two seater lounge, each with a glass.

'So, how was it?' she asked.

'It was incredibly erotic', I said with feeling.

'Do you think I made Charlie happy?' she asked with a smile.

'The happiest man on earth, I would have thought', I replied.

'Ha! You're very kind', she responded. 'Can I see where you watch me from?'

'This way. You go ahead', I said with obvious intent.

She ascended the stairs to the attic first, allowing me a look up her skirt to see glimpses of her white panties. It was obvious that she was enjoying her personal display.

'Well, well, well . . . You do have a good spot for watching, don't you? And all the gear'.

'I might as well get it right', I answered.

'Show me some photographs you've taken of me', she said.

I showed her a selection on the computer screen. I'd culled the fuzzy shots. She saw shots in clear focus, cropped and slightly enhanced.

'Hey, I don't look too bad in those', she said.

'You are a wonderful model', I told her.

'We might do a photo shoot some time', she volunteered.

'I'd love that', I replied. 'I might hold you to that offer'.

'I told Charlie you were watching'.

'What did he say?'

'He was happy to be watched. His only concern was that his face might turn up on the Internet as well as his cock. I told him that wasn't a problem. I said I'd cut your balls off if you betrayed my confidence'.

'I know that', I replied.

She finished her wine and rose to depart.

'Would you like to be in the room next time?' she asked.

'Oh my god, are you serious?'

'Never been more serious in my life. Yes or no?'

'Yes, of course'.

'Fine. Be at my place at 9 o'clock on Saturday night'.

For the second time Sue left me flabbergasted. She was very matter of fact yet what she was proposing was at the frontier of erotic experience for a voyeur.

At precisely 9 o'clock I knocked on her door, then I realized that it was ajar. I eased it open, entered then shut it.

'We're in here', she called.

A glass of wine was poured for me.

'Jack, this is Charlie. Charlie, meet Jack. He's going to watch us fuck'.

'How're you doin', man?' asked Charlie, extending his hand. On introduction he seemed a nice enough chap.

We chatted a while until we had drained our glasses. Sue, as always, led the way.

'Let's go into the bedroom', she declared and beckoned us to follow her.

There was a chair for me in a corner. Sue pointed me towards it before turning to Charlie to undress her. This time her thong was black.

Charlie's cock stuck out splendidly. His sizeable balls were tensed up, his ball sac tight.

The last thing Sue said to me before getting down to business with Charlie was:

'Take your clothes off. You can't watch us with clothes on'.

For ages they fucked every which way. Sue was completely uninhibited. She looked at me a couple of times, pointing to my cock and making wanking gestures with her hand, smiling broadly. I got her message and stroked my cock. To say it was hard would be the understatement of the century.

Sue got off several times before Charlie pinned her to the bed and had his cum. I marvelled at the amount of energy he expended as he came. He drove his cock into Sue, right through the action of his release, then flopped onto her body, exhausted.

Although I'd been working my cock I still hadn't cum. Realising this, Sue left the bed and knelt in front of me.

'Cum onto my tits!' she commanded. 'Get yourself off onto my tits!'

What a target her tits were! A few more pulls on my cock and I felt the inevitable male point of no return. I gave her three good shots and a few drops, right on target. She smiled her approval, massaged my cum onto her tits then left the bedroom, her gorgeous bum making its presence felt.

I nodded off in the chair. When I awoke Charlie had gone. I found Sue reading a book in the living room.

'You were asleep. I thought I'd leave you', she said, putting the book down.

'Where's Charlie?' I asked.

'He left', she said. 'He has a plane to catch in the morning. He's off to Singapore on business'.

'I guess I'd better be off', I ventured.

'Did you enjoy watching us?' she asked.

'Is the Pope a Catholic?' I replied. 'It was a fantastic experience'.

'Would you like to do it again?' she asked.

'See previous answer', I replied as I made towards the door.

Sue appeared late afternoon the next day, again armed with a bottle of white wine.

'You and I are an interesting mix', she said. 'You like to watch, I like to be watched'.

'True enough', I replied. 'I consider myself lucky to have found you. Not many women would do what you have done for me'.

'Maybe, but there might be more than you think', she said after some thought.

'I'm happy just to have you', I responded.

'I loved your cum on my tits', she said, out of nowhere. 'You shot a good load'.

'I'm happy to oblige', I replied. 'And I'm happy that you were happy'.

She took another sip of wine and put down her glass.

'Take him out', she instructed.

She proceeded to kneel before me and give me the BJ of all BJs. God was she good at it! She found places on my cock that I didn't know existed.

I warned her that she was taking me to the edge but that served only to encourage her. She got to me, I couldn't hold back any longer. She clamped her lips around my cockhead while I blew into her mouth, every drop I could muster. She took the lot without gagging, then kissed me, recycling my cum.

I sat back in the chair, wondering where the fuck I was, semi-dozing. When I finally shook myself awake Sue was nowhere to be seen. The front door was ajar. She'd gone.

A week later she announced that she was off to Italy for three months. Charlie seemed to have left the scene but she didn't offer herself to me in the interim. I volunteered to drive her to the airport. She pecked me on the cheek before entering the Customs Hall. It was a perfunctory kiss, without feeling.

She sent me a few emails from places like Positano and Milan. They were brief and essentially factual. If she was getting any sex over there she didn't say.

On her return I picked her up at the airport. We'd driven only a couple of kilometres when she suddenly went down on me, unzipping me and taking my cock in her mouth.

'That's a bit sudden', I remarked, trying to keep my mind on driving.

'You wait till we get to my place', she warned. She kept me hard during the drive.

I carried her bags into her house. I put them into her bedroom and returned to the living room to find her naked from the waist down and bent over a lounge chair.

'Just fuck me!' she said loudly. 'I need a fuck! Just get it in and fuck me!'

Sue presented plump, willing cunt lips. I went straight in, without subtlety or ceremony. She moaned and began thrusting hard against me, her head tossing around. Her fingers found her clit and soon brought her off, once, then twice. Both cums were big ones.

'Cum in me!' she commanded. She picked up her thrusting rhythm, ensuring that I wouldn't be able to last. I'd been without sex with a woman during her time away and my tank was full. She got the lot and loved it.

Sue is nothing if not pragmatist. After I'd pulled out she grabbed some tissues from her cabin bag and gave her cunt a wipe.

'Now for a shower', she declared, and took herself to the bathroom without inviting me to share the shower.

'Well then, welcome back to the land Down Under', she said when she emerged all fresh from the bathroom, wearing a t-shirt. 'How about a drink? There should be some in the fridge'.

We sipped and chatted for an hour or so. When I realised I was chatting to a sleeping woman I carried her to bed, then departed for my house.

I kept wondering if our relationship had developed beyond watching and being watched. Could we have become something more than voyeur and exhibitionist?

I asked this question of Sue's sister but she was non-committal. 'Ask Sue', was all she said.

When I summoned up the courage to ask Sue she answered by putting a finger to her lips to signal silence on the matter.

'You'll get your answer next Saturday night. Be watching, same time', she said.

At 9 o'clock that Saturday night Sue took on three men. Each of them had her twice. I went through a range of emotions, from dismay to nausea. When all was said and done, she was just an easy lay. Her display sent me that message. When they'd had their way with her she needed support to go to the bathroom. It was obvious that she'd had too much to drink.

I had never asked about her earlier life but her behaviour that night gave me a clue. I thought we might have warmed to each other but it was wishful thinking.

Her lease eventually expired and one day she was gone, without telling me.

Her sister cleaned the house after the removalist had left.

'Tell me, did I have a chance with Sue?' I asked.

'You're not the first man she's used', she told me, 'and you won't be the last. She's a slut. She can't help herself. That's what brought about her divorce. Her hubby found her in bed with two men. I knew of others. She can't keep her pants on with men around'.

I felt wistful for a time, then resolved to get on with my life.

Two gay men moved into the house next door. From that point I used my attic for storage.

In time I put the telescope on a web auction site. I got a fraction of what I'd paid for it.

Dinner Party

*T*he invitation came by email, to each of the couples who were well known to each other and utterly discreet. It read:

You are invited to a dinner party at the Stevens residence on 7 September. It is expected that you will attend. Dress formal. Ladies are asked to wear low necklines. Panties will be optional. Gentlemen are asked to wear dinner suits and black ties.

Pre-dinner drinks will be served at 6.30 pm.

Food and wine will be of the standard that you have come to expect at the Stevens residence.

The theme of the party will be hedonistic pursuit. Ladies are forewarned that their panty status may need to be verified. Gentlemen are forewarned that there will be an identification parade of an unconventional kind.

All guests are forewarned that they will be required in couples, after dinner, to do a photo shoot on the theme of 'Feeling Naughty'. All shots will then be shown on a big screen television for comment by the group and will in time be emailed to the group.

Following this there will be dancing, after which couples will be free to take themselves to one of the bedrooms for expression of their sexuality. Any couple choosing to remain in the living room for this should be aware that they may be observed. Any couple having sex in a bedroom with the door open and a bedside light on should realise that by doing so they are indicating that they are prepared to share.

RSVP by email by 31 August.

Brian and Mae Stevens were famous among their friends for hospitality. Nothing was too much trouble to ensure their guests were well provided for.

For this occasion they would spend hours planning the menu and choosing the wines. Their rambling old home was ideal for entertaining, wonderfully atmospheric. It had plenty of dark corners conducive to sexual adventurousness.

Five couples, including Brian and Mae, constituted the dinner party. Previous parties had all been convivial fun affairs but three of the women had decided to introduce an element of overt sexuality to spice things up. One or two expressed initial reservation but were soon persuaded by the others to abandon their inhibitions and to join in the spirit of the occasion.

Brian and Mae planned everything with meticulous attention to detail. Hors d'oeuvres would be oysters and pieces of lobster. The appetiser would be tomato and orange soup, which they had first encountered during a tour of France in the hillside village of Vezelay. The main course would be a piece of rare prime beef, served on a bed of minted pea mashed potato, garnished with parsley chips and a sauce made of pear and spinach. Dessert would be fresh fruit.

Chablis would accompany the hors d'oeuvres. Chardonnay would be served with the appetiser. The beef would be accompanied by a complex, earthy cabernet sauvignon. Dessert would be served with a small glass of sauternes.

The ladies did not disappoint with their dress. Breast flesh was displayed unabashedly, with blatant female pride. The men made no attempt to conceal their appraisal of the ladies' bodies. The women made it their business to check each other out.

Conversation over hors d'oeuvres was brisk and animated. There were no allusions to what might happen after dinner but the atmosphere was sexually charged. Though partner swapping was not necessarily on the agenda there was much flirting, suggestive eye contact and touching by hands. The enthusiasm for the evening was universal and strong.

Partners were separated for formal dining, the seating order having been determined by a draw from a hat. 'Soft' feeling under the table was allowed. Brian began by proposing a toast 'To friendship and the pursuit of hedonism' which everyone endorsed heartily.

After the soup Brian declared it time for upskirt photography to check on panty status. Andrew's name was drawn and he was given the job. Brian provided a digital camera. Mae instructed the ladies to pull up their skirts and to part their legs in order to ensure good shots of them. They shrieked with laughter.

Brian removed a couple of chairs to allow Andrew to crawl under the table. A series of camera flashes went off. He handed the camera to Brian. In a short time the shots were ready on the big tv screen.

Woman one wore no panties and had a trimmed bush with visible lips. She got a round of applause.

'Great shot, friend', said someone. 'How did you manage to keep your hand from shaking?'

'With difficulty', replied Andrew, taking a draught of red wine.

Woman two wore tiny white panties that just covered her bits and pieces. One of the men complained:

'Could we not take that shot again, without the white patch?'

Woman three got better, with no panties and a full wax. The camera lens did justice to her lips. There were audible sounds of admiration from both men and women.

Woman four wore black panties. The shot caught the pattern of the lace but no flesh was revealed.

Woman five had no panties and a full bush.

Andrew led the men's applause and proposed a toast:

'To the Ladies!'

Inevitably there were questions to the woman with the brazilian wax. The four other women had never had one and were keen to find out how it was done. The woman in question spoke without embarrassment, injecting humour into her account. The men also listened intently, their eyes drawn time and time again to the screen to see the sheer beauty of her smooth slit.

The meal proceeded to the main course. The ladies had done themselves proud with their necklines. Five gorgeous cleavages drew the eyes of the men constantly. The women also looked each other over.

After coffee everyone repaired to lounge chairs in the living room. The ladies were quick to demand payback for their photographs.

'Well, what have you got for us?' one demanded.

Brian was organised.

'Close your eyes, no looking, while I set something up', he said.

He produced two metal stands between which he put a length of thick dowel. On this he hung a white sheet, down to about belly level. Anything above the belly was not visible.

He turned to the men and said softly:

'Stand behind the sheet and drop your pants and underpants'.

He spoke to the ladies from behind the sheet.

'Your task is to identify which cock belongs to which man. You will find a pen and paper each on the little table'.

'It's called 'Pick the Prick!' declared one of the women, causing hilarity.

The description of the parade was provided by Mae in these terms:

'We opened our eyes and burst into laughter at the sight before us. We assured the men that their cocks weren't funny but the situation was.

Man one had a stubby little cock over low-hanging balls. He had thick hair on his lower belly.

Man two's cockhead hung lower than his balls. It had a lovely fleshy end on it. He had trimmed his body hair.

Man three was uncut, his foreskin giving the appearance of his having a longer cock than perhaps he had.

Man four had the biggest one, at least while soft. It had to be Brian.

Man five's cock had a huge knob on it. He also had the biggest balls, his left one lower than the right.

Fortunately for marital stability all the women were able to identify their hubbies' cocks correctly. One scored three out of five, three scored two out of five and one got only her hubby's cock correct.

'Turn around! Show us your bums!'

The women were all high-spirited.

'Only if you show us yours!' came the reply from a man.

'You first', said a woman's voice.

The men were all in middle age but none of their bottoms showed any sag. Indeed, all five bottoms were very firm and muscular. Three were smooth, one had hair all over it and the last had a thick strip of hair up the crack with a little tuft of hair on the lower back.

All of the women were able to identify their respective partners.

'Last show! Bend over! Show us your balls!'

Five sets of testicles hung on public view. The ladies appraised them carefully, murmuring approval.

The ladies broke into sustained applause and cheering to signal the end of the men's show. The men hauled up their pants, adjusted themselves and took the ladies' chairs.

'Front or back view first?' came the query from behind the sheet.

'Back view, then front view' came the instant answer.

The ladies were cooperative and the ones with panties took them off. Three of the bottoms were slim. Two were on the larger side though were decidedly voluptuous in their attractiveness. The bigger ladies wiggled mischievously, making sexy little ripples in their bum cheeks.

'Bend forward . . . You made us do it . . .'

Pussy lips came into full view, all of them plump and suggestive.

'Any chance of a feel?'

'You know the rules. No touching!'

'Front view now!'

All eyes went first to the hairless slit, understandably. There was no sign of redness or rash, simply a beautifully defined set of lips. The woman in black panties was revealed to sport a landing strip. All five ladies drew loud applause from the men.

Brian put on a CD, moody, soft big band jazz.

'Gentlemen, take your partners', he announced, 'but not your wives. Change partners when I tell you'.

Breasts were pressed into dinner suit fronts. Bodies swayed. Hands began to stray. Kisses were exchanged. Things were hotting up!

Brian had one last bit of fun to direct.

'Each present couple should take the camera into the guest bedroom and, as quickly as possible, take shots on the theme of 'Being Naughty'. When you've all finished I'll put them on the big screen'.

The results were hilarious, one shot fading to the next. Cock shots, cunt shots, bum shots, leg shots, tit shots, hands on cock and balls shots, hands in panties shots . . . Imaginations went wild, all in a spirit of fun.

By then it was time for things to get serious.

'Ladies and gents . . . There are four bedrooms at your disposal. You know where they are. Use them any which way you will, for however long you will, all night if you wish. If you remain in the living room, however, you should know that you might be observed. If you leave the bedroom door open with the bedside light on you should understand that indicates that you are willing to share. My last requirement is that all present couples enjoy—right now—a long romantic kiss before moving off'.

The kissing was very willing, in some cases going well beyond 'romantic'. Couples then moved off as then paired, none with their spouse.

Brian and partner (the waxed one) chose to remain in the living room, having decided previously that they would not mind being watched while having sex should anyone care to watch them. They discarded their clothing. She knelt on the floor, resting her arms on the sofa. Her knees were cushioned by two soft pillows. Her cunt lips were on prominent display.

One couple decided to stay and to watch them. In turn the other couple disrobed, sitting side by side but not themselves initially having intercourse. They both masturbated while watching Brian take his lady from behind, their eyes riveted on his thick cock parting her lips, his increasingly powerful thrusting's being met by her increasingly strong juttings of her bum.

She fingered herself to several orgasms then told Brian she wanted to feel him cum inside her. This led the other man to seek his partner's cunt and take her from behind.

Brian made a final series of thrusts and passed the point of no return, releasing his seed as far inside her body as he could get. He collapsed onto her back and remained there for some minutes until his cock subsided from her cunt, bringing with it a string of semen that found its way to the carpet. Brian's cum brought the other man off soon afterward.

When they'd all returned to reality they swapped partners and went off in search of a bed. Brian and his new partner (the landing strip) chose to share the big bed in the main bedroom with Mae and her partner, her second man for the night.

Four couples elected to sleep over. They took a bedroom each, not with their spouse. All bedroom doors remained open and Brian gained much satisfaction at the success of his planning when he looked into each room in the early morning and saw further sexual activity. He and 'airstrip' had also had it off upon waking.

Mae served breakfast, after which two more couples departed, leaving waxed woman and her hubby. Mae had deliberately arranged for them to remain behind. The shot of the smooth slit on the big screen had aroused Mae's bi side.

She despatched Brian and the other hubby (Andrew of the upskirt photos) to the billiard room while she and her friend went into the main bedroom and closed the door.

They had an hour or so of 'perfect woman to woman sex', in Mae's words.

When they'd gone, Brian opened a bottle of white wine and poured a glass each.

'How about that?' he exclaimed. 'I think we got it right'.

'I'll drink to that', said Mae, and raised her glass in a toast.

University Days

$\mathcal{M}$y time at university was filled with boozy parties, pissups in pubs, uninhibited sex including group sex, one night stands, the lot.

Well, no it wasn't! It was decidedly quiet on the sex scene during those four years. My first time was during a university vacation in my first year, at age 18. That lovely fellow and I had a couple of further meetings. Our times together were only brief. He was a skilled lover and a real gentleman, 25 years of age.

For the first two years I shared a house with three other girls. I had to get a part time job as a waitress to help pay my share of the rent. The house had only three bedrooms and we had to roster someone to sleep on the sofa. By the end of the two years I was the only original one left. During my third and fourth year I rented a room from an old couple who had a house near the university campus. That arrangement put a dampener on my social activities but it was more affordable and I could save money for a planned overseas trip at the completion of my studies.

In the house with the girls we had rules for visiting lovers and boyfriends:

- Don't bring drunks into the house.
- Visitors must not be naked when walking to the bathroom.
- Don't be too noisy in bed. Think of the others.

The rules worked well in the main. If the 'sofa person' got lucky she could arrange to have one of the bedrooms.

We vetted each new tenant carefully and got it right except for one girl who proved to be promiscuous. She lasted only a month before we asked her to leave. We weren't prudes but 2-3 men a week and noisy male and female cums became too intrusive for us. Besides, I woke on the sofa late one night to find a naked man looking at me, pulling on his cock.

'You're nice', he said.

'You're not', I replied, 'now fuck off out of here!'

That was the last straw for me. I took on the job of telling our friend that she had to go. She just shrugged her shoulders in acceptance.

There were occasional funny happenings. I remember going into a bedroom to get something, only to find one of my fellow tenants going hell for leather on top of a naked man.

'Shit! Sorry!' I said as I departed. I had no idea that she had brought a man home. She laughed about it later.

I've been trying to recollect any episodes of sex worth writing about. From memory I got laid occasionally during those two years, aside from times with the fellow who had initiated me into sex. Frankly, it's hard to remember details of lesser episodes whereas my memories of sex with my 25 year old remain vivid. He was damned good and had a cock memorable for its length and thickness. He was gentle and very attentive which is a lovely way for a young woman to discover the world of sex.

One of the three times I can recall is not worth writing about unless readers would enjoy an account of inept sex and hasty ejaculation, all to background classical music which was playing too loudly. You win some, you lose some and I sure as hell lost that one. He seemed a nice enough fellow, just clueless in bed.

Which for some reason brings to mind advice my mother gave me, bless her. She had a very liberal outlook for her time.

'If a man wants you to give him your body, make sure he is worthy of you.

You're the one who has to look herself in the mirror in the morning. Make sure you like and respect the person you see'.

I had a brief relationship with one of my tutors. These days I imagine that university staff are very wary of approaching female students for fear of being reported for misconduct but in those days it was taken for granted that some staff were predatory. My man wasn't predatory, merely attracted to me.

I could tell from the way he looked at me and spoke to me during tutorials. Personal contact was possible in a group of about fifteen. I attended his 'tute' once a week for two terms.

He kept me after class on some flimsy pretext one day, to discuss a minor point in a paper I had written. It was 4 o'clock and I had finished for the day. As it turned out, so had he. He invited me to a nearby pub for a drink.

'Why not?' I thought.

He was good company and not at all pushy or macho. He made no untoward advances. He didn't touch me, he didn't ogle me. He was a gentleman in his attitude and behaviour towards me which I appreciated.

We met the following week. He seemed hesitant but managed to ask me to dinner on the following Saturday evening. I was pleased to accept the invitation.

We went to his place afterward, a one-bedroom apartment near to the university. Dinner had been good, our mood was convivial. I kept waiting for him to make a move but he seemed hesitant so I resolved to take the action up to him.

My 25 year old sexual initiate had encouraged me to have confidence in my sexuality, to express myself, not to be backward if my instincts told me to be forward.

After we'd kissed and cuddled awhile I simply stood up and took off my clothes. The poor fellow nearly died with surprise.

'How about that?' I asked him.

'I've never seen anything more beautiful in my life', he replied, running his eyes from my tits to my cunt.

I turned and gave him a long look at my bum.

'Like it?' I asked smugly.

Why ask a question when you know the answer?

'I love it!' he said with genuine feeling.

We hit it off brilliantly in the kissing department. He didn't try to dislodge my front teeth. Our kissing was romantic, slow and sensual, simply a joy. If there is a sure way into my pants it is through slow and sensual, romantic kissing.

He didn't last the first time but I was able to resurrect his cock within a short time. Second time he lasted until he had brought me off several times, gloriously so. I needed a good fuck and I got one. I think he got a good fuck as well.

We followed the same routine for the next two consecutive Saturday nights. The sex got better each time, for both of us. I loved the way I could arouse him to being frantic. He'd be desperate to put his cock into my cunt, spiking the head of it at my opening. I had to be careful getting him in.

To be honest I thought he might propose marriage but I got that wrong. He was offered postgraduate work at an American university and took up the offer. He told me over a beer in 'our' pub. A squeeze of hands and a perfunctory kiss brought an end to our relationship. In retrospect, I have no regrets. He was part of the tapestry of my life. We weren't destined for each other in the sense of the long term.

My other uni lover was studying music. I met him at a concert at the U, put on for free by a music interest group.

His long, shoulder length hair was a turn-on. He had expressive eyes. His voice was rich and sensual.

There was no sensitivity in our two sessions of fucking. He just got on and fucked the living daylights out of me. I gave as good as I got!

We served a purpose for each other at the time. Cock up cunt, rewarding fuck, mutual cums, end of story.

I hardly made the grade as an easy lay, that's for sure! No matter, I made up for it in later years. I have an understanding with hubby that I can meet up with a man who appeals to me. So far I've met . . . let me see . . . one . . . two . . . three . . . over about ten years. That hardly makes me promiscuous but it's a good arrangement to have. I give hubby the same rein and he's told me about a one night stand at a conference.

Our marriage is strong enough to encompass a bit of adventure on the side. We're honest with each other.

A Tale of Sharing from an Old Friend

*I*f you want strenuous hardcore action, go elsewhere. If a human story with a touch of poignancy appeals to you, read on.

I will try to do justice to this account to accord respect to a woman friend of many years. I thought hard about writing it at all but then I realized how much my friend would have enjoyed sharing her story with others.

She and her long term lover (her husband was impotent and thoroughly approved of her lover) had spent occasional nights at our place. She had been an artist and art teacher during her professional career. In her teen years she had attended a dance school and was an exceptionally good dancer all her life. She also did life modelling for much of her life. We enjoyed some wonderful food and wine and some wonderfully decadent situations especially her dancing and her stripping when the champagne kicked in. Sadly she died of cancer a couple of years ago. I lent my hubby to her for a night of sex after her diagnosis. She'd had the hots for him for years but had had too much respect for me to make requests for his services.

I received a sealed letter from the executor of her estate. The letter was found recently among a pile of her papers. It was addressed to me but was meant for hubby as well, written by her. It contains an account of the night when successful final year art school students were celebrating their results, back in the 60s.

I will summarise events though the letter is several pages long. Her memory of events is remarkable but then she was a keen diarist.

In short, she had sex with no fewer than six of her fellow graduands at a party that night in the inner part of Sydney, twice with two of the men.

The party had thinned out, leaving only the six men and her. They were tipsy rather than drunk (though the men apparently continued to drink all night). They asked her to do a strip for them, knowing how good a dancer she was.

She'd had enough champagne and agreed, having a wicked sense of adventure.

Someone found a tape that was suitable and she gave them the works. Forget those tired old tarts who bump and grind their way in strip clubs. This girl had class. She did a few strips at our place in recent years after a couple of glasses of champagne and her body movements were fluid and gracefully erotic.

At the end of her strip she sat on their laps in turn, making no effort to put her clothes on again. She had the dancer's body and loved their eyes roving all over it. She had a liking for one chap in particular and suggested to him that they find the bedroom. He replied that he couldn't do that to his mates and suggested that she take them all on. To her own amazement, she agreed.

'The first one bent me over the end of the sofa. The second one took me up against a wall. He hardly got it in before he came. The other four had me in turn on the bed, every which way (though I refused anal). Two of them lined up for a second turn, also in bed. I had an audience for every fuck, each fellow with beer in one hand and cock in the other'.

She also discovered the stinging discomfort semen can cause if a man's cockhead puts a tiny rip at the entrance to the vagina. Her last man tried to prod his way into her rather than slip in, jabbed her roughly on the side of her opening and she scored a little tear. Ouch!

'I had eight loads in me. You have no idea how messy I was. I cleaned up with tissues and a hand towel of dubious cleanliness before showering in the grubbiest shower cubicle you could imagine', she wrote. Four of the men shared the dingy apartment and 'their housekeeping skills were not well developed'. They asked her to stay over but by then she'd had had enough of men and didn't want to be asked to provide further entertainment.

As far as I know, the night I offered hubby to her was the only other time she gave herself to someone other than her husband (before his problem) and her long time lover. Hubby and I 'soft shared' with her and her lover a few times but that was as far as it went. We also went to a nude beach with them a couple of times. Nudity with them was easy and natural.

Our old friend revelled in her sexuality and she was candidly uninhibited in expressing it. She was proudly female and loved being so.

They don't make them like her very often. What a zest for life she had! How warm and reliable was her friendship!

A Weekend

A girlfriend and I had a weekend away, to ourselves. No reason why, just a chance to get away from work for a couple of days.

We encountered two young men at a bar on our first night. Nothing unusual about that. It's always on the cards. Inevitably they made suggestions but we declined them, with a smile on our faces. They seemed nice fellows but they were assuming fast track into our pants and we thought it seemly to deny them. We were not the easy beats that they assumed we might be. Bad luck about that, fellas!

Next morning was gloriously sunny and warm, ideal for a beach walk.

We reached an isolated spot and sunbaked for a while. The water looked good. There was no one in sight so off came our bikinis.

The water was cool but wonderfully enveloping of our bodies. Our nips got taut.

The freedom of being naked in the water was overwhelming. Each breaking wave caressed our skin. We rejoiced at the feeling of surging water on flesh.

When we left the waves we found we had company, one of the fellows from the night before at the bar. He wore a brief swim suit that did little to disguise what he had to offer.

What do two naked ladies say to a man with his package almost all on view? Did we cover, coyly, seeking to hide our bits and pieces?

No, we stayed on full display, proudly so. His eyes took us both in and we enjoyed being on show.

His cock got hard and looked ridiculous in his swim suit.

'Take it off', said my girlfriend, without consulting me.

His cock was hard and, I'd have to say, impressive: thick shaft, big head, tensed up balls.

'What happens next?' I wondered.

'Let's all have a swim', my girlfriend announced and headed back into the waves.

We romped in the ocean, just having fun and enjoying being naked. When we got to shivering stage we retreated to lie on our towels. Nothing much was said. There was no touching or ogling.

I needed to pee. Why I didn't have one in the ocean I don't know. I walked into the sand dunes and did what I had to do.

When I returned, only minutes later, I found my girlfriend with his cock in her mouth.

'Mmm . . .' I thought. 'Where is this leading?'

I didn't have much time to consider the issue. The second young man from the night before appeared on the scene.

The scenario for me seemed to have mapped itself out!

My fellow was very hard and very eager. His thrusting into my mouth became too vigorous and I switched him to my hand. It was as though I was his first and last fuck on earth.

Neither man lasted. They were more interested in emptying the tank than giving us sustained pleasure.

They stood, thanked us, restored their swim suits, said their farewells and walked off.

My girlfriend and I put on our swim suits, looking at each other resignedly.

'Had it been worth it? We looked at each other as much to ask that question. Maybe, maybe not. Another lesson in life, perhaps?

The incoming tide washed around our feet.

As we left we saw a man with a camera above the sand dunes. We hoped he would obscure our faces on the Net.

Believe These or Not

(You'd better believe them because they're all true!)

Fulfilling His Fantasy.

I met a nice guy in a coffee shop on a sunny Sunday morning. I'd not had sex for a while and he appealed to me. I went feral and invited him to my apartment. We fucked, in safe style. He was no world beater but he fixed my problem and that was that, or so I thought.

He rang me a few nights later. He must have got my number from my phone index because I didn't give it to him.

'Would you help me realise a fantasy of mine?' he got around to asking.

'Shit, what's this all about?' I wondered, but curiosity overcame prudence and I agreed.

'Fantastic!' he said. 'I'll call by around 8 on Saturday night'.

'Any special requests?' I asked, thinking thong panties/no panties and the like.

'No, nothing in particular . . . . Well, maybe wear a skirt'.

A skirt, eh? Mmm . . . That didn't sound very kinky.

What he had in mind was definitely kinky!

We parked adjacent to the airport runway, where planes landed only metres from our vantage point, screaming their way to touchdown.

'What the fuck is this all about?' I wondered as we alighted from his shiny black beemer.

We kissed passionately, me leaning against the car, as the next plane landed.

He suddenly reached under my skirt and took off my panties, unceremoniously.

'Go steady, they cost a lot of money!' I thought to myself.

As the landing lights of the next plane approached he turned me around and went into my cunt from behind. His thrusting went up a level as the plane hit the runway.

'What is going on here?' I asked myself.

He lasted five landings before he came.

The aftermath was very matter of fact. He handed me a wad of tissues. The inference I drew was that he didn't want semen on the leather seat of his beemer.

He dropped me off home and departed, citing his need for an early night.

He rang a couple of days later and begged for a repeat episode.

I declined, with grace.

I never heard from him again.

Put that one down to experience!

Getting it Up.

In the aftermath of a rancorous divorce I somehow got involved with a much older man. 'Any port in a storm', perhaps? He had to be in his 70s.

He needed the blue pill and he told me so. I'd not experienced the man pill before so I wondered what would happen.

The foreplay was satisfactory but the wait for his erection was something else.

We must have lain for half an hour while waiting for the pill to work. My libido, which had been lively, dissipated. I found myself thinking about what I've give my daughter for her birthday!

'I'm ready now', my man of the moment announced. I'd lost interest but felt I had to let him get his rocks off, having taken him along this far.

He got on top and thrust away. I lay there and thought of Mother England. He shot off. It felt like a thimbleful.

I lay with him for a few minutes, then departed the scene.

'Write him off to experience', a friend advised.

'Yeah . . .' I thought, 'some experience!'

The Budgie

I found a seemingly great date on the Net, a divorced medical man in his 50s who sounded adventurous.

We clicked through email, then talked on the phone. He said he'd cook dinner for me at his apartment by the harbour.

'How good does that sound?' I opined.

I drove to his address. It had to be a million buck apartment.

The introductions were fine, living up to my expectations. My friend was the perfect host.

Not so his budgie!

For god's sake, he let a bloody budgerigar have the run of his apartment!

As I looked around I found the evidence. Budgie shit! All over the place!

When I put my glass of champagne to my lips, the frigging budgie tried to land on the lip of the glass!

When my friend put my dinner in front of me, the budgie landed on the edge of the plate and started picking at the potato! It then did its business on my serviette!

I went to the bathroom and retched.

I composed myself, made excuses and departed.

'But . . . I'd hoped we might make love', my date stammered.

I wrote the night off. I never saw him again.

Margaret in San Francisco

*T*hese events happened during a trip to San Francisco, USA, visiting friends. The background is that I was walking to shops one day when a woman in about her late 30s asked me to give her assistance to lift something. She was down from LA, staying at her sister's house for a few days. After the job was done she invited me to have a drink and produced a lovely white wine. Anyone who offers me a good wine becomes my friend instantly.

I had a second glass. By then I'd become aware that there was a developing dimension to our chat, that indeed Margaret seemed to be coming on to me. In a sense I felt flattered, being in my early 50s, but I was also wary. Margaret was a toucher and put her hand on my arm several times.

As I rose to leave she asked me if I'd like to visit again. I told her that my wife and I were staying locally with friends and that we had a busy schedule to attend to. She was persistent and extended her invitation to my wife. I muttered acknowledgement and took my leave of her.

'Think about it, I'm here for three days', she called after me. 'I'd love to have you both over'.

Jenny:

Alan told me about Margaret and expressed the view that she was seeking sex. He told me that she was a well-presented, well-spoken woman who seemed very nice.

Alan and I had experienced shared sex so that wasn't a problem. I'd also been with two other women and having it off with another one didn't faze me.

By 3.30 yesterday I had had enough of touristy things and Alan and I took up Margaret's offer to visit her. We both realised that our visit could eventuate in a three-way and that was quite ok by us, as we knew it would be by her.

We just wore track suit pants with a t shirt, under our raincoats. Margaret was dressed similarly, comfortable clothing for a day like that. We knocked on her door at about 4 pm.

I sat on a single lounge chair, Alan & Margaret sat together on the long lounge. Alan volunteered to pour the drinks. It was obvious from the start that sex could be on the agenda. I didn't need to be Einstein to work that out!

I suppose we chatted for 45-60 minutes. I had to duck off to the loo. When I returned I found Alan & Margaret kissing passionately. Each of them lost no time in putting a hand down the other's track suit pants. Hands got mutually busy. I was content for the moment to stroke my clit idly while watching their passion develop. I knew quickly that three-way action was what I felt like.

Margaret was on fire. She finally broke off the kissing and discarded her clothes, motioning us to follow her example. Alan's cock stuck out, lovely and long and thick. Margaret went straight down on him, working his cock with mouth and hands, murmuring her pleasure at its hardness and dimensions. Her spare hand cupped his balls. I slipped my hand between her thighs and put a finger along her slit, seeking her clit. She has a prominent clit when aroused and I was soon working it for her. Her first cum could not have taken more than a couple of minutes. She buried her face in Alan's lap and let out a series of loud moans and expletives, her body convulsing.

'I need you in me!' she declared, hoisting herself onto hands and knees on the long lounge and jutting out her bum & cunt. Alan stood behind her, stroked his vas to get some liquid, wet her, opened her cunt lips with one hand and inserted his cock with the other hand, straight in up to his balls. Margaret likes it that way. She tossed her head, pushed back onto his cock and made all manner of female noises. Alan put his hands on her hips to assist him in his thrusting.

I merely watched as Alan fucked her and she stroked her clit to a second orgasm of equal proportion to her first. I watched her face as she came. Agony or ecstasy? Ecstasy obviously but her face got contorted with the first waves of her orgasm.

She fell off Alan's cock onto the lounge and curled up. I sat Alan on the single lounge chair opposite and went down on him, enjoying the taste and scent of Margaret's cunt. I took him slowly, visiting all of his sensitive spots that I know so well.

Next thing I felt a tongue on my bum hole! Margaret had rejoined the action. Then she rubbed her tits on my bum cheeks, then presented them for Alan's hands. I reached down and brought myself off, my body shaking with the force of showing off my cum to another woman.

After a while Alan said quietly: 'You two go into the bedroom and start without me. I'll get another drink'.

Margaret & I lay breasts to breasts, legs intertwined, kissing woman-style, long and sensual. We took turns suckling each other's breasts. Our hands roved all over each other's body. Inevitably fingers found their way to cunts and clits.

Alan gave us plenty of time. When he returned I rolled away from Margaret and indicated with my hand that he should fuck her. He rolled her onto her back, parted her legs and went straight in.

I became fascinated by the body/cunt angles that she presented him with. I have always been conscious of my own instinct to get a man as deeply into me as his cock would reach but it was something special to see how another woman varied his angles of penetration. Margaret is fit so varying her legs does not present a problem for her. Spots of arthritis in my hips put constraints on me for some positions.

Alan's dicky knee eventually necessitated putting Margaret on top. Her cunt lips relinquished his cock reluctantly, or so it seemed to me.

She was quick to get it back in. Again I found myself enthralled by her variations of angle and pace. Alan's hands embraced her tits.

He slipped his cock out after a time and indicated that she should draw it over her clit. I was amazed as she had three cums in succession, in a matter of a few minutes, putting his cock back into her cunt each time she came. I couldn't resist putting a fingertip into her bum hole to feel her anal contractions and Alan's shaft. Beautiful!

I could tell that Alan was in need of having a cum of his own and whispered this to Margaret. She rolled off him and lay on her back next to me.

'Where do you want Alan to cum?' I asked her so that he could hear.

'On my tits, all on my tits!' she replied with enthusiasm.

Alan straddled her body and began to pull himself off as we girls watched the pressure and rhythm that he employed. His balls were tensed right up. Alan masturbates the head of his cock, not down the length of his shaft. He gets quite rough with it, especially near the point of no return. He made all the right man noises then leaned forward and let go in the requested spot. A little spurt, then his big one, another little one, then residual drops. Up till a few years ago he would shoot four good strong spurts plus the inevitable dribbly bits to finish. The smell of fresh semen delighted both of us girls. We took some each and stroked it onto our tits and around our nipples, making little sticky patches on our skin. There was a bit left and we shared tasting it. Both of us enjoyed its freshness and sweetness. Straight out of a man's body, spurting out of his hard cock, lovely and hot! Yum!!!

Alan collapsed, exhausted. We three all needed a break. I turned on my side, Margaret snuggled in behind me, Alan in behind her (I think!) We all dozed off to sleep. I loved the gentle pressure of Margaret's tits on my back!

I woke alone, I guess about an hour later. Alan & Margaret were having a glass of wine, seated on the big lounge. I thought I'd better duck back to base to check on things in case I was needed for kid minding. I wasn't required so returned to get myself a glass of wine. We didn't bother getting dressed.

Margaret suggested a girls' shower to freshen up. She produced two shower caps, thank goodness. I'd washed my hair that morning and didn't want to get it wet. Before she turned on the shower I told her to kneel down, then straddled her back and peed on her. She lamented the fact that she'd been to the loo not long before and couldn't manage another one for me.

We giggled our way under the shower, stroking each other with soapy hands. When she dropped the face washer and bent to retrieve it I stuck a finger in her bum, causing her to yelp. Soon after she deliberately dropped the washer again and told me to pick it up, with the same consequence for my bum. We dried each other off.

We were all hungry. Alan suggested that he get a takeout but we weren't certain that the place he had in mind would be open. Margaret volunteered to make us a ham omelette which she served with salad. Very tasty! She put on her track suit pants and t shirt for cooking purposes, wisely so in front of a hot stove. Alan & I threw on our clothes for dinner. We opened a bottle of lovely white wine.

When our food had settled our inclinations turned again to sex. We stripped off and returned to the big bed.

Alan started things off by lying on his back, gesturing to me to go down on him and gesturing to Margaret to sit astride his face, looking towards his feet. Margaret astounded me yet again by being able to achieve quick cums in succession, this time brought off by Alan's tongue on her clit. She & I then changed places and I had a couple while enjoying the attention of Alan's tongue while watching Margaret at work with his cock in her mouth.

Alan then left us again though he soon returned to watch. We took turns on top in 69ing each other without cumming, then cuddled up for more kisses and caresses. Our faces were both wet with each other's juices, causing us to giggle.

Alan had not yet fucked me but I found myself unconcerned by this. I was more than happy to play with Margaret and to watch her and hubby doing it. Margaret was more than happy not to share cunts with his cock, I suspect.

Alan rejoined us in bed and turned Margaret so she had her back to him and her front to me, meaning I could suck on her nipples while he fucked her. At one point I reached down for him. He must have felt my fingers seeking his cock as he pulled out and slipped his length along Margaret's slit. His size allowed me to manipulate his cockhead on her clit, another new experience for me and probably for all of us. She had another cum and he put his cock back inside her.

I was well and truly ready for another cum after that. I left Alan cuddled behind Margaret, still hard in her, and got onto my knees so they had a good view of me. I spread my thighs and proceeded to give a finger and clit show. Alan gave Margaret a few slow thrusts as he watched me. Once again, my sense of wicked display meant that my cum was a big one.

Alan wandered to the kitchen to open another bottle of wine. Margaret & I just lay with our eyes closed, holding hands, saying nothing.

'Turn over', she eventually said.

She opened a bedside drawer and took out a butt plug, her purple penis toy and a tube of gel.

'Plug first, to get you used to the feeling of something up your bum', she declared.

She eased my bum cheeks apart and I felt the tip of the plug begin to invade my bum hole. She slowly and gently put it all in. She then laid a hand on a bum cheek, just leaving it on my skin.

The toy was quite large and thick. I had an idea of what was about to happen as I've let two men, the larger one being Alan, fuck me in the bum. Alan's been in there quite a few times since we experimented with anal sex when I was about 32. There is really only one position that I find comfortable to take his size and that is lying on my side. I decided I'd let Margaret experiment with the latex penis and just see what happened.

After a short while she slipped the plug out and put the head of the toy inside my bum. She gave me plenty of time to adjust to its size. It was well coated with lube.

'Ok with that?' she inquired. 'Ready for some more?'

'Go very slowly', I told her. 'I'll tell you if there's a problem. This isn't the position I generally use for bum fucking. Be kind to my bottom'.

She got most of it in before I asked her to stop. She moved it gently and I found myself lifting my bum against it.

'Touch your clit', she said.

I took a long while this time to cum. When I did I thought I'd explode internally. The experience of a cum during bum sex can be overwhelming.

When I recovered I opened my eyes to see Alan seated near the bed, a glass of wine in his hand. He nodded to me and raised a thumb in approval. He'd seen the lot.

Margaret had further plans for Alan. She beckoned him back to bed and rolled onto her belly. I guessed what she had in mind.

'Fuck me in the ass!' she said with a smile. 'I'd like that'.

'Not so fast', Alan replied. 'Let's do that but let's take you along slowly'.

'I'm empty inside', she confided. 'I went to the bathroom after dinner'.

Alan winked at me and nodded his head in the direction of the bathroom. I knew what he wanted. I wet the wash cloth with warm water and cleansed around her bum hole, drying it with the dry corner of the cloth.

'Turn on your side, away from me', he directed.

He lay with his head towards her feet. He proceeded to give her an Alan special. He licked in and around her bum hole; he sucked gently on it, capturing her ring with his lips; and he used his thumb tip around and in her ring. When Margaret picked up the gentle rhythm and the sequence of anal pleasuring she murmured audibly, one would almost say purred. I slipped around the bed and used my hand and mouth on Alan's cock.

(Let me digress for a moment. I don't know why it happens but when Alan does this routine to me he induces a whole range of unique sensations, feelings that are very different from any that I feel in my cunt or clit. It would be an overstatement to call these 'an anal cum' but they put me in mind of that when my anus has little spasms and twitches without any direct stimulation elsewhere. This is what I knew Margaret would be feeling, possibly for the first time).

When Alan knew he had prepared her to his satisfaction he turned to me and nodded. I lubed up the butt plug (which, along with the toy, I had washed in the bathroom) and went to hand it to him for the next stage of getting her bum ready. He eased her bum cheeks apart and indicated that I should do the insertion. He then held her cheeks very gently together and softly massaged her cheeks. I could see her ring clenching on the plug.

I lubed the head of the toy and inserted it in place of the plug. I let her get accustomed to its more substantial penetration. She has a 'soft' bum hole and I was amazed at how easily she accommodated the bigger device.

I lubed Alan's cock and waited. I really would have preferred that he use a condom but I knew how much Margaret would appreciate him cumming in her bum so I let that one slip by. He'd have lots of lube on his cock and he'd shower afterward.

When he winked at me I slipped the toy out and put her hand on his cock, letting her make her own insertion. Her eyes were closed, the look on her face a mix of arousal and wonderment.

Alan stretched her slowly until he had his cockhead comfortably in. After that he went in slowly, inch at a time so to speak, all the time listening for and watching her responses. He eventually got it all in and flexed it for her. She cast her arms out in front of her and gave a series of prolonged cries, sighs and murmurs.

Alan took her along carefully.

'Tell me if and when you want it rougher', I heard him say to her. He did 'mini thrusts' into her, making her gasp each time.

I took one of her hands in mine and our fingers intertwined. From time to time she would squeeze my fingers.

'FUCK ME, CUM IN MY ASS!' she suddenly yelled, out of nowhere.

Alan picked up speed, holding her firmly by the hips. She thrashed about, tossing her head, her eyes shut. She lost the plot completely. Alan's pace became frantic and I could see by his face that he was close.

Out of left field he suddenly did some yelling of his own. He pushed right into her bum and held himself there. I saw his bum cheeks go all tense, then he unloaded into her. She joined in the noise and between them they would have woken the dead.

As with me, he took quite a time to wilt from her passage, perhaps because of the anal grip on the base of his cock. I watched closely—I mean, up close!—when he finally left her body. A dear little trickle of man cum came out. I couldn't resist licking it up.

Margaret reached for a pillow and hugged it for her life. I kissed her on the forehead. The darling had tears down her face. We covered her with a sheet and departed the room quietly.

Alan went off to shower, I found a half-glass of wine left in the bottle. We decided to wait until she surfaced which she did, bleary-eyed, maybe 30 minutes later.

'Thank you both, so much', she managed to say and gave us each a naked hug.

And with that, she expelled an audible fart, having had Alan pump air into her bum.

We broke into hilarious laughter, making a three-way hug as we did.

Bodies!

And that was that for the day. We'd made much of it, we thought. Alan and I slept soundly.

Two days later, Jenny again.

Margaret rang a short time ago. Her sister will be back on Thursday and she herself will return to LA on Friday. She wants us to have another three-way session before she leaves. She's also asked if she could borrow Alan for an hour this evening. I'll leave that decision up to him.

Alan.

I habitually wake early, around 4.30 am. About that time yesterday I made a call to Margaret's cell phone and told her I was available for a couple of hours.

'Give me fifteen minutes', was her reply. 'Don't bother to knock. I'll leave the door ajar'.

I bit off a fragment of a blue pill as insurance. I'd needed it with the two women!

I left a note for Jenny.

Margaret was in bed, all freshly-showered smelling.

We started out slowly but she soon became ravenous with her kissing, so much in fact that I had to restrain her lest she do me dental damage.

'Put it IN!' she soon demanded.

I've never slipped into a more willing cunt!

My knee lasted a couple of her cums, then I had to put her on top for the next couple. She rode me as if they were her last cums on earth, throwing her head back, getting very noisy, her tits jiggling wonderfully, her bum & hips vigorously active.

She lay on me after the last one, pressing her body down on mine, her tits squishing against me, her breathing gradually resuming its normal regular pattern.

We cuddled and dozed for some time, then her sexual restlessness exerted itself again. She reached for the bedside drawer and handed me the tube of gel.

'Put some up my bum', she said and rolled on her side to make it available. 'I've emptied my bum, don't worry'.

Such a frank admission! Those fifteen minutes she'd asked for had been well spent!

I used my middle finger to lube her back passage, then put a liberal quantity of lube on my cock shaft.

I got my cock in surprisingly easily. I gave her time to adjust to its penetration.

What followed was breathtaking. She took off, went nuts. It was all I could do to keep my cock in her. She thrashed about and had two very noisy serial cums, using her fingers on her clit, her legs very widely apart for the second cum. I had to try hard not to cum but in the finish I had no say in the matter. The tightness of her bum ring on the base of my cock did the trick.

I had to grip her firmly by the hips to ensure that my cock stayed deeply in her as I came.

Had the neighbours been awake they might have heard us. We might even have woken them!

I departed for the mandatory piss and shower, returning to snuggle up but not before asking Margaret to set the alarm. I sent her off to sleep with my mouth on a nipple and a hand splayed on a bum cheek.

Jenny.

He has taken both Margaret and me gently to the point where we can seriously contemplate FF sex. He is adamant that our first encounter should not involve his personal services. He is not insistent, either, at being present should we prefer our own company.

Margaret & I have established trust. I have no reservations about going down on her. I've studied her cunt closely. Her lips are perfectly formed, inner and outer.

Alan says he will continue to act as a facilitator for a brief time, then he insists that we should talk between ourselves about what happens from here. We're both confident enough to follow that path. It's a great leveller, is it not, to sip wine and chat with a fellow naked woman?

Margaret's sister has concluded her real estate matters in Florida much faster than expected and may return early. With that in mind, I propose to suggest to Margaret that we meet up soon, leaving open the possibility of Alan joining in on a second occasion should that appeal to us two girls. I get incredibly aroused by watching Alan with another woman.

A new twist to the story for Alan.

Margaret asked me if I would 'meet up with' Clare, a friend of hers from Vermont. Clare's sexual history was most unfortunate, as related by Margaret in confidence. Up to age 24 she'd had two men: the first who'd treated her brutally, tantamount to rape; and the second who'd been a premature ejaculator. So 'meet up with' Clare had a distinctly sexual connotation. Our meeting was to take place at the home of Margaret's sister.

I took an instant liking to Clare. She had a vibrant face with lovely eyes, a great smile and a trim but shapely body. She blushed when Margaret introduced us but a hug and a kiss on on her neck soon broke the ice. I took both her hands, stood back from her and showed (I hope) my appreciation of her with my eyes and smile.

Margaret had booked Clare and me into a local seafood restaurant for lunch, only a short walk away. The food there is excellent. We both had whiting fillet, beautifully cooked, and a glass of sauvignon blanc. We found conversation easy. I took her hands before our food arrived. She still seemed nervous but was gaining in confidence.

We held hands on our walk back to Margaret's place. I 'warned' her that I intended to kiss her as soon as we were inside.

'I hope that will be all right with you', I said.

Clare didn't reply but gave my hand a squeeze.

There was no sign of Margaret. The front door was not locked.

We kissed in the hallway.

Clare's lips had no 'give' in them. She pressed them onto mine, denying herself the sensuality of real kissing. Initially, her tongue was missing in action. My thinking was how to get her to relax and experiment without seeming critical. Her enthusiasm was without bounds.

A kiss or two more and she got the picture. Her tongue began to match mine. I let my hands stray to her bum which caused her to let out a little gasp. Gentle pressure from my hands soon had her pressing herself against me.

Margaret had turned down the big bed. I sat in the cane chair.

'I'd love you to undress for me', I said. 'It will be very exciting for me, I promise you'.

'You're not just saying that, are you?' asked Clare.

'Clare, you and I must be completely open and honest with each other', I said. 'We must say and do whatever comes to mind, holding nothing back. We must be ourselves and not try to be someone that we're not. I've told you how excited I'll be to watch you undress. Believe me, I meant it. I want you to feel proud of your body and its effect on me. You have already attracted me to you with your mind and your interesting conversation. Lunch was lovely and bed will be wonderful'.

With that I stood briefly and undid the top button of her blouse.

'There, I've started it, now you can finish the job'.

Blouse disappeared, followed by skirt. Black bra & panty set. I complimented her on how well she wore underwear.

She unclipped her bra and held it against her breasts until my head gestured for her to toss it aside.

'What beautiful breasts!' I exclaimed. That was no rehearsed or insincere statement. I meant it. Clare has perfectly shaped breasts, not very big but eye-catching.

'Turn around and take your panties off', I said.

She slipped them off and kicked them aside.

'Your back and bottom are gorgeous', I told her. 'Now you must turn around and show me your cunt. You must get used to me using words like 'fuck', 'cunt', 'cock' and 'bum'. I hope you will use them when you talk to me'.

Clare turned to reveal her smoothness. Her slit was visually prominent.

'What a joy you are to look at!' I said with genuine admiration. 'Come over here to me and give me a closer look'.

I took my time studying Clare's body, making sure I maintained contact with my hands throughout. My murmurings of appreciation were genuine.

'Now, I must undress for you', I said. 'Lie on the bed and watch. I'm not a young man of athletic build, remember'.

Clare laughed.

'You're doin' ok so far', she joked. It was good to see her loosened up. We were getting alone fine.

I'd taken the precaution of biting off a piece of a pill, just in case I didn't relate personally to Clare. In retrospect I needn't have bothered. She had strong sexual appeal and I told her so.

My cock was hard when I finished undressing. Clare's eyes were fixated on it.

'Like what you see?' I asked as I slipped into bed.

'I love it', she replied.

'Let's go slowly', I said. I want you to explore, express and enjoy your sexuality'.

We kissed, cuddled and felt each other up for ages. Her lips were now more sensually persuasive, her tongue learning to work in my mouth. Her nervousness had gone. She was enjoying just being herself in a sexually charged context which is exactly what I had hoped for her.

'Time for my mouth', I said eventually. I lay between her legs for her first cum, then shifted sideways for a couple of ensuing cums to allow her to hold my cock in her hand.

Clare's orgasms were amazing. She later told me they were her first in the company of a man, her others having all been self-induced. I tongued her clit directly for the first one, wanting her to get one out of her system. When I shifted position I started at her perineum and worked my way up, always sensitive to her responses which I encouraged and acknowledged. Jenny loves this technique as it allows her to experience all kinds of sensations along her slit. Clare also proved highly responsive as I touched her in various places.

By then she was more than ready for my cock.

'You put me in', I said as I positioned myself between her legs. I love the symbolism of a woman putting a man's cock into her body.

I slipped straight in, effortlessly due to Clare's extreme wetness. I told her to close her legs and just lay on and in her, stroking her face, telling her how good she felt (did she ever!)

'Is that good for you?' I asked.

'God, you're beautiful!' she said emphatically.

I took things slowly for a time, using my cockhead through her slit and on her clit for her to have another cum or two. I told her gently to tell me when she wanted me to fuck her hard.

It wasn't long before she said the magic words:

'Fuck me! Fuck me!'

Clare fairly flew and took me with her on a journey of sexual intensity. Her cunt had a good hold on me and was responsive to every thrust. It wasn't long before I felt familiar male feelings and I told her I was about to cum.

'Cum for me! Cum in me!' she said, her eyes closed, her arms locked around my neck.

She got every last drop that I could muster.

'God that feels good!' she said with feeling, pulling me down onto her body, taking my full weight, holding me until my cock softened.

It was all too much for her at that point. She snuggled into my chest and began weeping. I just held her until her moment had passed.

'Thank you, thank you!' she said as she pulled back and got some tissues to wipe her eyes. 'I'm sorry for crying'.

'Don't apologise for your responses', I told her. 'You are what you are and that's a fact'.

We lay for a while, holding hands, speaking only occasionally. I commented on the force and passion of Clare's cums.

'Now I know what I'm capable of', she said thoughtfully.

'You're only young, Clare, you'll have lots of pleasure ahead of you. You are a natural sensualist. You must realise that and enjoy it'.

It was time for another test for Clare. I wriggled down the bed and lay between her legs, my face up close to her cunt.

'I want to watch you stroke your clit with my cum', I told her. 'It's very exciting for me to watch a woman touch herself. Use your finger to get some cum for your clit'.

Unabashedly she used her finger to draw out cum. Her fingers worked her clit and brought her to yet another big one. She was panting at the energy expended. I let her recover then asked her to do it again for me. She readily complied with my request and found another cum.

'Rest time', I said. 'Time for a glass of good white wine'.

We sat on the lounge in the living room. Clare took the precaution of sitting on a towel, given the fabric lounge covering.

We were still in the living room, nakedly sipping good wine, when Margaret returned.

'Seems like you two are getting on well', she remarked with tongue in cheek.

'We've howdied and we've shook', I said.

Margaret poured herself a glass of wine and topped us up. We chatted for maybe 20 minutes, whereupon Margaret declared that she had shopping to do and left us. I'd wondered if she'd ask to join in but she seemed happy to leave it all to Clare.

We drained our glasses and I asked Clare to put her mouth on my cock. She kneeled on the carpet and gave me a marvellous time. She asked a couple of times if she was getting it right and I was able to assure her that she had me in frontierland.

When I sensed that her knees needed relief I eased her mouth off me and led her back to the bedroom.

I gave her what I call at home 'the Marvell effect': Lengthy sucking on her left nipple, with the ball of my hand on her clit, allowing her to set her own pace and rhythm for a cum; then the same on her right nipple, this time using my fingers on her clit for a second cum. She was purring in my arms afterward.

'Wow!' was all she said.

After a time I turned her onto her belly and took her from behind, complimenting her all the while on how good she felt and telling her what a lovely bum she could display for a man. For a while I pinned her wrists and legs but she didn't show much response to this and I abandoned the technique. She did react with a gasp, however, when I put a fingertip onto her bum hole.

I picked up the tempo. As I got progressively vigorous her pleasure noises became louder and more unrestrained. I waited for the magic words.

'Fuck me! Cum in my cunt!'

I really gave it to her from that moment.

'Cum in me!' she said again.

I lost it at that point. I had my customary massive orgasm without producing much cum.

We fell asleep after that, which is how Margaret found us when she returned home. It was time for me to show my presence back at base and I departed. Clare was still out to it.

'I hope you can make it back tonight', said Margaret at the door.

'I'll do my best', I replied, 'but I can't guarantee that my cock will work'.

'There's more to sex than a cock', said Margaret jokingly as she shut the door.

It was just on 10 pm when I was able to spirit myself away from base. My wife was onto it of course but the others thought I had turned in for the night.

I'd bitten off another fragment of pill which allowed me to get hard but I knew that another cum was out of the question for me. My tank was empty.

Margaret poured me a glass of her excellent white wine. She and Clare were sipping slowly on near-empty glasses.

I sat on one end of the lounge and invited Clare to lie with her head on my lap.

I held up my hand and told her to put it wherever she wanted it. She put it over a breast and gently pressed on it.

'Some people get all the attention', jested Margaret. 'Am I going to get a turn?'

Clare intervened, telling me quietly that her cunt was very tender and that Margaret deserved some attention.

'Will you watch us?' I asked.

'I'd love to. I've never watched people having sex'.

'Then let's all go into the bedroom', I said, and led them off.

I was honest with Margaret and told her that I wouldn't be able to cum even though I could get hard. That didn't bother her, she said.

Margaret and I did it slowly, shifting positions from time to time. Whenever I looked across at Clare, sitting on the cane chair, she was smiling broadly.

Margaret had a series of cums, one following on another quickly to Clare's delight.

'How beautiful!' she exclaimed at one point. 'Do I look like that when I cum?'

I was feeling drained of energy and was happy to call it quits for the night. I beckoned to Clare to join us in bed, between us.

We must all have dropped off quickly. When I woke for a comfort stop in the early hours the bedside lamp was still on. I left it that way.

I made a quiet exit around 6.30 am when I knew I could get in without being sprung. Thank god the dog didn't bark! She knows me.

I returned to the 'fray' around 9.30 am.

Clare gave me a long, wonderfully passionate kiss.

'My cunt is still very tender', she said. 'We'll have to find other ways'.

Her frankness was lovely. She'd gone through any barriers of communication that she might have anticipated.

'We'll think of something', I said with a smile as she went in for another long kiss.

The fact of her nakedness was not lost on me!

'Where's Margaret?' I inquired.

'She's gone into town for the day. We've got the place to ourselves'.

'That's nice', I said, leading her into the bedroom. I had plans for her.

I lay her on her belly then positioned myself between her spread legs.

She gave a little jump when my tongue first touched her bum hole.

'My god, what are you doing to me?'

'Trust me. Just lie there and see what happens. Any woman with a bum as good as yours is going to have a man wanting to explore it'.

I took my time, allowing Clare to experience the various sensations that the bum hole can provide. Tongue fucking became gentle finger fucking. At my suggestion she used her fingers on her clit. For each cum I inserted my thumb, feeling her strong contractions and allowing her to feel them.

'Time for a cock', I said eventually. I knew that Margaret had a tube of lube in the bedside table.

'God, will that thing fit in my bum?' she asked.

'We'll use lots of lube. You'll be fine. I'll go slowly to let your bum adjust. Make sure you tell me if you feel discomfort or pain'.

I put several fingerfuls into her passage and lubed her bum hole well before smearing some on my cock.

'Now, reach back and pull your bum cheeks apart to give me a good look at your bum hole'.

'I feel like a tart', she said with a laugh.

Not a hair in sight anywhere down below. The beautician had done a good job.

I took my time getting my cockhead in, watching and listening for Clare's responses.

'Tell me when you feel ready for more of it', I told her.

After maybe a minute she told me to go in all the way. I went in slowly, a bit at a time.

When fully in I remained still, only flexing for her. She quickly got the idea of squeezing herself on my cock. We played those little games for some time.

'Touch your clit', I said. Her fingers were soon at work, her fingertips occasionally brushing my shaft.

'My god, I'm going to cum!' she declared out of nowhere and promptly had a massive one. Her contractions on my cock were something else again.

'I need a rest after that', she said. I pulled out and lay beside her, holding her hand. She rolled onto her back.

I waited a minute or two before going off to the bathroom for a pee and a thorough wash in the shower.

On returning I sat astride her face and gave her eyelids, cheeks and breasts a balls massage. Her fingers strayed to her clit, stroking with a slow but deliberate rhythm. I loved watching her lips envelop her fingers.

By then I was confident I could produce cum so while she stroked, I stroked, still astride her face. She beat me to it, this time uttering a series of quiet moans. I came onto her tits, not much but enough for her to remark on the heat of it. I then lay beside her and massaged what cum there was around her nipples.

I had to appear again at base for a couple of hours. Clare kissed me at the door and said 'Thank you so much' as I departed.

An idea flashed into my mind.

'Be at the door at 2 o'clock. I have something else in mind that will spare your cunt and bum from further invasion'.

'Care to tell me what?' she asked.

'No. You'll have to wait to find out', I replied.

At 2 o'clock I gave her a full body massage, culminating in an internal massage that took her to a monster of a cum. From experience I can predict with certainty that a woman who has had say 45 minutes of full body massage will have a huge cum from a final internal massage.

'I think I'm all cummed out', said a voice somewhat later when she woke from the usual very deep sleep following massage and cum.

We showered together.

'When do you plan to go home?' I asked.

'First thing tomorrow morning', she replied. 'I've only taken a couple of days leave'.

We dozed a while before I suggested a final glass of wine to celebrate our time together.

'Do you have a man in mind for yourself?' I inquired.

'I do, actually', she replied after giving thought to my question. 'I've never felt confident about making my feelings known to him . . . And I've never felt confident about how I might make it happen for him in bed'.

'I hope you will now go back and make an approach to him', I said. 'Invite him to dinner at your place and see what happens. You might find yourself taking the initiative in bed, who knows? I reckon he will regard himself as a very lucky man'.

The time had arrived for me to leave Clare. I don't pretend to have 'tutored' her. I had merely facilitated the release of her sexual impulses, allowing her to find herself and to feel good about herself and her sexual attractiveness.

'You've got the glow about you', I told her, causing her to laugh, take my hand and spin around in two jive turns.

'Last kiss', I said.

It went on for ages, necessitating several breaks to catch our breath.

'Thank you so much', she said again.

'And thank you for allowing me to be part of your wonderful sexuality', I replied.

Our parting was starting to become awkward.

The words of Lady Macbeth came to mind, though not in a murderous context:

'If it were done when 'tis done, then 'twere well
It were done quickly'.

'Goodbye', I said, giving Clare's hand a final squeeze. I then turned and departed.

Jenny cracked me up with her comment on the next phase of things.

'It's more practical than panties!' She knows that I have a few pairs of women's panties to wear occasionally.

To explain:

I was walking back from the wine shop (surprise, surprise!) when Clare came out to greet me.

'Come inside for a second', she entreated me.

'Can't stay long', I said, having also been assigned a couple of items at the supermarket that were needed to prepare dinner.

'Two minutes', she said, leading the way.

Inside she handed me a parcel, gift wrapped, with a card.

'Open it', she insisted.

Inside was a classy red t-shirt, beautiful to feel. It was no cheapie, that's for sure.

'Margaret got your size while we were drinking wine without our clothes in the living room. She bought this today in town for me'.

I was gobsmacked.

'Now read the card', she told me.

'Red, the color of lust, which you have helped me find again. In college our women's supervisor warned us that the color red inflamed men's passions. I hope this shirt will hold that true for your lovely wife. Clare xxx'

'You darling', I said with conviction. 'After this we need another kiss'.

We had another long kiss, the front door open for anyone passing by to see.

It took all the will power I could muster to walk away.

I went so far as to ask if her cunt was still tender.

'Yes, you naughty man', she 'admonished' me.

Clare and Margaret plan to have dinner out tonight. I wonder if they will share each other afterward. I hope so.

I must say that I enjoyed Clare's company immensely. Margaret's idea of lunch was brilliant. We both knew what the purpose of the overall exercise was but having an hour over lunch really provided a time for acquaintanceship before we got down to business.

Margaret asked me to call in this morning before she departed. I'd been in the garden for an hour or two before deciding I needed a cold beer and, failing to find one in the fridge, I headed off to the liquor shop.

I called in on my way back. I was hoping like hell that she didn't have sex in mind as I was aching and all sweaty from the humidity. She was dressed for the drive home. Whew!

She told me that she and Clare did not bed together after their dinner but they did sit up late with a bottle of white wine, talking about what had happened.

I had made it a firm decision not to allude to the two unfortunate episodes of sex that had driven Clare into her shell and destroyed her confidence. Had she mentioned them I would have stopped her. She needed to look and think forward, not dwell on the past (though her initial time, 'tantamount to rape' in Margaret's words, must be hard to erase from her mind).

Clare was, in Margaret's words, 'bubbly' and 'positive about her sexuality'. She feels she can now handle sex with confidence, even with a sense of true adventure. While on this roll she's going back to invite her prospect to dinner at her place.

My primary satisfaction was in the trust that Clare bestowed on me to take her down paths that she had only fantasised. All her doubts about her body, her sexual appeal, her capacity to excite and satisfy a man have now been dispelled.

After about ten minutes I bid Margaret farewell. I resolved on my way to the gate that I would not see her again.

Eric the Artist

*D*arren, my husband, recently invited home Eric, a fellow to whom he'd been introduced at the local market. On the spur of the moment Darren rang me and we decided to invite Eric to stay over for a night,.

He arrived a bit earlier than expected. Darren was away doing some shopping for dinner. I was looking daggy in a t shirt and track suit pants. He'd caught me by surprise.

Eric was a delight. Like us in his 60s, he exhibited a love of life. Like us, he believed in the philosophy of *carpe diem* ('make the most of each day') and 'joie de Vivre' ('enjoy life').

I showed him through my studio to kill time. He made complimentary remarks about my drawings and paintings which I appreciated. He then suggested, out of nowhere, that he do a couple of drawings of me.

I had all the materials required.

'Why not?' I thought. I love the photographs that Darren takes of my body. Why not add some sketches to our collection?

The fire was going so there was no problem with freezing my tits off.

'Where would you like me?' I asked, having taken off my clothes.

'I'll do one vertical, one horizontal', he said. 'Stand or lie anywhere you like'.

The two sketches took only about thirty minutes. I was thrilled to pose.

Darren arrived home just before completion of the second sketch.

'The mundane walketh past the artistic', he remarked as he walked around my naked pose and the working artist, carting two bags of supermarket goods.

It was my first experience of life modelling and I loved it.

The two drawings were superb. He had an artistic talent, that's for sure. I couldn't believe that it was me! I love Darren's photographs of my body but it was uplifting to my spirits to have another man produce flattering sketches of me. At my age I'll accept all the visual and other compliments that come my way!

Darren took Eric to the pub and I got on with preparing dinner. Darren normally helps with cooking but I was happy to know that he was entertaining our guest. Darren and I pride ourselves on our hospitality.

During dinner I felt growing sexual interest in Eric. I was aware of his eyes appraising me. I looked at Darren and he winked and nodded his head. It was my call.

Even though I had been naked before Eric for some time I felt I needed to get Darren to make the suggestion of sex among the three of us. He was happy to do that. I went off to brew coffee, knowing that their conversation would be about me.

When I returned with the coffee a most extraordinary conversation occurred. Its frankness and honesty were astounding.

'Darling, Eric would love to join us but he needs the little blue pills and he doesn't have any with him'.

'You keep some for emergencies', I said.

'Yes I know and I've checked. I've got none at the moment'.

Mmm . . . had to think quickly about the situation. My clit was on red alert and so was I.

'This might help us work something out', I said after we had had our coffee, and I threw off my clothes.

'Anyone got any bright ideas?' I asked as I headed for the main bedroom, giving my bum a bit of a wiggle.

The next hour was incredible. Both Eric and Darren brought me off with their tongues and fingers. Darren provided a hard cock and a cunt full of cum. Eric couldn't get hard but managed a couple of spurts of hot male essence onto my belly after frantic masturbating. I'd never known that a man could cum with a softish cock. All in the mind, perhaps?

Darren went off to the guest bedroom, leaving Eric and me to sleep together.

Nothing happened until Darren returned in the morning and put his hard cock into my very willing cunt. Eric lay next to us and stroked his cock. Darren gave me a series of wonderful cums then released into me, a flood of biblical proportions. Eric put his mouth on me, supping on Darren's cum.

After all that, scrambled eggs seemed very anticlimactic!

Eric departed. He was wandering up the east coast of Australia, somehow keeping food on his table.

We invited him back, this time with a supply of man pills.

Eric got almost to Sydney before he rang up and told us of a change in his travel plan. Would it be ok with us, he asked, if he could stay over with us again on his revised route?

I took his phone call and readily agreed to have him as a house guest. I couldn't resist being mischievous and inquired if he would have 'supplies' with him on his return visit. It was obvious what he was up to, the scallywag. He wanted to get into my pants. There was a short silence, then he laughed and said:

'They're in my wallet. Do you think I'll get to use one?'

'I expect that you'll try but I might make you work hard to have me. And you'll have to wear a little raincoat, you know that'.

'I'll do what it takes', he replied.

He made the long trip in a single day, arriving on nightfall. He was very tired. After showering, a couple of beers and dinner with wine he excused himself and went to bed. He wasn't too tired, though, to look me over during dinner. He had a twinkle in his eye. I helped his cause by wearing a dress that showed off my shoulders and a bit of cleavage. We had our big heater on so baring some skin was no problem. He got his money's worth.

He and Darren put our billiard room to good use next morning while I did some shopping. On my return we had coffee and sandwiches for lunch. What had begun as an overcast day turned into a lovely sunny one and Darren suggested that I take Eric for a walk along the bay.

By the end of our walk, about forty minutes or so, we had progressed from holding hands to having an arm around each other. We both paint and we enjoyed the ease with which we could communicate, about art and other things. We arrived home in high spirits.

I needed to do some preparations for dinner so I sent both men off to the pub.

'Two beers at the most!' I insisted. 'I don't want drunks on my hands'. I was, of course, only joking.

'Ring me on the mobile as you are leaving the pub', I said quietly to Darren. 'You won't be disappointed when you get back. Tell Eric to take a pill at the pub'.

I got a casserole prepared, ready for the oven, then took a shower, trimmed down below and dabbed perfume on my neck and between my tits. I turned down the bed, checked the warmth of the room and put on a gown while waiting for the phone call.

'We're just leaving the pub. See you shortly'.

I took off the gown and lay on the bed, my back to the bedroom door. Even at 67 I've got a damned good body: smooth back, long legs, shapely hips, no cellulite on me. I'm not boasting, just stating the facts!

Our house is only a couple of minutes drive from the pub. I heard the front door close and the men's voices as they ascended the stairs. As soon as they turned into our living room I knew they would see me through the open bedroom door.

Within seconds I had two naked, erect men for company in bed, one either side of me. I turned onto my back, having each one in turn for a long, sensual kiss.

'Take a nipple each', I murmured, and felt the joy of having both nipples ministered to simultaneously. Each man caressed my body as well, sending into realms of bliss, into la-la land.

I took their cocks in my hands. I'm not into guessing size and I don't especially care to try. I know from measuring on our honeymoon that Darren has eight thick inches. Eric was not as big or not as thick but the pill had allowed him to get really hard. I felt I had to say something by way of compliment.

'You're wonderfully hard', I whispered to him. 'I'll need you in me soon'.

I say in passing that in my hubby's view the two sexiest things a woman can say to a man are 'Take off my panties' and 'I want you in me'.

Eric wanted more kissing. He kept making little noises of pleasure. We'd break for air, then he'd find my lips again. I felt his fingers seeking my slit and I parted my legs to make it easy for him. He inserted a finger, then said softly:

'You're very wet'.

'Tell me about it!' I thought.

On his earlier visit I'd had to give him some much-needed tuition in respect of my clit. He'd learned his lesson well. At precisely the right moment he put his finger down the length of my slit, gently parting my lips, touching my clit in the process.

Darren jokes that my idea of foreplay can be to have two or three cums in succession before settling down to serious lovemaking. As soon as Eric's finger touched my clit I knew I was in that frame of mind.

'Bring me off! I'm so close!' I said fervently to Eric. Darren's mouth went back to my nipple. I worked both cocks, both hands slick with their juices.

'Fuuuuuuuuuuuck!' I cried as I came, reaching down to hold Eric's finger on my clit. The orgasm had crept up on me quickly.

In a situation of high arousal my clit has a mind of her own. Darren knew what to do. He bent my knees and eased his head between them, using his tongue on me in artful fashion. Eric cuddled me and stroked my nipples, something that drives me crazy. There is a very direct line between my tit and my clit.

I had a second massive cum in a very short time. This one went forever. At the very last Darren provoked a few last little spasms by inserting a fingertip in my bum.

'Put your mouth on me', I said softly to Eric.

'You're amazing', he replied as he shifted down the bed to lie straight on between my legs.

The different positions adopted by my men gave me wonderfully different sets of sensations. Eric's tongue stroked and lapped from perineum to the very top of my slit. I'd give a little gasp each time his tongue passed over my clit. The naughty man occasionally let his tongue tip touch my bum hole as well.

I soon had another big cum, a noisy one from what Darren told me later.

'Whew, I need a rest', I said, after all the energy I had expended. 'Cuddle up to me'.

Darren got out of bed.

'I'll leave things to you two for a while. I'll be back to watch'.

After rest and recovery time I was ready to have Eric inside me.

'I want that hard cock in me', I said in my sexiest voice.

He reached for a condom. I heard a little snapping noise as he put it on.

I watched his face as he kneeled between my legs. His eyes were fixated on my cunt.

He just slipped in, thrust a few times then leaned forward to kiss me and to tell me how tight and wet I was. They were not tokenistic compliments. He meant them.

I returned the compliment, sincerely. He was very, very hard and I told him how good it felt.

We began with a slow rhythm but it soon became obvious that our need was mutually urgent and our rhythm picked up, reflecting the intensity of our arousal. At some point I saw something move and I guess it was Darren returning but I was increasingly off the planet.

'Sweetie, you're getting to me, I can't last much longer'.

'Let go when you have to', I said. 'You need to get the first one out of your system. Cum into me!!!'

Another dozen, frantic thrusts and Eric suddenly threw back his head, let out a long moan then went into me as far as he could. I put a hand on each bum cheek and pressed, to let him know that I wanted him in up to his balls.

He collapsed, physically and mentally, with the force of his ejaculation. He took a long time to soften, the pill again I suppose. When he took off his condom I asked him to hand it to me. I dislike the smell of condoms so I scooped a drop of semen from the little tip and smelt it, then tasted it before I wrapped the condom in tissues and put it aside. Darren came around to the bedside table and took the condom off to the bathroom. He had a glass of white wine in his hand.

I didn't know whether Darren would want his turn. I looked at him, asking with my eyes if he did. He gestured that he didn't, the nice man. He reads me perfectly. Eric was looking bleary-eyed. I snuggled up to him and pulled up the sheet.

'Wake me in an hour', I said to Darren.

When I woke the house was lovely and warm. Darren had the fire going. Things were very cosy.

Darren cooked us a lovely dinner, leaving me to chat with Eric over a glass of wine. At Darren's insistence I had put on a black silk top, black French knickers and black stay-up stockings. I enjoyed the sense of display. Eric kept staring at my legs.

After coffee we each did a reading, a customary practice at our place after a good dinner with guests. Darren did his specialty, the 'Seven Ages of Man' speech from 'As You Like It'. I followed with a passage from 'Lady Chatterley's Lover', one of the spicier bits.

Eric had nothing prepared so we gave him three erotic sonnets to read as his contribution. We were all pleased with our renditions. The atmosphere was jovial though there was clearly a strong sexual undercurrent.

Another of our habitual practices with guests is to cast off our shoes and to shuffle dance, a perfect incentive for sexual arousal. It was only a matter of time before hands started straying over my body. Darren led the way by putting his hand down my panties, spreading his hands on my bum cheeks. Eric got the message and he did the same thing during the next couple of songs.

I decided the time had come to take things a step further.

'Take off my panties', I murmured to Eric.

He kneeled as he drew them down, his eyes coming within a few inches of my trimmed cunt. I drew his head in against me. His tongue eased into my slit. I reached down and parted my cunt lips. He started lapping at my clit, increasing both his pressure and his pace. I look across at Darren who smiled and nodded. With his encouragement I let my instincts fly, succumbing to the delights of the situation, letting Nature take its course. My clit sang for me and I had a beautiful cum.

I flopped into a big armchair and wondered if I'd return to normality. I pressed my finger on my clit to finish myself off. I must have been flagrantly on show but I didn't care or hold back. I guess both my men were spectators but I didn't register. I was, you might say, preoccupied with my own state of mind and body.

An eternity later, it seemed, Darren took my hand and assisted me to my feet.

'Time to tango', he said.

Darren and I attended tango classes a couple of years ago, fulfilling a long-held ambition. Dancing the tango is like having sex in the vertical. The tango allows for individual interpretation and we have spent hours working on our own routines. Darren wore his dinner suit trousers and a white shirt, most of the buttons undone to reveal his chest. I wore only my black top and my black stay-up stockings, bare-bummed. The atmosphere was erotically charged.

Darren and I maintained provocative eye contact as we moved. Such is the nature of that dance.

Eric watched, entranced, stroking his cock, on the only occasion I looked in his direction. You have to realise the power of dancing the tango. It becomes all-consuming, challenging to one's sensual frontiers.

As always we finished our dance exhilarated.

What to do next?

Darren led me to a big lounge chair and unzipped himself to reveal his thick appendage.

'Put your mouth on me', he said.

To Eric he said: 'Take her from behind'.

I heard, vaguely, the sound of Eric putting on a condom. He inserted himself into me, a hard, pill-induced erection. I enjoyed the ministrations of both of my men, revelling in the power I was having over both of them. I reached between my thighs to stroke my clit.

None of us lasted long. It was humanly impossible to delay the inevitable. I got off first and my orgasm brought both men to the brink soon afterward. Eric thrust deeply into me and made all the right noises as he came. Darren filled my mouth soon afterward.

I waited until Eric's cock had wilted from my cunt before declaring that I was off to bed. I was, to use an expression, stuffed.

Darren was lying back on the lounge, eyes closed, exhausted. Eric was lying on the carpet, seemingly asleep, his filled condom clinging to his soft cock.

Neither man joined me in bed. I have no idea where they slept but I simply passed out, sexually sated.

Next morning Darren insisted that I have breakfast in my see-through white blouse and white g-string. In return I insisted that they eat naked. Our kitchen table has a clear glass top and I was able to see their male bits.

When our tummies had settled I changed and took Eric for a walk. We held hands along the way. The fresh air was lovely to breathe in deeply.

We got back home around 10 am. He was planning to leave after lunch. We had about two hours to kill.

I took the initiative. I took off my track suit pants and panties and sat on a single lounge chair.

'Come here, you two. Sit on the carpet in front of me and take out your cocks'.

I leaned back in the chair and lifted my knees, parting my legs to ensure they had a good view. Both men took out erections.

'Watch me', I 'instructed'.

I began to stroke my clit. Their faces showed astonishment at my blatant action. They were staring at my fingers, goggle-eyed at the way I worked my clit shaft, catching glimpses inside my cunt. Their hands were on their cocks.

The exhibitionist in me was in full cry. I didn't hold back. They got their money's worth when I came.

When I rejoined the land of the living I walked off to the main bedroom which has a king size bed. My men followed me.

Eric kissed me and stroked my breasts while Darren used his mouth on my cunt and clit. Between them they brought me to another massive orgasm. I had wondered what might happen during the morning. I needn't have. I was on for it and just let Nature dictate events.

I wanted Eric first, for a very practical reason. His cock is not as big as Darren's and I didn't know how he would feel if he were to have me after Darren stretched me. I'm still tight down below but I wanted to guarantee maximum pleasure from Eric. He was very hard from the man pill. I wondered if he'd had a top-up.

Darren's thick cock sticks straight out. It's very heavy in my hand and maybe its weight explains its angle when hard. Eric's cock, even in his 60s, still points upward.

Darren's cock fills me and reaches deeply into my cunt. I do not aspire to anything bigger. It would cause me discomfort and who wants discomfort during sex? Darren's size also means that I can't take him with my legs raised right up. There is also one angle of thrusting that he knows he must avoid when taking me from behind. It hurts! It's just the one angle, for some strange reason. Everything else from behind is fine, even the rough stuff.

Which is not to say that a smaller man was not able to satisfy me or give me pleasurable sensations. During our first threesome I was able to lift my legs in the vertical and enjoy our friend's cock at that angle. When Eric mounted me I found that his upwardly angled erection touched me differently inside from Darren's thickness. I found the same thing when Eric turned me over and took me from behind. Bodies are fascinating, are they not?

Darren joined us this time, putting his cock in my mouth. When Eric turned me over, Darren spread his legs and I continued with his cock in my mouth. When Eric quickened his pace, however, I found that his thrustings were forcing Darren's cock into my mouth, distractingly so. I held Darren's cock in my hand until Eric's arousal took him over the edge. He gripped me firmly by the hips and had a massive, noisy cum, holding his cock in as far as it would go. I thought he might pass out on me!

Eric fell back on the bed, worn out from his supreme effort. Darren took over, taking me from behind as well. I reached under and stroked my clit. The sensations of Darren's cock were so different! He waited until I had my cum then unloaded into me. Because he stretches me I can always feel the pulsations when he cums.

I went off to shower. No gauzy shirt and g-string this time, just a comfortable track suit and a favourite pair of old white cotton panties that would soak up any little accidents.

I've now been shared with three men and I've enjoyed each episode, finding out more about myself and my sexuality each time. I've enjoyed being naked with other men, relishing the visual effect of my body on them. I've enjoyed teasing them and testing my sexual attraction. I've enjoyed taking them into my cunt and into my bum as well. I've enjoyed indulging Darren's fantasy of seeing me fuck other men. I've enjoyed taking on two men and drawing their semen from them. I've enjoyed cumming in the company of other men.

Would I do it again? Maybe, but the man would need to be something special—*very special!* I'm not into charity fucking.

I am very contented with my Darren. He is imaginative, devilish, skilled, attentive, sensual and a dozen other things in lovemaking. His artistry in bed has led him to stray from time to time but not in recent years. I once found an email to him from a casual lover. It said 'Thank you for taking me places I could never have imagined'.

Darren and I make love pretty much every day in our retirement, sometimes twice a day if the mood takes us. I'm very satisfied with my lot in life including my sex life.

Now back into my studio to paint.

Sex has a close correlation with aesthetic stimulation in my world of things!

Skinny Dipping and Sharing . . .

*H*ow did this conservative-thinking, modest young wife come to go nude bathing in the pool of friends? And, god forbid, share her favours in the pool?

Alcohol assisted, I must confess. If I have a second glass of white wine I lose a layer of inhibition, maybe two layers. But to this point in my life I'd only allowed my imagination to find stimulation.

It was a warm summer evening. There were three couples present. We'd all parked our kids out for the night, with sitters.

My hubby and I didn't go there with the intention of sharing sex. It was the furthest thing from my mind and I think that was the case for the others, at least the women.

I was conscious all the while of my minimal state of dress. My dress was see-through and I had only thong panties underneath. I hadn't set out to be provocative, merely comfortable, but the more the wine took over, the more I enjoyed being visually on show. I began to notice the glances of the other husbands. The other women were showing plenty of leg.

The pool episode happened by chance. Well, maybe it was deliberate! The wife of the house posed herself on the edge of the pool then fell in, seemingly by accident. There was mirth all around. She emerged from the water with her tits all on show, her bum as well when she turned around.

'Let's all go in!' said her hubby, whereupon he stripped to display a deep suntan, his bottom white in contrast. He hit the water straight away.

I looked at my hubby for guidance. I needn't have bothered. He was divesting himself of his clothes at a hundred miles an hour. His big dick was flopping around but soft.

The other women were both nude by then. I felt silly being the only one with clothes on.

'WTF?' I thought and stripped off.

Well, I wondered, what do six naked people get up to in a swimming pool?

I swam a couple of lengths of the pool to see what might eventuate.

The host husband soon solved the problem for me. He came up behind me and put his arms around me. He pressed a hard cock against me.

'!!!@@@###$$$???' I thought.

The others had paired off and were getting on with things. Cocks were in cunts and there was action aplenty.

I had never before been in a situation of making my body available to another man in public. I felt his cock tip probing at my cunt, seeking to get in. Suddenly my demeanour changed. I went from being doubtful and apprehensive to being wanton and willing. I jutted my bum out to facilitate his entry. I was very, very wet and I don't mean from being in the pool!

The other couples were oblivious to us. They were going for it. Hubby was shafting the hostess. It was on for young and old.

The host gripped my hips and went about his business, giving it to me hard and fast. He made no attempt to get me off. It was all about him getting off.

He put what felt like a big load into me.

He softened and left my body. I looked around. The others had all done their thing and were separated.

We remained in the water afterward, chatting occasionally. I think we were all wondering what would happen next.

My hubby got hard again and went looking for the other wife. Her husband came looking for me, putting my hand on his cock to get him hard. The host and hostess sat on chairs on the pool's edge, drinking wine and watching. She was masturbating.

This fellow had a longer, thicker cock that he really knew how to use. He used the head of it to bring me off, once and then a second time before he lost his load in me. I must have put on a good show for the others but I wasn't really with it. I was somewhere 'out there', 'off with the fairies'.

I was vaguely aware of hubby's noisy cum into the other woman.

We two ladies headed off for the shower, only to be headed off by the hostess.

'I don't want to waste all that man cum', she announced. 'Let's go up to the house'.

She lay us on our backs, opened our legs and proceeded to lick the cum from our cunts. When I'd overcome my surprise I had a monster of a cum from her tongue, another first for me.

'Now you can shower', the hostess said when she'd finished with us.

Curiously, we then fell into normal conversation: about family, kids, everyday matters. I mean, fucking in the pool one minute, then chatting about run of the mill things the next!

We had another glass of wine then called it a night.

Bloody hell, some night! I could never have imagined it. Did it really happen? Could a clean-living, virtuous lady like me have impulsively fucked two other men in a swimming pool then get eaten out by another woman?

Being honest with myself, the fact is that I'd share myself again if the opportunity arose. When I masturbate my mind often drifts to that occasion.

I sometimes think of setting up a situation for it to happen again. I have a keen imagination and a thirst for more of life's experiences.

All I need is the guts to take the step. Wish me luck!

An Affair to Remember

I'd separated from my husband. I'd loved him once but he had given me lots and lots of reasons to 'unlove' him. I mean, how many pairs of cum-stained underpants does a wife have to wash before she says 'Enough is enough'?

Our sex life dwindled to an occasional fuck. I grew tired of being a convenient receptacle for his semen and finally denied my services.

'What's your problem?' he asked, naively.

'These', I replied, throwing his most recent offering to the laundry basket in his face. 'From now on you sleep in the second bedroom!'

Men can be so fucking stupid, can they not? How presumptuous, how arrogant of him to toss evidence of his serial infidelity into the basket for me to wash!

From that moment until I threw him out he washed his own underpants.

I worked in middle management in an insurance company. I liked my workmates and the boss was generous towards his employees. The atmosphere of mutual support in the office was a significant factor in how I coped with my marital split. I had two kids to support, after all.

One day I took a long phone call from one of our best clients. He'd obviously got out of bed on the wrong side (and perhaps had been drinking) because he became testy with me, even downright rude.

I drew on all my diplomatic skills and calmed him down but his manner had upset me. When our phone call terminated I rushed to the bathroom, locked myself into a cubicle and burst into tears. It did not help the cause that I was having a period. I was emotionally fragile.

'Shit', I thought. 'Get your act together!'

I had to pass the boss' office on the way back to my desk. He called me in and told me to shut the door.

'Your eyes are red', he said. 'Is there anything wrong?'

I told him of the client who had upset me. The client paid thousands in premiums each year and was one of our best.

'Don't worry about him', my boss said. 'I know what he's like. I play golf with him occasionally. I'll ring him. He'll wear it'.

He went on: 'Take the rest of the day off. You shouldn't have had to put up with that behaviour'.

Then something incredible happened, something amazing.

By way of comforting me he put his hands on my upper arms and drew me to him. There was nothing sexual in his manner. It was a gesture of human support. Then he lent his head forward and his lips came into contact with my neck.

'FUCK!!!!!!!!'

That single, simple touch sent a flow of arousal through my whole being. I can't explain the feeling easily. It was as though I suddenly had honey flowing through my veins instead of blood. Honey, from the top of my head to the tips of my toes!

He did not seek to prolong our embrace. He wished me well and opened his office door. I floated off to the train station, desperately trying to come to terms with my emotions. Something unique, something special had happened to my psyche. I was at a complete loss to account for what it was.

I remained intrigued (and excited, to be honest!) by my response for some weeks after. My contacts with the boss at work were incidental and professional. His office door remained open when

I was in discussion with him. My memory of the touch of his lips started to fade.

Then my name was included in a weekend training workshop at a classy hotel in the countryside. There were 15 of us on the list. We were assigned individual rooms.

The boss had the habit of attending these workshops, participating for a while and showing the company flag at the Saturday evening dinner.

A few days before the weekend I encountered him at the coffee dispenser.

'I see you're on the list for the workshop', he said.

'It sounds good', I replied.

'I'll be there for a time', he observed.

'Will I? Will I?' I thought to myself.

Then I threw caution to the winds.

'Will you be staying over?' I inquired.

'I hadn't planned to but I guess I could', he remarked. 'To be honest I don't enjoy the drive back after dinner and I don't like having to restrict my intake of wine. I'll think about staying over'.

On Thursday after work I had my hair and my nails done. As an afterthought I booked for a full wax. It was all a bit overwhelming, to be frank, but I adjudged the effort to be worth it. I confided in my beautician.

'Go for it, girl!' she said. Beauticians share so many secrets!

I knew there was chemistry happening between the boss and me but I wasn't sure what it was. I was certain that I had the hots for him!

He joined our group for the last session on the Saturday, then mixed around the group for drinks afterward. I sensed that he was looking at me but he refrained from making it obvious. I was getting aroused, that's for sure.

Dinner was a smorgasbord. The boss contrived to line up behind me, then to sit next to me. Those decisions could not have been accidental.

He took care to spread his conversation around the table during dinner, disguising what I felt to be his increasing attraction to me.

When the people either side of us went onto the dance floor he put his hand on my thigh.

'Do you think that we could meet later on?' he asked.

'Your room or mine?' I asked. 'I'd prefer mine'.

I smiled inwardly at that. My late mum would have been horrified at my making advances to a married man ('Married men can get you into awful trouble', she would counsel) but she would also have advised to 'fuck 'em on your own territory, not theirs. Better to throw a man out of your place rather than try to make a dignified exit from his place, when there might not be many cabs around.'

He squeezed my thigh before asking a colleague to dance.

I departed the scene not long afterward.

'Oh fuck', I thought, 'does he know my room number?'

No problem! All our rooms were listed on the conference agenda. My thinking was confused! Of course he would know it!'

A knock at the door came about 20 minutes later. I had decided to meet him fully clothed.

'God, you have no idea how much I want you!' he said with feeling as he took me into his arms. He had become instantly hard.

'And I feel the same about you', I told him.

We had a series of passionate kisses during which time our hands explored each other. Our passion became overwhelming. All I could think about was getting his cock into my cunt! Damn the niceties!

Common sense prevailed for a moment and I visited the bathroom, god knows why I hadn't done that before his arrival. When I returned he was lying naked on the bed with a hard-on pointing at the sky, definitely a size above economy class.

'Sit on it', he said, reading my eyes. 'I just need to get it in! It's like that, I'm afraid'.

I stripped for him. In my younger days I used to delight in doing a strip. At 47 I had reservations about my body, with my little mummy tummy and all.

'God, I hope I can still turn a man on', I thought as I discarded bits of clothing.

My answer to that doubt lay in his goggle eyes when he saw me naked. He gave his cock a couple of strokes. Confidence ran through my system. I hadn't lost my touch!!! Yes, yes, yes!

I mounted him straight off, damn the foreplay.

His cock was a cunt stretcher, all the way in. He began to thrust but I held up my hand to tell him to stop. I just wanted to enjoy the feeling of being filled. I flexed on his shaft to keep him interested. He took my tits in his hands. He had such a delicate touch. My nips were on fire.

I rode him to a couple of genuine vaginal orgasms. I'd not had sex for many moons and here I was fucking a man of huge sexual attraction. My cunt had never felt more receptive. It had surely never been wetter!

'I can't hold on', he admitted. 'I have to cum'.

'Just do it, I want your cum in me!' I replied.

A few more thrusts and he shot his load into me.

When he'd softened out of me I cuddled in against his chest and shed tears of sheer joy.

He drifted off for a while. I put my fingers into my cunt and drew out semen to smell and taste. For a man in his mid-50s he'd left a very respectable quantity. My inner thighs were all wet and sticky.

He eventually woke and had a bathroom visit. On returning he stood at the end of the bed and looked at me. In a blatant display I opened my legs, showing him everything I had. He tugged on his cock a couple of times to get hard then fell on me a second time. We rutted, furiously and mindlessly. It felt so good to have a man on top of me, losing the plot in his urgency of need. That hard thing of his kept ramming into me.

I curled against him afterward, smug in having his second load in my cunt. I'd been so aroused by having him want me so much but I also felt reassured of my sexual attraction. His chest smelt warm as I fell asleep. He had little clusters of hair around each nipple.

We woke suddenly in the morning and panicked at the clock. He threw on his clothes and departed for his own room. I had a hasty shower. I forgot about breakfast and just managed to make it for the first of the day's workshop activities. I hoped that I didn't look too much like a woman who'd spent a night on her back!

That was the first of several meetings, all of them involving highly passionate fucking. We experimented with techniques, always with success. I took him in my mouth, my cunt, my bum.

I broached with him the possibility of coming to live with me but he was bound to his wife who had health problems. I accepted the situation. I had to. I'd become so emotionally dependent on our relationship. Better to have him some of the time than not to have him at all.

He was so easy just to be with, fucking or not. I recall one time when we went to a local beach. We squatted in waist deep water. He put his arms around me and drew me to him. Our feelings were sensual, not sexual. His cock remained soft throughout. His hands felt wonderful around my waist, his hands gentle on my belly. We didn't speak. We didn't have to. The waves lapped softly around us. The sheer sensuality of the moment was memorable.

Was I in love with him? Yes, I believe I was but I had to put up a barrier to that notion in my mind. I knew he could never be mine. I shed tears at times but I had to accept the way things were between us.

I could go over many of our meetings over several years but I think I'll stick to just one, a time I ventured onto my dark side. A woman can go there with a man she knows and trusts. It involves total trust.

I was on annual leave, a few days before New Year's Eve. An unheralded email from my man popped up on my laptop. It pressed all my buttons! Role play!

'You don't know who I am and that doesn't matter. I have watched you and lusted after you for a long time, now I want to have you. My proposal is that you come to my apartment on New Year's Eve for dinner and for fucking. Be prepared to stay overnight. I make one proviso, that you will be under my total control once you walk through the door of the apartment. There will be no turning back, no chance of refusal of whatever I demand. If that arrangement is not to your liking, forget about the whole idea. Submit to my demands or don't turn up. Over to you. I expect an emailed reply within 24 hours. A yes will get you an address'.

Whew, what to think about that!!! He and I had talked about my dark side but we'd never gone far in exploring it. What did my man have in mind for me? I hadn't a clue.

A good friend was happy to have my two teenage kids at her place on the night.

'Half your luck', was all she said. 'You'll get more than I will on the night'.

Three days out a final email arrived.

'You agree to my terms, I see. Be at this address at seven o'clock sharp. Knock three times on the door. I require black stockings, black shoes and black underwear. You will need to provide me with evidence of those on arrival by lifting your skirt. Remember: by the act of entering the apartment you will be signifying your willingness to submit totally to my demands, however outrageous or demeaning they might be'. I wrote the address on a card and put it in my purse. I didn't really have to as I'd been there before but I felt I had to join in the spirit of the escapade.

I had the usual things done: hair, nails and a full wax. My long-time beautician pumped me for details. Her curiosity was salacious.

'I'm all excited for you', she said as she carefully rendered my cunt hairless. She's expert at her job (thank goodness!)

I ordered a cab on the night. I'd delivered the kids a couple of hours earlier, giving me time to tart myself up. I'd bought new undies and stockings. I felt really good by the time the cab pulled up. His apartment was about twenty minutes away. He mentioned that his wife was at her sister's place, in another city.

I pushed the button outside the exterior door to the apartment block. He said nothing, merely activated the door to open. I took the elevator to the third floor.

My heart was beating fast. I had no idea what I was about to subject myself to. I drew deep breaths then knocked on the door.

My man was impeccably attired in a dinner suit, black tie and white pocket handkerchief. He said nothing as he waved me inside and closed the door.

He sat on the lounge chair and took up a glass of white wine.

'Prove to me that you're wearing black panties', he said.

I lifted my skirt and displayed them.

'Hold your skirt up and come over here', he said in firm, authoritative tones.

He put his nose onto my panties and had several long sniffs. I always have a strong scent of arousal.

'Mmm . . . you don't disappoint me with your scent', he remarked. 'Get yourself a glass of wine. The bottle is in the fridge'.

We sat for a while. He directed me to have my skirt up so that he could see my panties. We had little conversation as such. He made occasional comments about my display and told me how 'fuckable' I was. During the last few minutes before we went to the dining table he made me put my hand down my panties.

He'd cooked a superb dinner: Onion soup, then a piece of beef that I could have cut with a butter knife, with beautifully done vegetables. He'd chosen a red wine of celestial quality, a merlot that in itself would have put any thinking woman in mind of sex.

We sat a while at the table after eating. We kissed, exchanging mouthfuls of merlot. His hands went to my breasts. When I reached for his cock he took my hand away.

'Not yet for that', he said firmly. 'I'll tell you when I want my cock touched'.

We finished the wine and rose from the table.

'Take off your panties', he ordered. 'Give them to me'.

I followed his directions.

I should emphasise that there was no sense of attraction or devotion in this role play. It reminded me of the atmosphere in 'The Story of O' where the men used O with mechanical intent.

'Now sit on the lounge with your dress up and cum for me'.

He stared intently at my cunt as I worked my clit to a couple of massive orgasms, one after the other.

I flopped, helplessly, afterward.

'Get on your knees and pull up your dress', he commanded.

Again, I complied.

He put a finger into my cunt, then a second finger, then a third, then a fourth. He expanded his fingers inside me, vertically then laterally, causing me to gasp as he stretched me to the point of tolerance. He did this three times.

Next thing I felt an object being put into my bum. I felt the flange of a butt plug.

'This will get your bum hole ready for my cock', he said in matter of fact tones. 'I'm going to fuck you in the bum'.

He kept me in this very exposed position for some minutes, sitting on a chair behind me, making occasional remarks about how my bum was getting him stirred up, reminding me of how much he wanted to fuck me there. When he relented and let me take out the plug I found him with his cock out of his pants, hard and ready.

'If you need to visit the bathroom, now's the time to go', he announced.

I took that to mean that he didn't want to encounter any little surprises up my bum. I'd taken care of that back home. I did, however, settle for a pee.

'Prepare yourself with this', he said, handing me a tube of lubricant.

He watched as I put several fingerfuls of lube into my bum.

'Now put some on my cock', he commanded.

He was very hard.

'Now . . . take your clothes off'.

I did as I was told.

'Turn around . . . give me a good look at you'.

'Now come into the bedroom'.

The bed clothes had been turned back. There was an old stocking tied to each of the cloth handles on the corners of the bed.

'Lie on your front'.

He proceeded to secure my wrists and ankles with the stockings, giving me a little bit of leeway, I suppose to let me fight against the ties.

I suddenly felt a series of stinging blows on my bum cheeks, caused I learned later by a set of little leather thongs tied together to make a kind of whip. He struck me slowly, perhaps 20-30 times. My bottom was smarting but the blows were not hard enough to really hurt.

A camera flash went off a couple of times. I'd get to receive the shots by email next day. They would show clearly the red marks left on my bum by the device.

Things happened in a hurry after that. He didn't bother to undress. I felt the wool of his suit against my skin. Fingers parted my bum cheeks and his cock made its presence felt pressing on, then into my bum hole. He got the head in, held still for a moment then muttered obscenities as he gave me his full length in a single thrust.

I pulled against the ties and made noises of 'protest' against being 'violated' in this way. I thought he might want me to respond in that way as part of the role play.

I'd used plenty of lube and his long, thick cock wasn't bothering me. I quickly realized that my 'struggling' and 'protests' were getting to him so I doubled my efforts.

Suddenly I had a man cumming into me! The tightness of my passage and my grip on his shaft allowed me to feel every flexing of his cock.

He took shots of my leaking bum hole before he released me from the ties.

'Game over', he said light-heartedly. 'I'll be back after I've had a shower'.

We made love in more conventional manner during the rest of the night, nodding off for a while, reawakening for renewed coupling. Mid-morning I wanted a last fuck but his cock wouldn't rise and I settled for his mouth.

I was so glad that I hadn't driven over. I'd have gone to sleep at the wheel on the way home.

We had full-on bum sex on only two further occasions. The first time had hilarious consequences. We were window shopping on our way from a restaurant to a hotel. Another couple stood next to us. Suddenly, precipitately, involuntarily I farted audibly, always a possibility after a cock has pumped air into your bum. The woman gave me a haughty, disdainful look and marched her husband away.

On our last occasion I'd had a gorgeous cum but my man hadn't had one. He went off to the shower to cleanse himself. When he returned he cuddled up and said 'We must do that again sometime'.

'How about right now?' I asked and jutted my bum out.

This time he got his, as well.

We saw each other after that with greater infrequency. Finally, when he retired and moved away, our relationship came to an end. He attempted to keep in contact by email but I could not find satisfaction at that level and told him that the show was over. I felt an emotional vacuum for a while but I had to get on with my life.

Episodes of Sex in Public Places

1 Paris 1991

*F*reda and I had enjoyed dinner in a lovely little restaurant on the Ile-St-Louis. Afterward, late night, we walked along the banks of the Seine, pausing only to admire the sights and to share long, romantic kisses on a beautiful, balmy night.

We stood on the wonderful Pont des Arts, a pedestrian bridge of visual perfection, along with perhaps a hundred other people, mostly couples of amorous intent. Freda leaned on the railing of the bridge and I stood behind her, cuddling in close as we admired the sky and the Seine. The nearest people were perhaps two metres from us.

Freda took my hand and moved it to the long slit in the back of her black skirt. Wickedness prevailed. She wore no panties! Her trip to the rest room of the restaurant had had a dual purpose!

I took out my cock and slipped it into her very wet cunt. We couldn't get very physical for obvious reasons so it was a matter of mutual flexing, very enjoyable in itself but also very arousing. After a while I whispered to her: 'Let's find some place. I've got to cum'.

We walked to the Left Bank and found the wonderfully named Rue du Chat qui Peche, the shortest street in Paris, more a kind of walkway between two busy thoroughfares. The risk of being sprung was high.

Freda lifted her skirt and bent forward.

'Be quick', she said.

After the pure eroticism on the bridge I had no choice other than to be quick. A few frantic thrusts and I was gone.

There was a funny side to the episode. As I started to cum my cock slipped out and I shot off down her black skirt and black stockings. Next morning she discarded the stockings as a lost cause but the skirt had to go to the cleaners. The lady on the desk at the cleaners gave Freda a meaningful look.

2 France 1995

We were driving through Central France through sparsely populated countryside on a lovely sunny day. We passed a deconsecrated church in an isolated spot.

'Let's go back there and fuck', suggested Freda.

We took a rug and walked some 70m to the church. Off came our clothes and we settled onto the rug for some passionate kissing.

The first European wasp appeared, followed by a second, then a third.

We grabbed clothes and rug and took off. Those mothers can do you damage.

We dressed in the safety of the Renault.

3 France 1995

We were in a hotel in St-Remy-de-Provence, in the South, following the easel trail of van Gogh. Around midnight a storm was looming. Freda threw on a shift and took us to the nearby majestic Roman Arch. As we got there the storm broke but the arch provided some shelter. She threw off her shift and I discarded my shorts and shirt. Our emotions matched the elements, wild and stormy. She had an intense and noisy cum, then dropped to her knees to bring me off with her mouth.

We ran naked through the rain to the hotel, putting on our wet clothes near the entrance. The night concierge gave us a strange look.

4 Tuscany 1997

A friend had rented an old farm house and had invited us to drop in during our wanderings. We found the place with great difficulty, down a potholed dirt road. Our friend was seemingly delayed so we strolled down to a disused mill adjacent to a picturesque little stream.

The sun was inviting so we stripped off and did what came naturally, firstly up against the wall of the mill, then on the lush, soft grass. Freda came first, then got onto her hands and knees and presented her gorgeous bum to me. Cunt and visuals got to me and I came in turn.

Then followed one of those images that stay in one's mind for life. A naked Freda squatted in the little stream and washed herself. She wandered around while her skin dried then we both dressed for the walk back up the hill. Just at that time our friend's car appeared in the distance.

5 Holiday by the sea

We took a rug into the sandhills late at night. We lasted only a couple of minutes. Some kind of buzzing insect took a liking to us, then a squadron of mosquitoes attacked. I wrote a sonnet about that episode, the couplet of which reads:

The only climax on that night of nights
Came when we put the lotion on our bites

6 Venice 2000

We were there for the whole of Carnevale, a once in a lifetime experience, masked ball and all. Our mood was joyous throughout. On our final night, after dinner in a wonderful restaurant we had discovered, Freda suddenly drew me down an alleyway to a little alcove adjacent to a canal. She had sussed out a suitable location.

She kissed me ardently and whispered 'Fuck me!'

She turned and lifted her skirt. No panties!

There were people passing nearby so we had to be quick. She squelched her way back to the Rialto Hotel. She revelled in semen runs down both thighs.

7 Paris, 1997.

We had a hotel room which overlooked a narrow passage way. We could see into the apartments opposite. Freda took in the early morning air on the little balcony. Her t shirt rode up, exposing her gorgeous bum. That did it for me! I slipped into her cunt from behind.

I noticed the curtains stirring in the apartment straight over. I drew Freda's attention to the movement and we both watched with interest. Sure enough, the curtains went further back and we could see a man masturbating.

I couldn't last. Freda departed for the shower. I gave a thumbs up to the man but he didn't respond. The curtains fell back into place.

We were scheduled to fly out of France that evening so there was no prospect of him becoming a pest.

Asian Lady

*I*t's funny how things happen in life, especially where sex is concerned.

Ben took a phone call a couple of nights ago from Robert, a fellow he had worked with professionally, if only briefly, just before retirement. Somehow Robert had found us and asked if we could join him and his wife for lunch. We agreed with alacrity. They would be the hosts on the day at a top restaurant.

Robert is in his mid 60s and now does only consultancy work from home. His wife is Japanese, I'd guess about 47. Since marrying Robert she has called herself Jenny. She says that people can remember that name whereas they could never remember her Japanese name. She is diminutive and very slim. Her face shows few signs of ageing. She might have had medical assistance in that.

The food and wine were top class and our conversation was lively, a thoroughly enjoyable occasion. As things were winding down Jenny beckoned me to join her to the rest room.

'Your husband is a handsome man', she said as we washed our hands and checked our makeup.

'Ha! He calls himself a rust bucket on the back lot of life!' I replied.

'I don't understand. What does that mean?'

'It's like he's calling himself an old used car that a dealer would keep in the back of the car yard where it couldn't be seen'.

Jenny laughed at that.

'He shouldn't think that about himself', she said, 'I think he is a handsome man'.

I smiled. Ben is pretty well preserved for his age, just 68, and his belly is firm. His voice is one of his strongest attractions. My friends always like it when he answers the phone.

'Ben has big feet', said Jenny out of nowhere. 'Is it true that big feet mean a big cock?'

'Uh oh', I thought. 'Where is this conversation going?

'It isn't small, that's for sure'.

'Does he still want to do it with you?'

'We do it often'.

'You are a lucky woman. Robert has lost interest in sex but I have two men whom I meet'.

'Does Robert know about them?'

'Oh yes, he actually found both of them for me', she replied. 'He watches us most times, sometimes takes photos or videos of us'.

'You lead an interesting life by the sound of it', I said somewhat lamely.

Jenny opened her big purse and withdrew a disk from it.

'Take this and have a look at it with Ben', she said. 'It's for your eyes only'.

With that we left the rest room.

After a couple of family phone calls that night Ben & I settled into single lounge chairs, tipped up the footrests and watched the disk that Jenny had given me. The good thing was the quality of the images. Robert obviously had good camera equipment and a sense of the importance of adequate lighting.

Jenny's lover was a very big man, 6'6" perhaps, with broad shoulders and a barrel chest. He had the nose of a man who had put his head into a lot of rugby scrums. He was sitting naked on a sofa, his cock already hard.

Jenny appeared, looking gorgeously sexy, in a dark blue pants suit. She did a slow, tantalizing strip for her man. Her bra, panties and stockings were the same colour as her pants suit. She wore no shoes. A thin gold necklace adorned her neck.

Her slim little body was breathtaking. Ben & I both exclaimed our admiration for its beauty. Small, shapely breasts, smooth skin, wonderfully contoured curves and the dearest little patch of very dark pubic hair.

'Fucking hell!' Ben exclaimed when she turned around to display her bottom. He is a bum man from way back.

Jenny took her man's hand and led him off to the bedroom, Robert filming all the time.

We watched in amazement the next twenty minutes or so of film. We both found it profoundly arousing to see a huge man fucking a diminutive woman. In one way her tiny body seemed so frail under his huge frame, his thick cock pounding into her relentlessly, driving her down into the bed with its thrustings. In another way she was claiming her man with her cunt, pleasuring him, rejoicing in her capacity to excite him.

Robert managed a close up of her delicate fingers working her clit. All of his shots were in perfect focus, making our viewing even more stimulating.

She came and her man followed soon afterward, his broad, muscled bum cheeks tightening up with his release. When he eventually softened Jenny sat astride his chest and we watched a close up shot of a runnel of cum leaving her body.

Sadly, the show ended there.

'I think we should see that again', Ben pronounced, and we did.

I sipped on my wine and reflected on the events of the day. Did they form part of a pattern? Questions about Ben & his sexual performance and the size of his cock . . . Admissions about Robert's loss of interest and his willingness to share . . . A disk showing Jenny in action with one of her lovers . . . Complimenting Ben on being handsome . . .

'Mmm', I thought. Jenny is nothing if not forward. I wonder if she has something in mind for Ben?'

I have never watched Ben with another woman. Was that what Jenny had in mind?

I've heard it said that every man would like to experience an Asian woman.

Jenny rang a couple of nights later. She was forthright in her request. Could she meet with Ben for a fuck of mutual convenience? Her Robert was fine with the idea.

I handed the phone to Ben. It was his call as far as I was concerned.

'Only if you join in', he said, covering the phone with his hand.

I nodded assent, on impulse.

We decided to combine an annual flower show with our meeting with Jenny. We left the show around 1 pm, exhilarated by a magnificent spectacle. Jenny hosted us to lunch at a nearby restaurant. We were back at her apartment by around 3.

We'd eaten and drunk well and I wondered if anything would happen. Jenny soon put paid to any thoughts of nothing happening. She simply stood up and took her clothes off, tossing the discarded garments aside. She paraded her nudity in all its magnificence. Her full bush was black and profuse in the Asian style. No trimming for her, that was for sure!

Ben and I undressed. Jenny once again took the initiative and went down on Ben. He was very hard and very appreciative of her ministrations. When she sensed he might blow she gripped the base of his cock with her fingers and squeezed, giving him respite. She took him to that point several times.

She smiled at me and pointed at her cunt. I put my mouth on her. She was earthy and fragrant, ripe for the taking. It took only a few lappings of my tongue for her to cum, her mouth still encompassing Ben's cock. She put her hands behind my head and kept my tongue in position for a couple more cums, one after the others, all of them powerful.

After some minutes, when we'd returned to something like normalcy, we went into the bedroom.

Jenny made her intentions clear by lying on her back and opening her legs. Ben got the message and went straight into her cunt. She raised her legs, then bent then back to enhance his angle of entry.

Ben went berserk in her, lifting himself, withdrawing his cock to its tip then ramming it into her yet again. I found myself incredibly aroused and my fingers went to work on my clit.

For perhaps an hour we 'did it' this way and that: man-woman, woman-woman, man-woman-woman. Jenny led the way with her seemingly insatiable appetite for sex.

She offered Ben her bum hole but he declined the offer, being carried away by the pleasurings of her tight cunt. He had a monster of a cum. She nearly ripped the sheet with her hands as he came into her. She pushed back against him to take his full length when he went off. She drained every drop he could offer her.

We cuddled for a while, then Jenny headed off to the shower, beckoning Ben to follow her. I didn't follow. He told me later that she'd brought herself off under the shower, smiling at him as she worked her clit. He again expressed admiration for her body. She touched his penis but he'd had such a big cum that it refused to respond. If she'd waited maybe thirty minutes it would have been a different story.

She climbed into bed and gave me a farewell kiss and snuggle. Our breasts felt beautiful pressed together.

Our feelings were muted as we departed in our different directions. It had been a brief but very intensely erotic episode. It seemed a shame to have our euphoria dispelled by the reality of crowds and the rumblings of passing trams.

Robert soon after was transferred to the Tokyo office of his company. Jenny rang, desperately seeking another meeting but we were unable to find a date before their departure. She wept as she entreated us to accommodate her but family matters simply made that impossible.

We have a standing invitation to stay with them in Tokyo.

A Week of Sharing

*T*his story is based upon a series of sharing episodes that took place over a period of seven days with four couples participating. We all know each other well and are good friends. This was not our first experience of shared sex, sometimes two couples, on occasion three couples. Our sharing is based on mutual respect, mutual friendship and mutual trust.

We stayed in the one house for the whole time, meaning that anything could happen at any time, day or night. The warm weather allowed for nakedness and all of us spent many hours interacting naturally and easily without clothes.

All four of us couples are in our sixties, our active sex lives giving the lie to the popularly held notion that sexual activity diminishes with advancing age.

Linda is an American email correspondent of mine. She and her group of friends are also into sharing. The episodes hereunder are taken from a series of emails to Linda detailing what happened during this week.

Now read on.

Hi again, Linda.

Well, what a panty parade we put on last evening! 3 pairs each, each parading two pairs individually then all of us showing the final pair which were of course our new ones.

The rule for pairs one and two was 'hands off!' We relented for pair no. three and let them touch us up, moving along the line so that they all got a feel of all of us.

The two thongs were ever so tiny but Beth and I got equal applause for our French knickers, proving that panties can be suggestive rather than minimalist to get a man's attention (or a woman's attention, for that matter). They are so, so stylish, worth every penny. I bought my first pair in Paris in 1991 and I've had other pairs since. The ancient black pair should probably be consigned as a cleaning rag but the white and cream pairs are a delight to wear and to tease with.

Then we sprang a surprise. Using a couple of metal stands, a length of thin wood and a sheet I improvised a cover for the men from the waist up.

'Now, we want a cock show', I demanded. 'Pants and undies off, all of you! I then added: 'And no socks!' I would never, ever have sex with a man who was wearing socks! I've had it fully clothed or just minus knickers myself but it is the height of tastelessness for a man to wear just socks. Not so for a woman to wear only stockings, of course! John is a stocking freak.

It was easy to identify the men by their equipment! Jim's balls gave him away, as did Angus' uncut cock. George's cock tends to shrivel up more than John's so that gave him away (his erection, however, is satisfactory!)

We ladies drank wine and made several bawdy comments, the kind that come to mind on a third glass of wine.

'Can we come out now?' a voice was heard to say from behind the sheet.

'No, we've got other plans for you', I replied.

'One each in our mouths, girls', I said. I then produced the four men's names on bits of paper I'd prepared and we had a draw. I won Angus, Beth got Jim, Edie got George and Ange got John.

'Now, which one of them will get hard first?'

It proved impossible to tell who got it up first but Angus didn't take long. As soon as my mouth took him in he was on the way. It was the fun of the occasion that mattered, not the 'competition'.

I had one last bit of mischief to go.

'Turn around', I ordered the men. Four bums appeared.

'OK girls, smacks on the bums for these naughty boys'.

They got their 'punishment' They joined in the spirit of things by letting out cries of 'pain'.

We collapsed laughing. We couldn't help ourselves. The men pulled their pants up and got themselves a drink. We couldn't keep a straight face let alone get into the mood for fucking. Imagine taking a man on board then bursting into laughter as he got going!

We girls slept in the big bed, comfortable for the four of us.

When we woke this morning Ange produced her penis toy and I used it in her bum while Edie and Beth watched. I put in a bit more than usual but not to her discomfort. She had a couple of cums before I took it out.

Edie then asked if she could have it in her bum. I washed the device and lubed her up for it. I then handed the thing to Beth and told her to look after Edie. I departed to the kitchen to sort out breakfast. After a shower Edie came to help in the kitchen. She confided in me how much she had enjoyed Beth's ministrations.

Camille.

ps My other pet aversion is men who keep on their wrist watches during sex. A man cannot be termed 'naked' if he's wearing a watch! A man would be desexed on the spot if he tried to get into bed with me wearing a watch lol!

Hi again Linda on Wednesday.

Beth and Jim are with us until they depart for Sydney next Saturday.

Edie, Beth and I called a rest day today. Ange was in no mood for respite and had the men in succession during the late morning. Got to admire her stamina! John was last and he reported that he had no difficulty getting in it lol. We didn't watch. As one man left the bedroom the next one entered. The bedroom door was open but we didn't hear any noises of sexual activity, unusual for Ange. I think she must have settled for being the object of desire for four men and not seeking cums for herself.

Despite calling a rest day we couldn't resist playing games with Jim's balls. John, George and Angus went to the pub but we told Jim to stay. We all took off our clothes to make it more interesting.

(A note from John. It should be noted here that Jim has exceptionally big balls. Think of the biggest pair you've seen then double the size. He achieved fame in the showers at high school. We used to joke that his balls kept him out of the first grade rugby team because their size wouldn't let him run fast enough).

Ange had arrived at the idea of each of us in turn taking his massive left ball into our mouths for a timed minute, the idea being not to gag on it. I got our kitchen clock and we took turns in timing the minute.

We put Jim on his hands and knees, allowing his balls to hang low. And when I say 'low', I mean low! Jim wears only support underpants and I can understand why. A man could get tired carting those things around unsupported lol!

We took turns in lying under his rear end with that big left one not far above.

Edie went first and got the giggles, having to break away in order not to do damage to Jim.

She was embarrassed at perhaps having made fun of him and she apologized, just saying that she had never encountered a ball as big as that before.

Ange, Beth and I made the minute without a problem.

We then insisted that Edie have a second try. I ran the clock on her and cheated, making her last two minutes. She made it but was all wide-eyed at the effort. She gasped when I finally called 'time'.

To that moment none of us had touched Jim's cock. The poor man was sticking out and obviously in need of a cum. What man in the presence of four naked women wouldn't feel like a cum?

Edie got the nod to use her hand on him. She would have stroked him only about a dozen times before his bum cheeks flexed and he made man noises before unloading into Edie's hand. He then collapsed onto the bed.

Edie held up her hand. What to do with his cum?

I pointed at Beth and winked. She licked the lot from Edie's hand. She of course is accustomed to the taste and scent of Jim's emissions.

We left Jim asleep and opened a bottle of white wine.

We ladies are scheming for one more sharing session before on Friday.

On 'respite night' I think I'll bed down with the girls and the men can use the guest bedroom, the big lounge and the study bed. I could use some gentleness this time around and I would guess that Beth would feel the same way.

Beth laughed heartily when I called Jim's balls 'bum bruisers'.

Camille.

Final episode before our NYC guests departed for their Saturday morning flight to Sydney.

We decided to meet up again for lunch on Friday. George, Jim and Angus took us all to lunch as a gesture of thanks to John and me for setting things up. George brought along a half dozen magnificent wines from his cellar. We drank a couple over lunch. We were all dressed smart casual for the occasion. I stuck to oysters as I didn't want to over eat, knowing what was likely to happen.

When we got back to base John put on a slow dance CD, the rule being 'dance with anyone other than your partner'. George was standing near me so I claimed him for dancing, took off my shoes and got in close.

All of us girls were in only our panties by the 4th track. I don't know about the other men but George was hard and I used my hand to give him encouragement. We had a few slow, romantic kisses and he lost no time in putting his hands on my bum cheeks.

Having got ourselves going it seemed logical for me to fuck George first up. I wanted the comfort of a bed but had a quick look at the others before leading George into the main bedroom. Beth was working John's cock on her clit. Ange was up close and friendly with Angus and Edie was looking after Jim with her hand. Edie and Jim joined George and me in the big bed shortly afterward. George was already in me, having declared a need that I'd created during our shuffling dance.

I wanted him to last and he did, thank goodness. We did it in various ways and I would have hit double figures. Convivial lunches and dinners can get my cunt screaming for attention. When I needed a rest I went down on him and by then he was ready. He blew in my mouth and I kept him there while he went soft. Edie by then was on top of Jim and used his cockhead to advantage on her clit. Jim got the big thrusts and shot his load into her cunt.

I shared George's cum with Edie with a long kiss. She and I then took turns going down on each other, for just one each.

I was exhausted and curled up for a snooze. Edie did the same. The men disappeared somewhere. I later ascertained that they'd gone to play snooker while their cocks got fresh energy. Even with the blue pills it seems they need recovery time. They're not youngsters, after all!

Beth and Ange appeared, smiling but looking tired. We chatted away, all lying on the big bed. I think I may have dropped off again to sleep. I woke to find a naked Angus pressed up against my back and bottom, his cock sneaking its way between my legs, his hand on my tit. John appeared shortly afterward and joined Edie with us in the big bed. The others must have taken themselves off elsewhere.

Angus took me from behind which I appreciated, not having the energy to lift my legs again. He's a lovely talker during sex, murmuring his appreciation of my body. I used his cockhead to have another cum before he had his. His hands were gripping my hips and his thrusting was vigorous. I don't think he shot much.

I thought he deserved something more so I took his thumb and positioned it on my bum hole, then pushed back to get it in before playing my 'bum games' on it. He kept gasping his amazement. When

I'd played enough I opened my legs and used my fingers. John says that my 'bum cums' are likely to break his thumb and I can believe it.

'My God!' was all Angus could say when my throbs started.

I wasn't aware that Jim had entered the room for my thumb cum, having my back to the door.

'Can I have one of those?' he asked nicely when Angus had removed his thumb.

I didn't have the heart to refuse him. He was leaving next morning, after all.

I put saliva on my bum hole and guided his thumb in. When I began to use my fingers he put his face where he could see them working my clit. If anything my cum for him was bigger than the one for Angus. He, too, expressed amazement at my throbs. Tell me about them!

That was IT for the time, for me anyway lol! I set the alarm, knowing that I'd need to rise early to organise breakfast. I hadn't a clue who my sleeping partners were but discovered John, Angus and Edie still there in the morning. The alarm woke us all.

Saturday morning.

John has driven them to the local airport. The others have departed.

Nice people, Beth and Jim, as are Ange and George, Edie and Angus. I think we are, too!

I'll be sleeping this afternoon and John needn't make any approaches. I doubt that he will, having stayed the distance yesterday.

Sunday will most certainly be a day of cunt and bum respite.

Camille.

(No cocks in bums? Only an occasional thumb and a toy? I checked with Ange and Edie who both said no. I thought Ange would have been a sure starter. No one even suggested a two-man or a three-man job. It's funny how things turn out!)

One week later.

Hi Linda.

Edie, Ange and I made up the deficit from last week by taking turns this afternoon, each having one of your 'three holers' while the other two looked on. The men were gentle and patient with us. Edie went last and took their loads of cum. She then shared it with us. We're all a bit tender down below. You would know the feeling!

Hey, we're supposed to be slowing down, are we not?

Camille.

My One and Only Time with Another Woman

*W*e met in a lesbian bar. Normally I don't frequent bars but I went to this one with a friend who is lesbian and she assured me it was highly regarded among her friends of like persuasion. 'Hard' butches went to other bars, she assured me. She astounded me by telling of some of the things the hard butches did to each other.

I went there out of curiosity, not to be picked up. The idea was for us to have a few drinks, sample the atmosphere and just observe.

My mum was staying with me for a couple of weeks so she could sit the kids and I had the chance to get out and socialise. I had long since divorced my asshole husband.

It was a Friday evening and the place was packed. Fortunately the music was not loud enough to prevent conversation. I ordered a gin and tonic, we found a table and settled in to watch the action.

There was a small dance floor which was crowded but no one cared. Most girl couples were dancing apart but there were a few very torrid encounters going on. Deep kissing, blatant feeling up and in one spectacular instance, two young women with their hands down their panties, masturbating for each other while moving to the music. No one took any notice of them.

'Do you like it here?' asked my friend.

'It certainly has its moments', I replied, 'and it's only eight o'clock. What must it be like at midnight?'

My friend went off to the loo. She took a while due to the queue. I just sat there, by then on my second g & t. I became aware of someone's presence and looked around. Standing near me was a woman of perhaps 40. She smiled at me and said: 'I've been watching you. I really find you attractive. Would you mind if I joined you and your friend?'

'Go ahead', I replied. She was dressed well and well presented. I guessed she was in professional life, a guess that turned out to be correct. She had her own law practice. Most of her work consisted of getting a fair deal for women clients in divorce cases. That put her onside with me right away!

The three of us chatted for perhaps an hour before I had had enough and decided to go home. It had been an interesting evening and I was glad that I had gone along. As I declared my intention the lawyer, whom I'll call Evelyn, touched me on the arm and said: 'I'd like to take you to dinner tomorrow night. What do you say to that?'

There was something about Evelyn that I liked. She wasn't your classical beauty but she had a lovely warm manner, expressive eyes and a disarming smile.

'I'd love that', I replied.

She gave me her card and wrote her home phone number on the back of it.

'If I'm not home, ring my mobile number', she said. 'I'll let you know the arrangements'.

My friend drove me home.

'You've been hit on, you know that, don't you?' she remarked.

'I'm not naïve in these matters. I've always wondered what it would be like to have sex with another woman. Maybe I'm about to find out'.

Next evening I took a cab to the address Evelyn gave me over the phone. She greeted me with a smile and a kiss on either cheek in the European manner and gave me a quick tour of her stylish terrace house. The tour included the main bedroom which had a vase of red roses in one corner.

We dined at a Vietnamese restaurant nearby. She was a regular, going by the reception she got from the owner and the window table we were assigned. It was a BYO and Evelyn produced a bottle of white wine that I knew to be one of the best.

The food was beautiful, our conversation lively. We had lots of laughs. I was also aware of occasional touches of her leg against mine.

'Let's go back to my place for coffee', she suggested. The bill arrived, I opened my purse to pay half but she waved me away.

'This is on me', she said.

As we waited for a traffic light to turn green for a pedestrian crossing she took my hand and our fingers intertwined. By the time we had crossed the road we had an arm around each other.

Her place was all class. The path to her front steps was in caramel and white tiles. Her front door had a wonderfully colourful stained glass panel. The interior flooring was polished wood with big patterned rugs. The whole house showed her attention to detail. No companion, no kids, her own practice meant that she had money to spend and it showed.

She shut the door, took me in her arms and gave me a long, lingering kiss. I responded. Our breasts pressed together. I was acutely aware of her perfume. I was really getting turned on by this new adventure in my life.

We broke the kiss, took a long look at each other before Evelyn declared: 'Coffee time'.

'You and I have something significant in common', I remarked.

'Oh, what would that be?' she asked.

'We have the same coffee machine'.

We had a laugh about the coincidence.

'Let me guess, you bought yours from Mario'.

'I did'.

'So did I', she exclaimed.

Mario was a dear old Italian man who sold coffee and everything to do with making coffee. When I had told him that I wanted the best machine he had for domestic purposes he had led me across his shop and had said: 'This is the one you want'. He had said the same to Evelyn. The machine did not come cheaply but I thought damn the expense. My divorce had come through at that time and I needed some self-indulgence.

Evelyn and I each had a strong flat white. We sat in separate lounge chairs in her living room, feet up on the extended footrests. She put on a medley CD of classical music and dimmed the lights. We sipped our coffee, eyes closed, relaxed by the music.

'Let's move over here', she said, moving to a 3-seater lounge of soft leather, the same as the two single chairs. 'Put your feet up and put your head in my lap'.

I kicked off my shoes and lay on the lounge, head in her lap as suggested.

"I'm loving this', she murmured as she stroked my hair and face. I kept my eyes closed, enjoying the music, adoring her attentive stroking. This went on until the end of the CD. There was no talk, only touching of an incredibly sensual kind.

'We'll have one more CD then go upstairs', she said. She selected Chopin and kept the volume low.

She returned to the lounge with a big smile.

'I'd love to undress you', she said.

'I'd love you to undress me', I replied, getting up from the lounge.

I had a slim body, of very good proportions. My breasts aren't big but they are very shapely and finely contoured. My belly had survived the ravages of two kids and I was happy with my bum and legs. Evelyn's eyes lit up as my nakedness came into view. She remained fully clothed.

'We'll leave on your panties and stockings for now', she decided, then drew me back onto the lounge as before.

This time her hands stroked my breasts with exquisite tenderness. I simply floated away to some distant place, at peace with myself, at peace with the developing situation, trusting Evelyn implicitly.

Chopin came to an end.

'Let's go up to my bedroom', Evelyn said. 'I'll carry your clothes and shoes. You go ahead of me up the stairs so I can enjoy the view'.

I wore black stay-up stockings and a classy pair of French knickers which just kissed my skin as I walked. I could feel Evelyn's eyes on me all the while.

'You undress me', she said.

Her black pants suit would have cost a fortune, as would her bra and panties, both with gorgeous lace panels. I unclipped her bra and we stood before each other, dressed identically. Her breasts were bigger than mine and she had a bit of a tummy ('from good living' she told me). We embraced and I rejoiced in the way our breasts pressed together. Our kisses were long and romantic.

She drew down the bedclothes and took off her panties. I followed suit with mine. She had had a full wax and her slit looked stunning. I had trimmed right back and my slit was on show.

'I'll do a turn, then you do one', she said, doing a slow full circle so that I could appraise her body. She had strong, full curves on her hips and bottom, the shape of a real woman.

I then did a turn for her.

We lay on the bed, facing each other, quickly falling into a close embrace., breasts, bellies, legs pressing together. We shared a series of little kisses before she rose on her elbow and assumed the leading role, taking our kissing to the next level of arousal. Our tongues were soon active in each other's mouth, our feelings for each other and for the wonderment of the occasion rising in their intensity.

'Open your legs for me', she said between kisses.

As soon as she began stroking my clit I came. I just couldn't help myself. It just happened, and so quickly.

'Please don't stop', I whispered.

She brought me off once again with her fingers, then went down on me for a long period of expert tongue ministration. Two, three (?) more cums and I felt I should do something special for her.

'I want you to', she said, 'but let's just cuddle awhile until you've returned to the land of the living'. How considerate of her! We kissed again. She tasted of me.

In time I asked 'What would you like me to do for you?'

'I'd love your lips on my nipples, then your mouth on my cunt', she replied.

I spent ages on each of her firm, beautifully structured nipples. I knew I had the right pressure when she murmured aloud her pleasure. I stroked her face, kissed her again then wriggled down the bed and lay between her thighs.

The visual beauty of her slit was matched by the scent and juiciness of her cunt. I could not believe the sensations I got from her smoothness. Her lips were plumped up. When I finally got to her clit, which was prominent, I knew I was in heaven. I tried to emulate the techniques she had used on me and they worked. It did not take long for me to experience the joys of a woman cumming. She did not hold back, following my example.

"More, please . . .' she said almost inaudibly, her eyes closed, her inner thighs still quivering.

She had three more cums in quick succession, within the space of a few minutes.

'I need a cuddle', she murmured.

We cuddled and dozed. Eventually nature called and I went off to the bathroom. Evelyn followed soon afterward. I noticed a clock. It was heading towards midnight.

She put her arms around me, gave me a gentle kiss and said 'Let's go downstairs and have another glass of wine. We have all night'.

I chose to have white wine. She produced another bottle of the best. We sat, naked except for our stockings, on the individual lounge chairs. We spoke little, mostly kept our eyes closed, meditating and sipping. We finished about half the bottle, putting the rest in the fridge for later on.

'Time to go back up to the bedroom', she ventured. I nodded assent.

She turned on a bedside lamp to allow us to enjoy our bodies visually. A mirrored door on her wardrobe allowed us yet another perspective on our bodies and the action between us.

She reached into her bedside table and took out a latex penis, a butt plug and a tube of lubricant.

'You are the perfect person to do something really special for me', she said with a smile.

I watched as she put lube on a finger and inserted the finger into her bum hole, using the full length of the finger to get the lube right inside her. Her rounded bum cheeks were a delight to the eye, her crack and her dear little opening completely hairless. She reached back and pulled apart her bum cheeks.

'Put the plug in', she said.

I eased it in as far as the little flange would allow, thrilled at the sight of her bum ring expanding to accommodate the plug.

'Now put the other one in my cunt', she said.

The 'other one' was a substantial device, long and thick, with the moulded head of a penis. I parted her lips carefully and inserted the end of it.

'Fuck me with it!' Evelyn demanded. 'Stick it up my cunt!'

She lifted herself from the bed enough to get her fingers onto her clit. This was obviously one of her 'things'. She just let go, caution to the winds, body thrashing around, making all kinds of noises, thrusting back onto the device. When she came her body shuddered, she tossed her head, her bum cheeks jiggled, everything imaginable happened.

She fell forward, panting, gasping for breath, moaning her fulfillment. I simply waited, wondering what she would want next. It didn't take her long to tell me.

'Do that again', she said assertively. 'Harder this time!'

So I did, feeling a bit hesitant about the force I was using in her cunt. This time her cum was if anything more overpowering. I was amazed at how she could surrender herself to her dark side, a woman in sexual overdrive, abandoning herself to her instincts, blatant and joyous in her presentation of her body.

I withdrew both devices and set them aside, allowing me to cuddle Evelyn. She so obviously needed a sanctuary, a place of emotional refuge. She found it in my arms, she found it pressed against my breasts.

We dozed in each other's arms. Some time in the early hours she woke and her stirring woke me as well.

She went to her wardrobe and produced a strap-on device.

'Would you like me to use this on you?' she asked.

'No thanks', I replied, 'but I would love you to use your mouth on me again'.

So in the hours before dawn I lay on the bed, legs wide apart, enjoying the skilled mouth of a woman very attuned to my needs and likes. I had a series of cums, all of them very forceful, rolling from one to the other. After each one she pressed on my clit with her tongue and waited until my responses had finished. And all through these cums the wicked woman had a fingertip in my bum. Somehow she managed to do it without her manicured fingernail doing me damage.

We woke around 9 am and showered separately. Our breakfast consisted of the last of the white wine from the night before. I declined the suggestion of coffee.

She rang me several times in following days, seeking a repeat episode. Work and domestic responsibilities, however, were overwhelming during that time and I was unable to make any time for her. Several weeks passed before a window of opportunity opened. I rang her office number to be told by her secretary that Evelyn was overseas. I wonder still if my unavailability had anything to do with her decision to leave the country.

I resolved to leave it to her to call me on her return but she never did.

Given that experience, would I have sex with a woman again? Yes, I would, if someone of Evelyn's class were to come into my life. She gave me something very special that night. I think I gave her something special, as well.

A Passionate Relationship

I'll tell you all you need to know about me. I'm Chuck (not my real name); I'm a lawyer in New York City; I'm separated from my wife; she has the home and the two teenage kids; and I rent an apartment adjacent to Central Park. Oh, and I'm almost fifty years of age.

For several years, until recently, I had a passionate casual relationship with a woman I'll call Lesley (not her real name).

My long time lover Lesley is a divorcee. She lives in an ex-nunnery, a simply magnificent old brick home with a slate roof. It contains one particular room that I christened The Room. It is the only room I have ever entered that put me immediately in mind of sex.

The Room is long and wide with a polished wooden floor; high pressed patterned ceiling with chandelier; fireplace, bay window; black grand piano; sofa and a specially purchased single easy chair, of which more below.

Lesley and I have had many sexual adventures, not one of them unsatisfactory. I will detail a few that come to mind from our times together.

1 Lesley left work early and met me at my place feeling mightily pissed off over events that day at work where she held a management role in real estate. I knew immediately what to do to relieve her tension. I took her into the foyer and shut the door. I reefed off her panties, jammed my forearm between her legs and said: 'Now get off,

quickly!' She came within a minute or two, a massive one. I had to support her afterward. After that she was fine and we repaired to her water bed.

2 She had a day off work. We spoke by phone and she said: 'You know what I've talked about having you do to me? Well today's the day'. She opened the front door of her place, naked, and led me to The Room. She leaned against the door, facing me. I knew from memory what she wanted. I stripped off then unceremoniously went straight into her cunt, fucking her like fury. Lesley is capable of vaginal orgasms and she had a monster of a cum. Without losing momentum she turned around and made her bum available to me. I went straight up her little hole which she had lubed up beforehand. This time she fingered her clit to a second massive orgasm. I lost my load this time. After that it was shower time and wine in the sun in her garden. Her mood was very subdued.

3 I found her front door ajar. I entered The Room to find her dressed only in a tiny g-string. We kissed with great passion, then I turned her around, pulled the string aside and did the deed in vigorous fashion. Having got that out of our system it was onto the water bed.

4 Lesley is a gourmet cook and a wine connoisseuse whose palate is far superior to mine. She had set up a table and chairs in The Room and had prepared a lovely lunch which she served with one of her best wines. There was lots of touching, smiling, eye contact. When we'd eaten I directed her to take off her panties, sit on the sofa and get herself off for me, not taking her eyes off mine, while I unzipped and stroked my cock while sipping the last of my wine and rubbing her panties on my face. She is a very strong-willed woman but sometimes she just likes to be told what to do, to have someone else make the decisions, especially in bed. She became very intensely aroused by being told to keep her eyes on mine as she worked her clit to a big and noisy cum.

I then led her to the special chair, a single one with a curved back, nicely upholstered, a genuine antique. She kneeled on it, facing away from me. I pulled up her flimsy russet coloured dress, my favourite of hers, and took her from behind, her gorgeous bum all on show. We took our time. She had two or three orgasms before I found myself passing the point of no return. We then showered together, taking turns to piss on each other, she down my leg, me pulling her bum cheeks apart and pissing on her bum hole, drawing a shriek of laughter from her.

5 We arrived at her house at the appointed time. She sent me off to the kitchen to open a bottle of NZ sauvignon blanc and to fetch two glasses. As I walked towards the door of The Room I could hear the first movement of Beethoven's 'Moonlight' Sonata. I entered The Room to find her clad only in tiny black panties at the keyboard. I took a seat and watched while sipping on the white. We finished a glass each then ripped into each other, standing up, on the single chair, in her bed.

5 Funny one: how to lose a bet. We were in a Vegas hotel room for a weekend. We'd taken a limo to the hotel from the airport and had kissed and cuddled and groped in adolescent fashion all the way. In the hotel room things heated up and Lesley took my cock in her hand. We were both in need of dinner but fooled around for a few minutes before going out. We both became aware of a long strand of prostate fluid making its way towards the carpet. We stopped kissing and just watched, fascinated. Lesley bet me the cost of dinner that it would not reach the floor without breaking. I said it would as it passed my knee, unbroken. About a foot from the carpet it broke off, to her hilarity. Bet lost! She made sure she ordered a very good wine.

6 Lesley & I had our first fuck in the Marriott Marquis on Broadway, where I was meeting a client for a social drink. The client couldn't stay long and Lesley rang me, saying she needed company. I took a room. It was a Friday and I didn't have to go into the office next day.

We did all the usual acts of passion and had a great time. Her sexual appetite is phenomenal. I'll mention a lesser happening, however, for its fun. We were enjoying a beer in a bar and were close enough for me to slip my hand up her skirt for a feel. Sipping on a beer, stroking a woman through her panties, watching her eyes for signs of appreciative response . . . How good was that?

We became aware of a fellow having his dinner across from us, showing the signs of having had one beer too many. He must have had a clear view of what we were doing. He nearly choked on his food and his eyes got all wide and stary. We laughed about it and kept the show going until we had finished our beers.

7 Once every so often Lesley likes a cock up her delightful bum. Her need for bum sex is impulsive. It just happens for her. I had to learn to understand this impulse and to accommodate its urgency. Fortunately she was very easy to enter through the back door. We rarely used lube.

The erotic potential of her bum hole was almost beyond male comprehension. Even a slight finger touch there would draw a spasming response from her.

8 We both sleep fitfully and for that reason will wake at say 4 am and have it off. She adores the sensations when I practise the noble art of clit lifting, an art I have perfected simply through practice. If practice improves a golf swing, why should it not improve skills with the clit?

9 I can recall vividly one dark early morning when Lesley reached behind her for my cock, got me hard, slipped me into her cunt . . . and promptly fell asleep again, as did I. We can still get a giggle out of that occasion. Sex has many memorable moments that don't involve frenzied thrusting and momentous orgasms.

10 We would sometimes picnic at a special spot in Central Park. It was of course far too public for anything other than a stolen kiss or two. Lesley would, however, compensate by sitting up the grassy slope a bit from me and lifting her skirt so that I could look up it. She is a lingerie freak so I had many a look at expensive panties, some of them ridiculously small.

11 Flying back to NYC after a weekend in Vegas where she calculated we had spent 22 hours in bed in a hotel, Lesley coughed

and had a cum leak. She sat in a big wet spot for about half the flight. She ducked into a toilet at JFK. When she emerged she stuffed the panties into my coat pocket and hissed:

'You messed them, you wash them!'.

12 Lesley does marvellous panty parades for me, otherwise dressed in only black stay-up stockings and black leather shoes (2 of my other fetishes). She parades 5 pairs, making me close my eyes until she is ready to appear and parade herself. Mostly we do this before going out to dinner. It is my choice which pair she will wear. I find it incredibly exciting to make the choice, then to sit knowingly through dinner, then to take them off. Shivers!

13 Lesley catered to all my fetishes (7 in all), one of which was my need for mild dominance. Lesley had an antique dish of great beauty that she bought for me to wash her panties in. I only ever got to do it a few times but the emotional impact on me was nearly overwhelming. She would come in the door of my apartment, take her panties off and toss them to me in an abrupt manner saying: 'I'll get myself a glass of wine. You get busy washing these'. She would watch as I washed, chatting away. I would get my glass of wine only when the panties had been rinsed and placed on a special little line in a shaded place on the balcony.

14 A variation was for her to order me to lie down, whereupon she would raise her skirt and press her panties onto my face, sometimes almost to the point of 'smothering'. The rest of our ritual would then proceed.

15 Lesley had a high stress, high performance job. She supervised a staff and was involved in negotiating some pretty big property deals. Sometimes this strong-willed woman just needed to be told what to do, to be almost submissive.

It's great that memories can flood back. Nice to have memories in the first place!

Afterthought on the notion of female permissiveness, again from a woman in a high performance role. I fucked her twice, once in LA and a second time in London. I had never encountered a true sub before and I wasn't certain how to deal with this one. I won't dwell on details but she repeatedly called me 'Master' as she plaintively responded to her body being used in, shall I say, somewhat unconventional ways including objects.

It takes all types, it does. I thought that I'd experienced just about everything about sex, admittedly an egoistic thought. How wrong I was!

Working Woman

*W*hen the company where I'd worked for 14 years went belly-up I found myself looking for a job. I had 2 kids to support and an ex who was not paying support regularly and whose whereabouts were unknown. I was 35.

I had a string of interviews without success. Maybe if I'd taken my education more seriously I would not have found myself in this position.

By chance I saw an advertisement seeking women 'of all ages' to work in an 'escort agency'. My bank account was running down fast and I needed something in a hurry so I rang the number and was invited for an interview.

I'd looked after my body and was reasonably good looking and I thought I could fill the bill. A friend styled my hair. I put on my little black number and went off feeling confident. Frankly, I had to be as this was the only alternative I could see to life on welfare, something I did not wish to contemplate.

A blonde woman of around 50 interviewed me. She put me at ease and encouraged me to speak my mind and not to be nervous. She was very frank about the requirements of the job. I would have to be flexible in my hours to suit the clients. I would have to be open minded about some of the things I'd be asked to do. Safe sex was guaranteed. Some of the clients would be downright kinky though that would involve things I would do to them, not them to me.

Some jobs would require me to travel to a venue, generally a hotel, but most jobs would be on the premises. I was given a tour of the facilities. There were rooms and ensuites set up for action. I was introduced to the girls working the day shift, seven in all. Most looked younger than I though one of them was older. The boss explained that she had several older women on the books, all of whom were in demand from clients.

'You'd be surprised how many men ask for an older woman', she told me.

The money on offer sounded good to me. Cash up front or pre-paid by credit card to a neutral-sounding business name. I was happy with my share. I had no choice.

I'd be provided with a personal alarm and a phone number for security. The woman told me that they rarely had problems with clients. Anyone who caused trouble was immediately ejected by a security guard.

'I run a tight ship, for the girls and the clients', she said. 'Please understand that'.

'That's fine by me', I replied.

'When can you start?' she asked.

'Whenever you like', I said. 'The only thing is that I have two kids and I'd prefer not to work too much in their time at home. Day work would suit me better. Is that possible?'

'We get lots of requests from day clients, mostly married guys whose wives are not giving them what they want. Let's see how things pan out for you. Tell me if you find yourself inconvenienced. I'm sure we'll work something out'.

She briefed me on hours, clothing requirements and pay conditions . . . oh, and no kissing or unprotected sex. Meals were provided. Alcohol was limited to socialising with clients who preferred to get comfortable by having a drink. I was advised to limit myself to sipping.

I filled out a form with my details and handed it to the woman on the front desk.

John Boase

'Give yourself a couple of days to sort out your home routines', the boss said. 'Let's say that you turn up here 3 days from now. I'll start you on 10 till 3'.

'Thanks. I'll be here'.

I had my very first client at 10.30 on day one. He looked the businessman type, all suited up. I was told that he was a regular. The boss chose me for him, telling him I was new to the scene and that he would enjoy my company. He ran his eyes over me, liked what he saw and started up the stairs, obviously knowing where he was going.

My heart was thumping. How would things start? Would I make the first move or would he?

He solved my problem by undressing forthwith. I suppressed a giggle at his snowy white singlet and y-fronts. Oh, so conventional!

I followed him, stripping as he sat on a chair and watched. His penis was hard, average size, his balls the same.

'Bend over onto the bed', he instructed, rising from the chair and rolling on a condom.

He took me from behind, with a sense of urgency.

It was all over quickly! He grunted a couple of times as he came, then pulled out and put the condom in the container provided. He dressed and thanked me, telling me he would ask for me next time. The boss told me that he turned up every Thursday before going to the office.

'He's a fast one, isn't he?' she said with a laugh.

'That's the easiest money I've ever made!' I replied.

'He sometimes likes it up the bum, I have to tell you. Is that a problem for you?'

'No, but I might baulk at a really big cock up my bum'.

'That's ok. I don't force any girl to do something against her will. I've got girls who'll take the big ones, in either hole'.

I serviced two other clients during my shift. The first was a retired gentleman of very distinguished appearance.

'Look after him', the boss confided. 'He's a widower. He uses Viagra but might take a while to get it up. He likes to talk about his daughters and grandkids. He's popular with the girls. He's very gentle'.

He was frank about his cock.

'I take a while', he confessed with a smile, 'but I do enjoy chatting with a naked woman'.

After 15-20 minutes he asked me to put my hand on his cock. It responded with a couple of strokes. He looked pleased with himself.

'How do you want me?' I asked.

'Would you get on top of me?' he inquired as he rolled on the mandatory protection.

I rode him slowly to start. He put his hands on my tits and stared at them. He complimented me constantly, telling me how good my cunt felt (he didn't actually use the word 'cunt').

'I can take a long while to cum', he said. 'I hope you don't mind'.

I smiled at his remark.

'Let's take you along and see how you go', I replied. 'Now you get on top'.

I got lively as soon as he was in. I 'talked the talk' to him, telling him how much I wanted his cum inside me. He picked up the pace but I really think it was the talk that got to him. He suddenly tensed up, tossed his head and rammed his cock right in.

'Dear god!' he exclaimed as he came.

We lay still, side by side, for a few minutes afterward. He kept thanking me for giving him such a good time.

'I'll ask for you next time I visit', he said as he dressed. 'I loved the way you talked to me. Oh, and this is a little something for you'.

He handed me a hundred dollar note.

I wondered about accepting it, house rules being what they were.

'It's ok, Elaine (the boss) knows that I give tips. She won't ask you about it'.

The whole episode had taken around 45 minutes. I was warming to this work!

My other client on the day dropped in during his lunch hour. Elaine steered him to me, telling him that I was new and pretty willing. He was middle aged, balding and physically overweight, very unattractive. I undressed for him. He gazed at my body for a minute or so then undressed to reveal a stiff, funny little willy poking out from under a hairy beer belly.

He sat on the bed and motioned me to put on his condom. Without further ado he got between my legs and put his cock in. I smiled inwardly. Is it in, I thought idly? I could hardly feel his little fellow frisking around inside!

He grunted and thrust around. I felt I had to give him the hurry-up so I used the talk routine again. Guess what? It worked! He upped the ante as soon as I started talking, the coarser the words, the more worked up he got. Maybe I had discovered something!

A couple of big grunts and he came. He flopped on top of me, an experience I could have done without. I'm not into obese men but a client is a client. Conscious of the time he climbed off me and walked his hairy bum to the bathroom, then got dressed. He'd dropped the condom on the carpet. I picked it up gingerly with tissues, hating to have to do it. It was full of cum. He'd had a big one.

I offered to escort him downstairs but he waved me off. I guess he know his way out.

I asked Elaine if she could direct him to someone else next time.

'I can try', she said, 'but if he wants to pay his money for you, that's the deal'.

I loved the money I was making. Elaine was a generous boss, always solicitous of the welfare of her women. When I proved my worth and gained my regulars she and I enjoyed a warm relationship.

As a favour to her I did a few evening jobs, usually at short notice. She always paid me extra for those times. She even paid me for a house sitter so the kids would have company. I guess the expense went on the bill for the client.

I learned about my clients, what they liked, what they didn't like, what their fantasies were. Most of them were married men. I never felt that I was party to cheating. Elaine was providing a service and these men were availing themselves of it, simple as that. If the men weren't getting it at home, I could provide it.

My regulars included the older man I've talked of and two others, one a widower, the other whose wife suffered dementia and lived in a nursing home. He visited her every day. He used to talk about her to me. One time we didn't even fuck, just talked of his life with her. Tears came into his eyes as he spoke.

'I still need sex', he would tell me. 'I hope you don't think I'm going behind my wife's back with you'.

'I'm sure I'd approve of our arrangement if I were in her position', I assured him. 'She'd want you to be happy'.

He was a fifty dollar tipper, cash in the hand, each fortnight that he visited.

I could go on and on about clients but frankly it would sound repetitive. I masturbated for some, I faked plenty of cums, I gave lots of hand jobs. I found myself more involved with my older men, really feeling well disposed towards them personally. With many of them I would feign goodwill but let my mind wander elsewhere. One chap I used to think of as my 'shopping list man'. I'd make noises of encouragement as he fucked while working out what I needed at the supermarket after work!

I did anal for a few but not for big cocks. Elaine knew that and directed the big ones to other girls. I lubed myself well and took things carefully. The good part of anal was that they didn't last long. My record was about three thrusts before he came. He was gone as soon as he got in. I wondered if that was his first time in a woman's bum. Dollar per minute he was excellent value for the house and my purse, that's for sure.

I'll mention only one other client for whom I did a couple of calls at his home where he lived alone, his wife having divorced him. Elaine had told me he was into bondage and gave me the option of not doing the home visit.

'Is he safe to be with?' I asked. 'I'm not into heavy stuff myself but I'm happy to do it for clients'.

'See what you think', she said and gave me his address. 'He's a real sub, believe me'.

JOHN BOASE

Was he ever! He greeted me cordially and led me to his cellar. On one side was a huge wine rack, full of bottles. On the other side, embedded into the bricks, were handcuffs and ankle braces.

'Please be rough with me', he said when naked, sporting a very big erection. 'I have been a very, very naughty boy and I need to be punished'.

I stripped down to my panties.

'Please leave on your high heels', he said plaintively, 'and your stockings'.

'Fine by me', I thought as I cuffed him and restrained his ankles, his face to the wall.

The toys for his punishment were in a rack. I selected a whip with three long leather strands with knots on the ends.

'Have you been bad? Confess if you have been so that I can punish you!'

He was on the verge of weeping as he confessed.

'Shit', I thought. 'What have I got myself into here?'

Oh well, not to think, just get down to work and role playing.

I used the whip on his flabby hairless buttocks, each time leaving red marks, each time eliciting cries of helplessness and contrition. I whipped his back and thighs for good measure.

'Now, you fucking worthless excuse for a man, I want you to pull yourself off while I watch'.

'Oh, please mistress, please let me cum!'

I'd read the situation correctly!

I released him from his shackles and ordered him to sit on a chair. He really did have an impressively sized cock, I thought to myself. He'd have been a 'no way' for my bum, that's for sure!

He started pulling himself while on the chair but I had another idea.

'Get on your knees, you wretched piece of humanity! Pull yourself off and cum on the floor where your cum belongs'.

'Yes mistress, yes, yes, yes!' he whimpered as he obeyed my command.

'Pull on it! Get yourself off! Don't waste my time! Don't be any more pathetic than you have to be!'

I watched as he pulled on his cock, weeping as he did so.

'You're taking too long! Get yourself off!' I demanded, having looked at my watch.

'Aaaaaahhhhhhh!!!' he cried loudly as he went over the top.

He laid three good spurts on the carpet then followed up by squeezing out a few drops.

'Eat your cum!' I told him. 'Lick it off the floor!'

He did as he was told, gasping in submission.

I was relentless with him.

'Turn around. Get on your knees!'

'Yes, mistress. Anything you say!'

I gave his bum another whipping. His balls were hanging low and I reckon the tips of the whip would have made them sting as well.

He eventually fell forward onto the chair, his body heaving.

I got dressed.

'I'm leaving now. Don't you think—don't think!—of being a naughty boy again or I'll have to punish you again, you know that, don't you?'

'Yes, mistress', he whispered in reply.

I found my own way out of the house.

'What did you do to him?' asked Elaine a week or so later when she showed me his obituary. His death was ascribed to 'a heart attack'. I did wonder if I had contributed!

I did three years in the working mode before Elaine offered me the management of the business. I've now been in that role for two years and I love my work.

My mortgage is paid off and I've got a new man in my life, in fact one of my regular clients.

The kids are fine and life has never been better!

Elaine has broached the subject of selling the business. I've got first offer. She's prepared to lend me the money. She's not short of a buck.

It's worth a thought. I could be a Madam!

Hubby's Friends

*I*f what you seek is a story of conventional, squeaky good wifely behaviour then you'd better look elsewhere. What follows is a candid account of my sex life and an honest analysis of where my sex drive has taken me.

Does what follows qualify me to be a slut wife? Judge for yourself.

Am I proud of where I've gone and where I'm going? Not particularly, but then I don't despise myself either. Everyone gets driven by circumstance. I'm no different. My circumstances will become apparent.

Some months back my husband and three of his friends had their monthly Saturday night card game at our house. For the previous couple of meetings hubby had prevailed on me to greet his friends on arrival, dressed only in an apron and thong. I feel a bit funny clad in that combination but I was told that's what they wanted. It was also my job to keep up the supply of beers and snack food to them. I had to make sure they got a look at my tits when I bent forward, as well as the obvious look at my bum exposed by the apron. Hubby rehearsed me to make sure I got all the angles right.

Until that night they had only looked. That night, however, one of them came into the living room where I was watching tv and made sexual advances to me. By 'advances' I mean putting his hands on my tits and making drunkenly suggestive remarks. I fobbed him off, nicely but firmly, and he returned to the game.

When I took the next lot of beers and pretzels into the game that night I got a different reception than the usual expressions of ribald appreciation. One man led the way in putting his hands on my bum cheeks and was followed in turn by the others. I looked at hubby for guidance. All he did was smile, lift his beer as if proposing a toast and wink encouragement.

'Take it all off', came the suggestion. 'Let's see everything you've got'. That comment provoked whistling and clapping.

Hubby again winked his assent.

Hesitating momentarily, I went ahead and took off the apron to renewed applause. I'm not your slender, willowy young thing and I carry plenty of padding but I've got big tits and I present, in hubby's words, as 'a real woman'.

'Take your panties off too', came the cry when they'd had a look at my body.

'I'll take them off for you', declared one of the men and dropped on his knees to do the deed. He got a loud cheer when he put a kiss on my mound.

'Turn around slowly', someone said.

'Jeez, I'd like a piece of that action', said another voice.

'Me, too', said yet another voice.

'Can I land my plane on that landing strip?' said another.

It was crude talk but something about it hit the spot with me. I didn't, however, let on. They could earn their way into my pants, if that were to be the case.

I took their empty beer cans on a tray and caught hubby's eye, nodding my head to indicate that I wanted to speak with him privately.

'What the fuck is going on?' I asked. 'Am I being set up for sex?

'Would you like to have sex with them?' he asked with a leer. 'They're pretty keen. They've told me so for ages. What do you think?'

'I need to think about it', I said. 'Maybe I will but not this time'.

With that I took myself off to bed. If they wanted more beers they could serve themselves.

Here I need to provide some background information so you can understand the context of my sex life.

Hubby and I had been married for seventeen years. We had two kids, both of whom were having sleepovers that night. Hubby's sex drive had gone off the boil, due mainly to his increasing dependence on alcohol. He was too damned stupid to seek help for his growing addiction and too damned proud to ask the doctor for the blue pill. In his terms that would have meant confessing to diminished masculinity which would have been acutely embarrassing, demeaning of his manhood.

'They're for old men', he said when I broached the subject. He didn't want to talk about his declining sexual interest or performance. He'd simply walk away, physically and mentally. Sex was off the agenda for discussion, except it seemed when it came to his mates.

I'd found myself increasingly reliant on self-help. That's fine to a point as it is for most women but I felt hurt at being deprived of an urgent, thrusting man on top of me, being able to excite him to the point of cumming, rejoicing in the feeling of a load in my cunt. And I tired of feeding my arousal with fantasies instead of responding to a real body in a real life situation. Heck, I wasn't 40 and I was experiencing the sex life of what I imagined a woman twice my age would have.

More confessions! I'm not a classical beauty (!) I came to know this during high school days, when my approaches from the opposite sex were few. In my last year, out of desperation to feel sexy and wanted, I gave three boys a blow job when one of them had the run of his family home for a day. I swallowed the load from each of them, wantonly so. I let them finger me but not fuck me. A friend of mine had found herself pregnant after a tipsy fling and I had enough sense not to take risks. Unfortunately one of the boys boasted about their 'success' with me and word got around the senior school, earning me the reputation as a girl of sluttish disposition. It was fine, it seemed, to fuck a boy (as many of the girls had) but to take on more than one was to be a 'slut'.

I had the prospect of exploring my capacity to excite three men—though they were influenced by alcohol—and to gain the sexual satisfaction I so desperately needed and wanted . . . or, to continue my journey of frustration and, frankly, heartache. Stupidly or not I was starting to be conscious of my age and starting to lose confidence in my ability to attract and excite a man.

So . . . in this situation I found myself having to come to terms with a lot of things!

In the ensuing month until their next game I thought a lot about the prospect of servicing three men. I knew them all. That was a big plus, as was the fact that I quite liked them all. None of them had the looks of Cary Grant but their faces were pleasant. They all had lively personalities, especially when they'd had a beer or two. They all had hard bodies, the product of physical work in their jobs.

Importantly for me they were all clean shaven. One thing was sure: if I agreed to take them on they would need to have smooth faces. I'm not into whisker rash!

I revived my memories of the three boys at high school. In all honesty, I had to admit that I had enjoyed the sense of power that I had exercised over those lads. I had relished the satisfaction of drawing sperm from each of them. I had loved the smell and taste of semen. And I had loved the feeling of their hands on my tits and bum and their fingers in my cunt.

Hubby kept at me for an answer. I got the impression that he was getting his jollies from wanting to be seen as the provider of services. He didn't always say so in words. Sometimes he would simply put on a silly grin and raise his eyebrows. I knew what he meant.

In that month hubby and I had sex only once. It was a disaster. He couldn't stay hard. He rolled off and went to sleep. When he started snoring I went into the second bedroom and shut the door. I cried myself to sleep.

My sense of self worth was at rock bottom. I kept asking myself if I'd contributed to the mess that our marriage had become. Had I not told him often enough that I loved him? Had I done something to upset him? Was his growing reliance on alcohol in response to shortcomings on my part? Was I no good in bed? I was beset by self-doubt.

I concealed my despair from the kids, of course. I gave them no hint of my feelings. Fortunately hubby never let them see him under the influence of grog.

It was those last few beers or glasses of wine that did the trick. Many's the time I'd had to wake him with the telly still on. He'd never be too far gone and could always make his own way to bed. Mind you, he blotted his copybook with me the time that he woke with a big patch of piss on the front of his shorts. Thank god none of it got onto the lounge! I made sure that he used the toilet after that before getting into bed!

Would giving myself to his friends be a tacit admission of low self-esteem, a cowardly and sleazy way of evading the truth? Or on the other hand, would it be a way of regaining hubby's love and respect, being seen to be willing to fulfil a dream for him? Or would it take our relationship further down the path it was on? I'd read that shared sex will never save a marriage but sometimes one's mental and emotional state doesn't heed advice. One's thinking is not always rational.

From my point of view I had to admit that I'd loved the sense of adventure I'd experienced with the three boys in school days. Should I approach this present matter from that angle and see it as some kind of self-indulgence, for me and only me? Could it not put a spark into my life at a time when there were no sexual sparks? 'Why not?' could perhaps be the way to think about it. I could be the user rather than the used!

'The lads are keen to know your answer', said hubby a few nights out from Saturday's game. 'So am I. Go on, be a devil!'

I told him I'd give my answer by the Thursday night.

I sat through Thursday going over everything, knowing that decision time had arrived. I went through a bottle of white wine in the process. I needed all the help I could get!

When the kids had gone to bed I joined hubby in the lounge room. I turned down the telly sound and made my announcement without delay or explanation.

'I'll do it', I said, 'but no one should assume that it will happen a second time. Make sure they all understand that'.

'Wow!' exclaimed hubby and went off to the phone. No 'Thank you', no kiss on the cheek, no show of gratitude, just 'Wow!'

On the Friday I felt some misgivings and doubts but I had made up my mind and that was that! I resolved to think only of the potential adventures involved, not to dwell on anything else.

Two of them were married but I'd never met their wives. I felt no sense of remorse at betraying a fellow woman. All men think with their dicks and these guys would not be the first to go looking for nookie away from the marital bed.

I resolved not to insist on condoms. I thought I could trust the guys and I really wanted to feel their cum inside me, not caught up in a little bubble to be flushed away. Let's face it, I'd not known the feeling of cum for a long time.

I spent a lot of time on my makeup and grooming. I don't have film star looks but I can still tart up to make myself feel good. I enjoyed this part of the exercise. It had been a long time since I had last dressed for effect.

What to wear? Certainly not an apron! How tacky had that been? I chose a cream top, a long black skirt, black bra and panties, black high heeled shoes and black stockings.

As an afterthought I had my hair done on the Saturday afternoon. I couldn't remember the last time I'd been to a hairdresser. I felt wonderful as I showed my new hair to the world. Hubby didn't notice, needless to say, but our daughter thought it looked really good, bless her.

I sat outside in the sun at home and did my nails. I'd trimmed my pubes the day before but not closely enough for them to be prickly.

This girl was going to present as the complete package!

Before taking a bath I put fresh linen on the big bed. Hubby drove the kids to their friends' houses where they would spend the night.

I'd told hubby of certain requirements, without which there would be no action:

clean fingernails, smoothly shaven, smart casual clothes, hair to be tidy, freshly showered with a touch of aftershave, must wear shoes. I didn't want much, did I?

Josh arrived first, just before seven. Check shirt, fawn pants, brown casual shoes all met my approval. He winked and held out his hands for me to check his nails. I made much of inspecting them before nodding my satisfaction. He's tall and blonde, has mischievous blue eyes and short hair.

'Been to the barber recently?' I asked. 'Today, perhaps?'

'You got it', he replied.

I eased against his body and kissed him on the lips. He wanted to go on with it, there and then, but I put a finger on his lips and told him to be patient as I had two others to greet. His pants were sticking out in the right place. He hadn't taken long! Hey, that was encouraging, I could still stir a man!

Andy and Joe arrived together.

'She'll want to see your fingernails', called out Josh.

Both men dutifully held out their hands for inspection. Both made the grade.

'How did you know that white shirts turn me on?' I said to Joe before giving him a welcome kiss.

Andy looked good in a short-sleeved red shirt with grey pants and black casual shoes. He'd used more after shave than the others. All three men smelt sexy.

We sat around in the lounge room. Joe and I had white wine, the others drank beer. I'd told hubby that I wouldn't allow them to drink beer from a can or bottle. It had to be out of a glass. I hope it doesn't sound as if I was being too bossy. I'd made up my mind that we were going to do everything properly. The men would have to shape up socially as well as sexually.

When we'd finished our drinks hubby produced a deck of cards. As always he'd set up a card table in the living room.

'Do we really need those?' asked Josh whose horny response to my kiss at the door had obviously got to him.

'Maybe not for long', I said with a laugh. Having gone to all the trouble I had, I certainly wasn't going to play seconds to a pack of cards. I smiled to myself. I was holding all the aces!

I waited for thirty minutes. I was really in the mood for some fun and some good sex. It had been a long time since I had felt this way. My nipples were brushing against my bra and my thong was giving my clit a good time. It was the longest half hour of my life.

I was determined to orchestrate events. I appeared in the living room and said to 'fold 'em' forthwith. I used the hand control to start a CD of big band jazz, slow moody pieces.

I shut my eyes and pointed in the direction of the men.

'Whoever I'm pointing out, come here and dance with me'.

Andy took me into his arms and we shuffled around on the carpet. I put my head against his chest, my arms around him. He whispered a compliment about my perfume (I didn't tell him that I'd had difficulty finding the bottle, so long had it been since I'd used it!). He insisted on a second track. I could feel his hard-on.

Josh took tracks three and four. I think he was hard before he got to me! During the second track his hands strayed to my bum. He knew instantly that I was wearing a thong and murmured his appreciation.

Joe was hard by the end of the first track. He took his lead from Josh and put his hands on my bum cheeks, drawing me into his body.

Hubby's turn?

No, he had told me beforehand that he only wanted to watch, not take part.

It was stripping time!

'Take out your cocks', I instructed, in my warmest, sexiest tones.

Whooska! Three hard ones emerged.

I used the next couple of tracks to gradually reveal the goods. I'm a reasonable dancer so my movements and rhythms were natural, not affected.

Things really hotted up when I took off my bra. As I've said, my tits are pretty big and pretty good, if I do say so myself. I tailored my movements to make them sway provocatively. Three sets of eyes were riveted on them.

I kept on my stockings and thong.

Josh—the horny devil!—pleaded to be allowed to take off my panties but I wagged my finger at him and told him to wait. He was the one who'd taken off my panties at the previous game. He was showing up as a panty man for sure!

I went down on each man in turn, just enough to get them attuned to the mood I was in. They were all moany and groany, poor chappies. I thought of the three boys of earlier years, how easy I had found it to control them with my mouth.

'Gotcha!' I said inwardly as each man surrendered to me in body and mind.

'Clothes off and lie side by side on the carpet. Leave a little space between you'.

I kneeled and fondled eack cock with my hand. All were wonderfully hard and eager looking. John and Joe were of average size, looking businesslike. Andy was the surprise packet, with an inch or more on the others. He was also thicker, mouthwateringly so. I debated with myself whether to have him first or last.

All sets of balls were tight and tense, a cum freak's delight.

I took off my thong and draped it over Andy's big one. I then 69d each man, loving the sensations of their tongues on cunt, clit and bum hole, loving their hands spread on my bum cheeks. When Andy's turn came I told the others to share play with my thong.

'Bed time', I announced when I'd got up from Andy. I chanced to look over at hubby, having virtually eliminated him from the moment. He had a grin on his face and a hand on his cock. He was having no trouble sustaining hardness in this context.

I led them upstairs, giving an exaggerated and perhaps silly waggle of my hips and bum.

'What the hell', I thought. 'In for a penny . . .'

'I need to visit the bathroom', I said. 'Leave room for me down the middle of the bed'.

I emerged to find Andy and Joe on the bed with Josh standing at the foot of the bed. All three had their hands on their cocks. Within seconds I had a mouth on each nipple and two sets of hands stroking my body. Then Josh moved my legs apart and went down on me.

Andy, then Joe kissed me, Andy with more urgency. I could feel his tongue talking to me!

Josh's tongue was in overdrive on my clit. The pent-up sexual tension in me had to find release and it did—twice—blowing away body and soul.

I had to have cock!

'I want you in me', I whispered into Joe's ear. I'd decided to leave the biggest until last.

Josh took Joe's place alongside me. Joe got into position then eased his cock into me.

A cock in my cunt, a mouth on each nipple, hands going everywhere! How good was this? I imagined that hubby was watching but I didn't bother to look for him. I was having too much fun!

I was prepared for the men to show different staying power. Dear Joe couldn't hold back for long. He told me over and over how good I felt, how tight my cunt was, how he'd dreamed of fucking me. The poor man just needed to unload! I helped his cause by murmuring into his ear:

'I want your cum!'

A few more thrusts and he lost his load. It felt like a big one but then, I'd not taken a load for a long time and perhaps it was just my imagination! Maybe a dribble would have felt like a big one!

'You next', I told Josh. He lasted longer but I still could sense the urgency of his need. I guess he'd also been aroused by watching Joe in action. His thrusting was strong and energetic.

When Josh pulled out I was very, very conscious of having a cuntful. Andy was eager to have his turn but I begged for a few minutes for recovery. Keeping my legs elevated for two men in turn had taken its toll, a nice toll perhaps but a toll nonetheless.

Andy's bigger cock felt incredible. I'd thought that my cunt might go all slack after Joe and Josh had had their way with me (or after I had had my way with them?). I don't know if that were the case but Andy's size made the question irrelevant. He stretched me and he felt fantastic!

'I'm sorry . . .' he said after he got wound up. 'I can't hold back . . . I'm sorry . . .'

He went berserk with his thrusting, grunting loudly. His hard, muscled thighs and bum cheeks were driving his cock into me. He let go with an enormous burst of energy.

Hubby got his jollies by jacking off onto my feet, then using his semen to massage them.

Whew! Where to go from there? What was the orchestrator to orchestrate next?

'Lick the cum from my cunt', I ordered hubby. 'There's plenty of it'.

As an afterthought I added:

'They're loads from real men who can get it up and in and fill a woman's cunt with cum. So lick it and feel how fucking hopeless you are'.

'Yes, yes, yes!' he cried as his tongue sought their semen.

Bloody hell, I had hit a chord with hubby! Years of marriage and I hadn't cottoned on to his fetish! He wanted to be a cuckold! I had my first cum from his tongue in many years.

Josh soon came seeking me with a reinvigorated hard one but I kept him at bay.

'I need a rest', I said genuinely. 'Get me a glass of white wine'.

I put a hand towel under my cunt. I'd prepared well!

Josh and Andy took me again, both in my cunt, Andy from behind. This time around I used their cockheads for my own advantage, stroking my clit with them.

Joe inquired about taking me in the bum. He'd hinted at this earlier.

'The lube's in the drawer over there', I told him. I'd anticipated this request and had bought a tube of gel.

'Get my bum ready for Joe', I told hubby. 'Use plenty!'

'Yes . . . yes . . . yes . . . !' was all he could say as he put several fingerfuls inside.

Joe was gentle with my bum which I appreciated. I was comfortable with him in there and we worked up a rhythm that we both enjoyed. He kept telling me how tight I felt on his cock. He left a big load in my passage. Hubby finished off a second time on my bum cheeks, self-induced of course.

'I can't speak for you lot but I'm all fucked out', I announced. 'Let's all have a last drink downstairs'.

I gave my cunt and bum a wipe with a hand towel and threw on a robe.

I'd wondered how I'd feel in their company, after having fucked them each twice. I soon found the answer. I felt contented, even smug. I'd scored three strikes. I felt no diffidence or embarrassment whatsoever. Inwardly I was smiling.

All three gave me a hug and a kiss on departure, thanking me profusely for what Joe called 'an unforgettable night'.

Hubby cuddled up in bed and repeated:

'Thank you! Thank you!'

'Would you do it again with them?' hubby asked a couple of weeks later.

'No, I wouldn't', I replied. 'They were good but I wouldn't want to go around again with them'.

'Would you consider something else?' hubby asked.

'I might. What do you have in mind?' I inquired.

'Dogging', he responded.

I'll keep this phase brief. Out of curiosity a couple of weeks later we drove to a popular spot for dogging. We gave the signal for 'Watch, look in and touch' but I was not prepared to alight from the car to signal my availability for penetrative sex. I let hubby get me naked, then invite strangers to reach through the passenger window to feel me up or finger me. I lost interest rapidly and told hubby to get me out of there. It proved a sensible decision. Soon after we had left police raided the site and made arrests. I could have been one of them!

The anonymity and the riskiness of dogging were not my scene. I can still feel revulsion at the memory of even the limited participation that I allowed. I'd done it to see what was involved but I wished I hadn't. I had found it degrading.

Hubby then proposed a gang bang.

This was 'a giant leap for mankind' if ever there was one!

Hubby was jumping around like a dog begging for a meaty bone. He was doing everything but leave puddles of saliva and pre-cum on the floor.

To keep him happy and at bay I agreed to him exploring the possibilities—no more than that guaranteed! It would give him something to do and shut him up for a while.

He went onto a couple of swingers sites, then signed up with the one that looked more promising. He placed this ad:

'Couple, late thirties, seeking to arrange a GB involving the wife. Proposal is to meet at a high class city hotel, cost to be shared. Prior personal vetting of candidates will be necessary. Please, only genuine applicants, no wankers. Initial contact per email at (address given). Preferred age range thirty-five to-forty-five. Must be clean, well presented personally, of good character. Dimensions of manhood not important. If you meet these criteria and are attracted to this ad then get in touch. Those who are chosen will not be disappointed with the lady'.

The replies started arriving within the hour. Within a day we had over 30 expressions of interest, then 20 more on the second day. Hubby posted 'No more messages will be acknowledged'. He had enough to go on, he thought.

I found the process mildly amusing. I wasn't sure I was prepared to go along with it and I felt it misleading for him to be holding out an opportunity that might not even exist.

He showed me a printout of the list of those aspiring to get into my pants. He'd marked them 'Maybe' or 'No'.

43 of the 57 were clearly 'No'. They stamped themselves that way: by marginal literacy, by crudeness, by cock boasting and the like. I'd heard that the Internet is full of wankers and here was the evidence.

Hubby sent messages to the remaining fourteen seeking more information. Two didn't reply and thus eliminated themselves. Four showed their real selves and were crossed off the list.

He asked the remaining eight to provide a recent photograph. One said he didn't have a shot, which may or may not have been true. Hubby crossed him off.

I studied with interest the seven mug shots. The tired looking old baldy would have to look elsewhere, I declared. The first principle of sending a shot to get a woman's attention is surely to smile. The fresh faced young fellow would have to keep living in hope, however much he claimed to want sex with a married woman. The remaining five looked passable.

Hubby then asked each of them to state why they wanted to take part in a gangbang and what their attitude would be towards me. He requested a body shot and a cock shot and all of them met his request. Hubby put the shots on the telly screen and we studied all shots carefully: face, body, cock.

By this stage I was getting caught up in the exercise. Far from being a dalliance to keep hubby happy it was becoming a source of genuine arousal for me, so much so that when hubby went to a mate's place next day I looked again at the shots. My hand found its way into my panties for a couple of big cums.

It is, to say the least, a fascinating thing to look closely at the face of a man (the face that will hover over you during fucking); the body of a man (that will cover you); the cock of a man (that will go into your body); and the balls of a man (that will unload into your body).

Hubby decided not to meet the fellows, merely to contact them by phone. He put the phone on speaker so that I could listen. They all sounded ok, well spoken and courteous. They gave their ages: 53, 47, 45, 38 and 36. That sounded like a good range!

The final step was for me to speak to each of them. By then I was committed to going ahead. I was finding the exercise increasingly a bigger turn-on.

It took three evenings to make the calls. Each man just wanted to talk and to prolong the chat, never less than 30 minutes, in one case nearly an hour. Three of them owned up to being married, the other two were divorced. A couple of them started to tell me their life stories but I cut them off. The last thing I needed to know was what led to their divorce.

I told them of the need for unconditional discretion and they sought that assurance from me.

Each asked if he could have a photo of me.

'No, you'll have to wait for the real person', I replied. I stressed the need for safe sex and all said that they had expected that and had no problem with it. I surmised that the fellow who'd sent the side-on cock shot, with his knob hanging well below his ball sac, would have to wear 'large'.

We needed to set a date of mutual convenience. The married men preferred day time so as not to arouse the suspicions of their wives. The other two were happy with that arrangement. Hubby booked a room for a Friday on the day rate at a 5 star hotel, 10 am to 4 pm.

I prepared as before, with one additional step: at hubby's request I got myself waxed. We'd watched a few GB videos on a web site, seemingly a truly amateur site, and I'd noticed the frequency of brazilians. Hubby was thrilled when I showed it to him. He didn't, however, do anything about it.

On the drive to the hotel I reaffirmed my resolve to control the situation, certainly the tone and atmosphere of the happening. The men had all given a commitment to pleasuring me and I felt I could trust them.

Hubby and I arrived first and organised the room and the wine. The men arrived within minutes of each other. I greeted them with a kiss and a hug. They seemed pleased with what they saw, especially my big tits! No harm in that!

None of us was in the mood for extended conversation, especially yours truly. I finished my glass and ordered hubby to undress me, thus establishing his cuck status right from the beginning. His hands were shaking as he went about his task.

Their eyes nearly popped out of their heads when they got to see my tits. Funny about that! I'm happy with them. So were they, it seemed! Nothing wrong with that in the circumstances!

I did a short parade around the room in stockings and panties, giving them every reason to put their hands where it mattered to them at the time.

'Clothes off!' I ordered.

It was amusing to watch five men undressing simultaneously. Shoes, socks, shirts, underpants flying all over the place, piles of discarded items.

It was clit stimulating to see five naked men, each displaying a hard one.

My lascivious eyes sought the man who'd sent the side-on shot. Wow, his cock was impressive! His was the stand-out erection (sorry for the pun!) That biggie would make its presence felt, for sure! The others, however, did not disappoint and were true to their photos. This girl's cunt and clit were on fire!

My account of what followed has taken ages to reconstruct, sometimes from only fragments of memory. It's not easy to stay of rational mind when having sex with five men with one's cuck husband watching! If you doubt me, try it!

I sat them along the edge of the bed and put my mouth on each cock in turn, at the same time holding the cocks on each side with my hand. My palms soon became slippery with pre-cum. Each man gasped loudly as I put my mouth on him. I felt surges of arousal as I sensed the control I was exerting.

When I'd given the last one his introductory treat I took off my panties and showed my smooth slit.

'I can't take much more of this', I heard one of them say. 'This is fucking incredible'.

'Are you trying to tell me something?' I asked. 'Is there something on your mind?'

Hands were working cocks. I realized that I had to stop the tease and let them enjoy my body.

I crawled onto the bed, lay on my back and opened my legs. The atmosphere I had created had no room for foreplay.

'You first', I said, pointing at one of them. 'And you . . . and you . . . take a tit each'.

They rode me, condom clad, one after the other, each time in missionary mode. One would pull out, the next would go in.

There is an expression called 'cum bucket', a most inelegant phrase for a woman who is prepared to accept semen from several men at the one meeting, with or without condoms. I dislike the connotations of the word 'bucket'. I would, however, own up happily to be called a cum lover.

Which brings to mind another point. I do not share the turn-on that some women get from being slagged during group sex, being derided as a 'fucking slut', a 'fucking bitch' or the like. Each to her own, I guess, and I'm not criticizing my fellow females for having those preferences. Personally, I enjoy my sense of control over men. I would get nothing from being put down.

We're all different, aren't we? And that's how it should be in this life of ours!

The bedside clock said 11.50 am and I had extracted the semen of 5 men. 5 filled condoms lay on a tray next to the bed. No way was I going to let all their good stuff go to waste!

'Put their cum on my tits and belly', I instructed hubby.

He obeyed, meekly, squeezing the cum out of each condom.

'Now . . . massage me with it', I told him.

'Yes . . . yes . . .' he replied plaintively, his dick pointing north.

My fingers flew to my clit. A cum massage! Five cums to play with! I brought myself off twice, big ones. The men were sitting on the bed, watching.

'Now get yourself off!' I ordered hubby. 'Cum on my tits!'

I had learned quickly how worked up cucks become when watching their partners have it off with other men. Apparently not every cuck can keep it up in the presence of other men but hubby's need to cum was desperate.

'Oh fuck!' he yelled a minute or so afterward.

I lifted my head to watch his cock spurting onto my belly and tits.

From neck to belly button I was smeared with the cum of 6 men. The smell of cum was pervasive.

Things quietened down as we all took stock of the situation. A couple were showing signs of renewed interest but I needed a break. The physical effort involved in fucking several men is rarely mentioned in the literature. I had found from my limited experience that it is a major factor for the woman!

'Get me a drink, someone', I said as I took one of the chairs, sitting on a hand towel. A nice wrinkly-cocked waiter served me. He had a droplet of fluid in his dear little cock hole. I wiped it with a fingertip and rubbed it on my nose.

What followed, unrehearsed and unexpected, was an hour of chat, all of us uninhibitedly naked. Hubby rang room service for sandwiches. He took delivery at the door, dressed in his pants and shirt.

It was an interesting question for me, how to make things happen after lunch.

My lower back and hips were showing the signs of the workout they had had. I know we women are supposed to lay it on, full on, all the time but in practical terms our bodies can't always cope with prolonged sexual effort. Which is not to say that I didn't want more. I did! There would just have to be variations to man on top, woman's legs pointed upward!

One after the other they took me from behind, two of them with me on my side.

One inquired about bum sex but I wasn't in the mood for it and told him to get on with things in my cunt.

Bum sex is interesting, is it not? I can take it in my bum but I have to be disposed towards it. Was I a spoilsport, a traitor to my slut status, a coward when it came to the big question? Maybe, and who cares? 'Horses for courses, on the day', was my rationale.

Hubby repeated the massage, this time spreading freshly-shot cum all down my back and on my bum cheeks. Once again I felt a surge of female triumphalism.

The next hour or so was lost on me. I fell asleep, waking only when hubby shook my shoulder.

'Whass up? What's happening?' I asked, only half awake.

'They've gone', he said. It's a quarter to four and we have to be out of here by four'.

'Shit!' I thought, 'best have a shower'.

In the days following I had to come to terms with lots of things. Hubby kept telling me that 'the boys' wanted another go at me, and soon.

'Tell them to take a cold shower', I advised. 'I might be cooperative but I'm not the town bike'.

Hubby pestered me for days. I finally sat him down and gave him an ultimatum.

'I'll think about doing it again but only on these conditions:

'Cut down on the booze and get your manhood back. If you can't get it back within a month, go see the doc. Furthermore, pay more attention to me and get back to looking after my needs. We used to have a good sex life, in recent months it's been non-existent. If you do all of those things I'll think about having another bunch of men for you to watch'.

I thought he might baulk at my conditions but, to my surprise, he agreed to them all. I doled out a weekly drinking budget to ensure that he couldn't drink on the sly. As soon as he cut back on booze his libido returned and his cock performed as of yore.

I gather from what I read that our experience of using a gangbang to restore marital harmony is not the norm.

I'm not complaining.

It's worked for me.

It's shown me new dimensions on life.

And tomorrow is another day.

Fulfilling a Fantasy

Two girlfriends and I were chatting one evening over dinner and a glass of wine. The conversation turned to favourite female fantasies. On our second glass we agreed to share each other's favourites.

One fantasised being tied to a bed, even blindfolded as well, to experience the sense of helplessness as a man took her roughly.

The second wanted to have sex with one or two other women.

It came my turn to tell. My fantasy involved having several men touch me, kiss me, even fuck me. We would all be stylishly dressed to start, the men in black ties. They would be older men, distinguished looking. We would be in a beautiful old home with extensive grounds. I would be the only woman present.

'How many men do you think to have involved?' I was asked.

I'd never considered a precise number and I had to give the question much thought, finally answering 'Maybe 5 . . . or 6 . . .' In my fantasy world I thought I could handle that number.

Inevitably the question arose if we'd seek to realise our fantasies one day or simply cherish them to be imagined in private moments.

We sat in silence for a couple of minutes, trying to make up our minds about our true intentions.

I broke the silence.

'Tell you what, let's all commit to making it happen . . . say, within the next three years. Let's report back in three years, on this table in this restaurant. Let's make it a mutual dare'.

We looked at each other then burst into laughter.

'Well?' I asked and held out a hand to each of the others. We joined hands.

'Let's say 'Yes' together on a count of three'.

'1-2-3 . . . 'Yes!'

I took out my diary and recorded our pledge on the date of that day.

Several months passed before I began exploring web sites. It took ages but I finally identified two sites that looked promising. Both claimed to feature men of mature age with a disposition to group adventures.

Unfortunately one of them proved to be only a front for a paid dating site. The second site, however, seemed authentic. I set up a false identity and a discrete email address then sent a message to the address provided.

'I am an attractive woman, 27 years of age, unattached at the moment. I could be interested in having discussions with your people about a possible meeting. Get in touch if you wish. No fakes, please. Emily'.

I had a reply within a day.

'We are a group of older men who get together a couple of times each year for a formal dinner at one of our homes. Our fourth such dinner is scheduled for eight weeks time. We've hired a stripper for each of our previous dinners. Are you a stripper? Is stripping what you have in mind? Let me know so we can talk, initially by email. We would require you to be very discreet as we are all married men and some of us are well known in the community. We would pay you handsomely for your services, of course. Jack'.

I wrote straight back to Jack.

'Dear Jack. Your dinners sound interesting. You could be assured of my discretion. No, I'm not a stripper and stripping isn't quite what I had in mind though I would not be averse to the idea. If we establish mutual trust I'll share my ideas with you to see if they fit in with the thinking of your group. Payment sounds good to me! How much would you have in mind? Emily'.

'Dear Emily. We paid our strippers $500, I think. I didn't make the payment but I put in $300 on the night, to cover everything: food, wine and table service. Let's assume $500 until we negotiate what you have in mind. Who knows, you might be worth more! Talk to me soon if our next dinner date suits you. We'd provide transport to and from the venue. It will be a Saturday night. Jack'.

Whew, the time had arrived to declare myself! My feet got cold at times and I even thought of postponing but determination took over and I resolved to put forward my idea.

'Dear Jack. I have had a long standing fantasy of being in the company of several men ('in the company of' would include sex with the men). I envisage all of us in stylish, formal dress, black ties for the men, a long dress for myself. I would move around the table during dinner, sitting with each man in turn. When our dinner had settled I would imagine us repairing to a living room, then a bedroom. If the night were warm—as it should be for your next dinner—I could see us even going outside into the garden. I would feel more secure if I could meet up with you for coffee. If our meeting is satisfactory I would share further thoughts with you. I'm happy for you to convey my sentiments to your friends. Emily'.

We met for coffee the following Sunday morning, at a venue of my suggestion, not far from my apartment (though I didn't tell that to Jack).

He was tall, silvery haired, straight backed, good looking, well spoken. He had deep brown eyes that never left mine. I could sense him appraising my body.

We chatted about lots of things including his prize roses. He had the typical hand scratches of a rose person. The skin, however, wasn't unsightly. He was impeccably dressed in quality casual clothes. We hit it off well from the start.

'Would you consider $1000 sufficient as payment?' he asked. The six of us are happy to put that figure up to talk about'.

'Let me think about it', I replied before changing the topic. Inwardly I was chortling at the thought of a double whammy: realizing my fantasy and getting well paid for it!

'Dear Emily. Let me tell you how much I enjoyed your company. You have a lively, vivacious personality, a keen intelligence, a lovely figure and a gorgeous face. My friends are delighted to have found such a wonderful prospect for our next dinner. Oh, by the way, we've decided to offer $1500, hoping that it might prove persuasive. Let me know. I've told you the time and date. I hope they will suit. Jack'.

'Dear Jack. $1500 sounds good to me! The time and date both suit. Here's hoping for good health! How would you like us to proceed from here on? Emily'.

'Dear Emily. Great! We 6 are all thrilled to bits! I'll tell you transport arrangements a day or two before the day. It will be by hire car, door to door both ways. The meal will have 3 courses: a seafood appetiser, beef for the main and my favourite caramel tart for dessert. White wine will be served with the appetiser, red with the main. Let me know if you would prefer something else and I'll arrange it. One of my friends suggested that you be asked to provide a photograph to us before the event but the rest of us said no, preferring you to be a surprise. I've assured them that they will indeed get a big surprise when they get to meet you! How would you prefer payment? My suggestion would be by bank transfer, in advance of the dinner. If giving out your account details presents a problem, we could pay in cash if carrying that amount doesn't worry you. Jack'.

'Dear Jack. I'm happy to be paid by transfer. I'll get my details to you before the day. Emily'.

'Dear Emily. Whoops, forgot to ask if your fantasies would necessarily involve anything specific that we might need to know about? Or would the situation itself be sufficient to get things going? Jack.'

'Dear Jack. I think the situation will take care of my wishes. Things will happen, events will evolve naturally. I'm happy with that if you are. By the way, how old are your friends? Emily'.

'Dear Emily. I'm 67. The others are 71, 70, 69, 68 and 64. All old codgers, you see! Dirty old men? We hope so! We're all married but our wives haven't a clue about the nature of our dinners. 3 of us have retired from professional life and the others have retirement in mind. I hope that answers your question. Jack'.

'Dear Jack. I have to raise the issue of safe sex, much as I dislike the limitations posed by condoms. My fantasy has always envisaged being flooded with cum, a thought which sends shivers down my spine. I'm open to that idea if I can trust each fellow. I don't know where they've been or whom they've been with. Emily'.

'Dear Emily. These are all close friends of mine. We have shared confidences, frankly and honestly, for many years. Our sharing has included detailed revelations about our sex lives. I can vouch for all of us as clean and trustworthy.

I do know where they've been and what they've done. If you are not happy with that, we will of course use condoms. Is there anything else you'd like to know beforehand? Jack'.

'Dear Jack. I've had a couple of drinks and ask this question out of mischief. Is there anything I should know about the size of the men's cocks lol? Only kidding! Well, maybe I should be forewarned if I need to be mentally prepared for a really big one! I've getting very excited as the day approaches. Emily'.

'Dear Emily. Loved your question and the spirit in which you asked it! I've seen their dicks when showering after a round at the golf club where we've all been members for 30 years. We're all around average, at least in the flaccid state. One gent, however, may give promise of above average size if he hardens in proportion to his softness. I'll share my mirth at your inquiry with the others. Jack'.

So far we had not given out phone numbers or addresses. Obviously, I had to provide my address to the hire car company but Jack didn't ask for it, nor did he seek my phone number.

We exchanged final emails.

'Dear Emily. This will be my last message. You should arrive around 7 pm on Saturday night. I can't begin to tell you how thrilled I am personally and how thrilled my friends are at the prospect of your company. The time can't come fast enough! Jack'.

'Dear Jack. My feelings echo yours. I'm keeping one little secret from you which I know will delight you all when revealed. See you all on Saturday evening. Oh, and the bank transfer has gone through ok. Thanks. Emily'.

I had my hair and nails done on the Saturday morning. My beautician picked up on my buoyant mood and quizzed me, knowingly. I fended off her curiosity with a smile.

My 'little secret", you may wonder? A full brazilian, done late afternoon on the preceding Wednesday.

I went away from wearing a dress and decided to wear a classy top and a long, dark green skirt, to allow flexibility in the process of undressing. Black high heels, black stay-up stockings, black bra and black French knickers. Ring, plain gold necklace, drop earrings.

I was ready a few minutes before the hire car driver rang the doorbell. His manner was very professional, very attentive.

The drive lasted about 30 minutes. I recognised the destination neighbourhood, one of the city's top suburbs. We pulled into a long pebbled driveway that led to a magnificent old two storeyed mansion which proved to be right on the waterfront.

Jack came out to meet me. He looked handsome in his dinner suit, black tie and white pocket handkerchief. He lifted my hand and kissed it.

'Welcome to our dinner', he said with enthusiasm. His face showed appreciation at what he was seeing. To be honest, I felt pretty good about myself!

'Thank you. I'm delighted to be here', I said sincerely.

He took my arm and escorted me into a grand foyer and hallway where the five other men were waiting. He introduced me to each in turn. Each one smiled greetings, lifted my hand and placed a kiss on it. Each one bent forward slightly from the waist, in a really old fashioned gesture. Within seconds I felt that I was part of their group.

We took sherry in a drawing room before a maid announced that dinner was served. My god, what a dining room! Dark wood walls, high ceiling with chandelier, dimmed lights, a table that could have accommodated maybe 16, high-backed chairs, three sets of candles.

Two attractive young maids provided discreet, expert table service. If they were musing about my role on the night they weren't giving their thoughts away. I got no meaningful looks from them. They left after they'd cleaned up.

The food and wines were superb, the only word for them. The portions were perfect. I didn't want to over-indulge, given what the night would bring.

I shifted chairs during dinner to ensure personal contact with each man. They were all fit-looking for their age, not a big belly among them. Their grooming was in keeping with their projection of a sense of natural gentlemanliness. Moving around allowed me to have individual conversations with each man. All of them complimented me on my appearance. Four of them put a hand on my thigh as we talked. I put my hand over theirs, for encouragement.

One, a very handsome fellow, leaned over and whispered:

'You are stunningly beautiful, a joy to look at', he confided.

I pressed on his hand in response. The occasion had already surpassed my fantasy wishes.

We had coffee back in the adjacent drawing room. I declined the offer of port. Two glasses of fine wine had put me in good spirits.

Two of the men went elsewhere for a cigar.

The conversation went on for a while but it was obvious that something had to happen to get things going. We all knew why I was there! I decided to take the lead.

I gave each of the four men a lingering, passionate kiss, leaving each with a look of disbelief and wonderment on his face. I did the same for the smokers when they returned. They tasted of cigar, which I don't mind (don't ask me about cigarettes, however, I don't kiss ash trays!)

I waved them to take a seat on the leather chairs in the drawing room.

'Unzip!' I said with a leering smile. 'Take him out!'

Four of the cocks were already hard. All of the men had their hands on their cocks.

I proceeded to slip out of my skirt, handing it to them, directing them to pass it around. They brushed the fabric on their faces as they stared at my black panties, stockinged legs and the silken gap between stocking tops and panties. I stood before each man in turn, doing a slow 360 degree turn, giving them a good look at everything on offer.

'My god, how lovely!' I heard one gasp.

'This time down the line you can touch', I told them, and repeated my movements, again slowly.

Each man put his hands on my bum, my thighs, my hips, my cunt. One tried to slip a finger into me but I chided him gently, telling him to be patient.

My top and bra were next to go. I tossed my bra to them to pass around. One put it to his nose, sniffing the warmth of skin.

All six cocks were hard by then!

When I opened my arms to reveal my breasts there were audible sounds of admiration. I moved again along the line, allowing each man to see them up close and to touch them. This time I reached down and felt each hard-on. Two men closed their eyes in ecstasy.

Think of a number between 1 and 10', I said. 'The winner gets to take my panties off'.

The man who chose 7 got the job. I stood with my back to him, giving them first look at my bum (I've got a good one that I can show with confidence). I moved along, letting each man get up close to it and to feel it. Two of them put a fingertip to my bum hole. One rubbed his face on my bum cheeks.

I was enjoying my hold over them and I was getting very, very wet!

'Show time!' I announced, and turned to reveal my smooth cunt. I knew I'd get a result but I was not prepared for the result I got! They were wide-eyed, staring intently. Again I moved along the line. Each one felt my lips, eyes right up close. One ran fingers down either side of my slit.

I decided to leave on my stockings, shoes and necklace. I took off the earrings.

I gave each cock another touch before I put two thin cushions on a low coffee table and knelt on them, my bum and cunt stuck out.

'Fingers and mouths first, two of you at a time, we'll see about cocks after that', I said in honeyed tones. I was well and truly running the show!

The pairs worked well. One man stroked my breasts while the other put fingers and tongue into my cunt, then they changed around. I found myself tremendously aroused by knowing that the other men were watching and enjoying my nakedness.

Jack moved things on by suggesting that we go up to a bedroom. It had a king sized bed and several leather chairs. Jack turned down the bed linen.

'Bring the chairs up to the foot of the bed, then sit and watch', I said.

I had long since lost any inhibitions I might have had. I was flying and loving it!

With all six men watching up close I used my fingers on my clit to get myself off, twice. They were gasping audibly.

I then wriggled up the bed and lay on my back, legs apart.

'Now . . . I need a cock in me', I declared. 'Who's going first?'

'Let's go by age . . . oldest first', said Jack.

None of them lasted long. I didn't expect them to. Hey, I would have been disappointed if they hadn't responded to me! The longest would have been a few minutes, the quickest about a minute.

They might have been older men but I sure knew that I had 6 loads of cum in my cunt. I let them watch me play with myself, using their cum, for another couple of strong orgasms.

'Your choice this time around', I announced when I observed a couple of renewed erections. 'I'll do it any way you want, anyhow you want'.

'Other way around this time', said Jack. 'Youngest goes first, oldest last'.

Man 1 wanted me on my hands and knees to give him entry from behind. He got a firm grip on my hips and quickly picked up his thrusting. He had the longest cock and went all the way in. By the time he came—my 7th load—there was semen everywhere.

Man 2 asked about anal sex. I said yes and used my fingers to lube my hole and passage with abundant cum. His cock was a good size for my back door and I felt no discomfort even when he was all the way in and was thrusting. I gave him some physical and verbal encouragement and he didn't take long.

Man 3 took me missionary for his second time. He lifted my legs to the vertical and went for it, moaning his pleasure all the while. I used my fingers on my clit which helped him to go over the edge in a very noisy fashion. Whew, load no 9!

Man 4 said he had a knee problem and turned me on my side, facing away from him. He had no problem getting in, that's for sure! One slippery thrust and he was in up to his balls. He kept making complimentary remarks about my 'lovely bum' before he unloaded no 10.

Man 5 also took me from behind, in the same manner. He declared loudly that my bum had got to him, just before he dispensed no 11.

Man 6 lasted longest of all, maybe 10 minutes. I was awash.

I reckon they'd all taken a man pill. They were very virile for their age!

I needed respite from my labours. I asked Jack to point me the way to the bathroom but he elected to walk with me. A second man joined us. I cupped my hand over my cunt to avoid leakage. By the time we reached the bathroom I had cum running down both thighs. The men had done themselves proud with their volumes. Having access to a stylish younger woman had got their old nuts working overtime!

Jack returned to the bedroom but the other man remained. He seemed hesitant.

'Do you want to watch me pee?' I asked him. I couldn't think of another reason for him to remain there.

'Would you mind?

'Not at all. Come over close', I said as I lowered myself onto the seat and parted my knees to give him a good look.

He kneeled on the tiles and stared at my stream, frowning with concentration.

'Now watch something else', I said, and used fingers to spread my lips. A runnel of cum fell into the bowl.

'How beautiful was that!' he said as he got back to his feet. 'Thank you, thank you, thank you!' His voice was faltering. I swear he had tears in his eyes.

We walked together back to the bedroom. I still had my shoes on! I took them off and lay on the bed.

'Now . . . I want all of you to touch my body, all over, do anything you like. I just want to feel what it's like to have 12 hands stroking me'.

Within seconds I was in a state of bliss. It had been fun to excite and experience 6 cocks and to realise my ambition of being flooded with cum but the sensations from 12 hands sent me over the moon. Hands gently touching and stroking, on feet, calves, thighs, belly, breasts, chin, cheeks, forehead, eyelids. I floated away to some distant, wonderful place where I found peace, pleasure and fulfillment.

'Let's turn her over', I vaguely heard someone say. Hands turned me. I hardly knew where I was.

Hands stroked me from my neck to the soles of my feet. Someone massaged around my bum hole with a finger.

It's hard to describe how I felt. I felt stimulated beyond belief, all my skin pores alive. In one sense I was relaxed, yet at the same time incredibly aroused. Somewhere in the back of my mind was a feeling of smugness at the show I was putting on for these lovely men. I felt a maelstrom of emotions, simultaneously.

They left me to rest awhile, I guess returning to the drawing room for another glass of wine. I dozed for a bit then thought I better get back to giving them their money's worth. I wasn't finished with my own fantasies, either!

I appeared in only stockings in the drawing room.

'I want you two at a time', I said. 'Tongues and hands'.

Jack stuck to his age criterion.

'Oldest and youngest pairings now', he announced with a grin. 'Get along now!'

I knew their cocks would be spent and it wasn't cock that I had in mind.

They took turns, one using his tongue on my clit, the other kissing me and stroking my breasts. I had a wonderful cum.

The second pairing did the same, as did the third, with the same result for me both times.

By then I was all fucked out! Common sense dictated that I shower before dressing for departure.

The man were so, so appreciative in their farewells, so gentlemanly in the old school manner. Each one gave me a hug and a kiss on the cheek. Each one murmured his heartfelt thanks for a memorable time.

I sat on a wad of tissues during the drive home. The same driver delivered me to my apartment and saw me to the door. I went to tip him but he waved away my offer.

'It's already been taken care of', he said with a smile. How could I have doubted that?

An email arrived next day from Jack:

'Dear Emily. I speak for us all. Words could not do justice to the joy and pleasure you brought into our lives on Saturday night. You were so natural, so wonderfully female, so generous with your mind and your body. And so artful in the way you took us along with your teasing. For our part, we hope we allowed you to fulfil and enjoy your personal fantasy of entertaining several men. If ever you would like to join us again for dinner, don't hesitate to ask. With much gratitude and affection. Jack'.

When next I met my woman friends I asked, inquisitively:

'Well, has there been any progress with organizing for your fantasies to happen?'

'Not from me', said one.

'Nor from me', added the other. 'What about you?'

I smiled broadly.

'Mission accomplished', I declared as their jaws dropped.

'Tell us all about it!' one demanded.

'Not here, in a public place. Let's say next weekend, at my place. I'll provide lunch and good wine. You won't be disappointed with my story'.

And they weren't disappointed. Nor was I, in recounting events with relish.

Would I do it again? Maybe, maybe not. Sometimes one should perhaps be content with fond memories of a perfect fulfilment of fantasy and not try to have perfection repeat itself.

No, I think I'll be satisfied with my memories, all the while waiting for the other two to play catch-up. I wonder if they will?

A Night I Cheated

his happened in 1986. I only shared it with my husband
Mick recently. He had guessed what had happened when
I opened my purse and he caught a glimpse of folded-up panties but
I'll get to that later.

We lived in an apartment close to Sydney Casino. I found it
convenient to meet my close woman friend there for a drink. On this
particular day I was waiting for her when she rang to say she couldn't
make it. I still had a glass of wine to finish so I sat back and surveyed
the scene.

A well-dressed gentleman entered the bar, saw me sitting alone
and took the table next to me. He'd have been around 50, tall and
straight, good looking in a rugged kind of way. He looked me over.
It was a frank and bold appraisal. I was then 42 and had a very good
body, even after 3 kids. I went along with his game and made sure he
had a good look at my legs.

I finished my drink and reached for my handbag, making to
leave.

'Let me buy you another drink', he said.

'All right, I will', I replied with a smile. 'And you might as well
join me'.

By the time we had finished the second drink he had asked me to
have dinner with him. He had a room in the casino hotel and was in
town from interstate to visit a client of his law firm. We both knew

that 'dinner' implied sex. We had established that kind of rapport in a very short period.

It was 5.45 pm.

'Book at a restaurant here', I said. 'Make it for 7. I live close by. I'll meet you in the foyer just before 7'.

I reached out and touched him on the arm as I rose to leave. I felt his eyes on me as I walked away.

I had cheated on Mick once before, 3 years earlier, firstly at a conference that a chap and I were both attending and thereafter twice in the apartment of the fellow's ex-wife. It took a couple of years for me to tell John about these episodes. I knew of Mick's indiscretions and my conscience was clear. I wondered how he would respond but he asked for every detail and finally admitted: 'I wish I'd been there to watch'.

That brought a smile to my face. You see, on the second occasion in the ex-wife's apartment the arrangement was for the ex to leave. After we'd all shared a bottle of good wine she suddenly leaned across and asked me if she could watch us.

'I've always wanted to see a couple have sex', she confided as the man took the glasses to the kitchen.

I wondered if she wanted to participate physically but she said she only wanted to watch. She would sit in a corner and be discreet. I found myself very aroused by her presence and didn't feel inhibited. I only looked across at her once in the hour or so we were at it. She had her hand in her panties and her eyes were riveted on us. She must have cum at least once but she suppressed her noises.

Back to the story. I rang my woman friend and told her about dinner with the nice man. She agreed to provide a cover for me. I found Mick in the apartment and told him that I was having dinner with my woman friend. I showered and dressed. Mick chatted with me all the while. I left off a bra but that did not surprise him. I put on a pair of white French knickers but slipped a high-cut sexy black pair of panties into my purse. I would swap pairs in a casino washroom.

Mick pecked me on the cheek and settled in to watch the news. I was a few minutes late to the casino rendezvous. My man friend was resplendent in grey slacks and a classy dark blue jacket. His white cotton shirt was eye-catching.

'You look stunning', he said with apparent sincerity. I smiled back. Like all women I'll accept a compliment, especially when I've tried to look my best.

'I've got a surprise', he said. We walked past the restaurant entrance and reached a bank of lifts.

'Trust me', he said as he pressed 13. I remember hoping that the number would not prove unlucky.

We entered his room which had spectacular views of the city and harbour.

He laid out the room service menu on a little table.

'I've already decided what I'm having. You choose what you want and I'll choose a wine for us'.

I'm normally averse to room service food but the casino's reputation for cuisine was very good. We both knew that sex would follow on the menu and it made sense for us to let the fun begin in private.

He rang through the order and asked for the wine to be brought up immediately. We looked at the view while waiting for the knock on the door.

He poured us a glass each and we continued to look out at the lights.

'You know something, I need to kiss you', he remarked with a smile, putting both our glasses aside.

'And I'm waiting to be kissed', I said genuinely.

We started kissing gently but quickly progressed into high passion.

We broke off only to regain our breath.

'God you can kiss!' he said with feeling. Then we got back to business.

By the time the food arrived he had me up against the wall, with his hand up my dress and down my panties. We were kissing mindlessly, urgently, lips and tongues working mutual magic. At some stage I felt for his cock and was very pleased with what I found.

I went to the bathroom while the waitress laid out dinner. My lipstick was smudged but I had some in my purse for when I went home.

'Let's eat', he said.

'Food first, then you can eat me', I thought to myself.

The food and wine were a wonderful combination. I'd only ordered an appetiser as I don't enjoy sex on a full stomach. It was a seafood dish, beautifully cooked. We chatted away about anything as we ate and drank. There were lots of meaningful looks and smiles of wicked intent.

He poured the last of the wine.

'I think we should make things more interesting', I said and took off my dress, leaving on black stay-up stockings and black panties. He stripped to his brief underpants but he looked so silly with his hard cock stuck in them that I told him to take them off.

I'm not into guessing cock length (though I did measure Mick's on our honeymoon) and I can't see the purpose of it. What a man has is what he's been given, like tits for women. I surmised that this man's cock was not as long as Mick's but it looked to be thick which I like. I enjoy having my cunt stretched.

We finished our wine sitting on the sofa, holding hands. His cock remained hard and leaking throughout. My nipples were prominent. He hadn't touched my breasts but his eyes went to them constantly. I could feel how wet I was. Even now at 67 I still juice up well.

I put my glass down and went to the bed, pulling bedclothes down to the sheets. I walked back over to him and said in my sexiest voice:

'Take my panties off'.

He got an eyeful as he drew them down my legs. I'd trimmed it for the occasion but had been careful not to create any rash. He put his hands on my bum and drew me to his face, putting a lingering kiss on my bush and easing just the end of his tongue into my upper slit. I couldn't get him into bed fast enough.

I was on the pill so that was not a concern but for reasons I can't to this day account for I played what John calls 'genetic roulette' with the man, not insisting that he use a condom. I spent some sleepless nights afterward wondering how I could have been so bloody stupid. I feigned a minor infection to keep John away until I felt sure that I was all right. Stupid!

I should mention at this point that the man and I had agreed not to reveal our names or our personal details. The sex was to be completely anonymous, a fuck of mutual convenience, a true one night stand.

He brought me off twice with his mouth before mounting me. He just slipped in! My sheath was tight on his cock and we both felt every tiny movement and impulse. We started slowly but soon gave full rein to our lust and simply fucked our brains out, noisily and joyously. The anonymity of our coupling made it more exciting for both of us.

I was amazed and thrilled at his volume of semen. He thrust in as far as he could and let go, noisily. I felt myself being flooded with his lovely warm man juice. He took a long while to finish and his cock took a long while to go soft and leave my body. I had his body weight on top of me which I loved. His breathing pattern against my neck gradually slowed and became less frantic.

We cuddled and dozed for a while, enjoying skin on skin, kissing occasionally, stroking our bodies.

His erection returned in a surprisingly short time. I found his heavy balls drawn up and tense again.

'How do you want to have me?' I asked with his balls in my hand.

'Turn over', he directed.

He pinned my wrists with his hands and pinned my legs apart with his legs, rendering me helpless. Again he started slowly but soon got worked up, putting a finger in my bum and fucking me with vigour. I met the challenge of his wild thrustings, lifting my bum to meet him as best I could while being held. We both knew that this was our final fuck and we were both determined to make the most of it. I came once then had another cum in concert with my man.

Again he unloaded a profuse volume of semen into me. His angle of entry was of course different and I felt different sensations because of this. I felt every shot of his second flood.

By then I had to leave so as not to arouse suspicion back at base. I sponged alone and freshened my makeup. I figured Mick would be asleep so kept on the black panties. Between sitting on the toilet and sponging I thought I had let gravity remove most of my friend's semen from my body. Mmm . . . how wrong I was.

I pecked his cheek goodbye, thanked him for a lively evening and departed for home.

I had walked only about 50 metres from the casino steps when a big flow of cum made my black panties wet and uncomfortable. I stepped into a dark little alleyway and took them off, stowing them in my purse. I put the white pair back on.

Surprisingly Mick was still up and about. I made small talk with him but at one point made a mistake. I opened my purse within his eyeshot and he apparently caught a glimpse of the black panties. He said nothing but I found out only recently, when I confessed to my night of indiscretion, that he had seen them and had looked in the washing basket for them after I had gone to bed. They were in a hell of a mess, soaked with semen.

It was Mick's idea that I should share this account with others. Our own 'sharing' of the brief liaison took over 20 years to eventuate but we have both found ourselves aroused by it. Our two successful threesomes in recent years have enabled us to put the casino episode into perspective.

I count myself fortunate to have had 3 heavy cummers in my life, apart from squirters: Mick, my anonymous man at the casino and a friend, Jim. If you like drawing semen from a man as much as I do, you enjoy a good volume in you or on you.

I thought I could rely on Mick to accept that it was fair enough for me to have some fun of my own, knowing that he had stepped over the line with a woman or two.

I don't regret not having further contact with the man. That could have led to complications and the last thing I needed was complications. I'm very happy with my lot in life.

Four Women: a Tale of Self-indulgence

*I*t was my husband who first broached the idea that I and three women friends should have time to ourselves in elegant Melbourne. It didn't take me long to consider it a good idea and I was quickly on the phone to the others. Their responses were predictably enthusiastic.

Hubby had an ulterior motive. For some time he had been suggesting that I explore my sexuality with another woman. There's nothing lacking in his stamina and technique but he felt that there were woman-woman elements for me to explore and discover.

I was amenable to the notion and was candid in suggesting sex to my friends. All were agreeable. We're all in our late forties and are all in pretty good shape. We share a love of mischief, a love of good times.

I'd had two episodes with other females in earlier days, both only brief but both highly arousing. In late high school my best friend Jane and I (I'm Kerry) had taken advantage of my mother's absence on a shopping trip to strip off, display and explore our bodies. I've remained in contact with her. Indeed, she would be one of 'The Four'. She has great tits. She and I used to get many an envious glance when changing after PE in high school.

The other time was overnight at a two-day conference, in my early thirties. A well dressed, attractive woman began to pay particular attention to me over drinks, then seated herself next to me at dinner. I soon realized that she was hitting on me.

She was upfront about it. As we rose from dinner she invited me to her room. Just like that! I thought for a second or two, then agreed. We spent the night together. She had a penis toy and we used it on each other as well as doing most other things. She asked to continue meeting but I declined, not needing to possibly complicate my life. I couldn't risk her becoming a nuisance.

We four had a planning meeting over lunch. Martin had suggested a forthcoming long weekend, with two nights in a five star hotel. He thought we should have plenty of time, not only for sex but also for shopping, restaurants, visiting the markets, seeing a Monet exhibition at the art gallery, walking in the Botanic Gardens . . .

Martin did the hotel booking. The men would transport us to our local railway station and we would take the train into Melbourne, about an hour's journey.

A bit about us. Jane is on her second marriage, her first husband having succumbed to cancer. She has two married daughters who are tardy in giving her grandchildren.

Hubby and I have three kids and, so far, three grandkids. We've enjoyed a long and happy marriage. Our intention is to retire from the work force as soon as possible and get on with other things in our lives.

Wendy is divorced but in another, happier relationship. She discovered that her husband and his golf partner were closet gays. Luckily her new man is an attentive and devoted lover. She has no children.

Veronica (or 'Ronny' as we know her) is satisfied in the company of her affable, likeable husband of many years. She says 'He keeps me happy', whatever that might mean. He has a great sense of humour and a twinkle in his eye for the ladies.

Now to the events!

We'd checked the weather in advance. Brilliant! The temperatures would be warm and pleasant, the sky clear.

Saturday, Saturday night, Sunday, Sunday night, then a train home on Monday afternoon.

We all booked into a beautician and got the works including a full wax. Four smoothies! Our men were impressed.

We all had our hair done at the same time. The staff are all good cutters and we were pleased with the results.

There was an air of hilarity on our train trip into Melbourne. Our fellow travelers had every reason to think we were a bunch of nutters, giggling away but also excited at what we were about to experience. We expressed mutual admiration of our clothes. I'd sneaked off to buy a dark green pants suit and smart black shoes. Hubby might get a surprise when the next credit card bill turned up.

We had an eleven thirty check-in which meant we could go straight from the central train station to the hotel. Our room was up high with sweeping views over the city. We had a king sized bed and a queen sized bed. It was a classy suite. Our complimentary champagne was in the bar fridge.

'Well it's there, we should drink it!' someone declared.

I'm hopeless at uncorking champagne but Ronny said she'd had plenty of practice. Four glasses of bubbly were soon poured into long flutes.

'We should have a toast', I said.

'And let's make it interesting', said Wendy, and promptly stripped to her panties.

A flurry of undressing followed a burst of laughter. We'd all agreed to wear our good stuff. Jane had gorgeous pair of dark blue 'boy style' which were cut to highlight her hips. Ronny being Ronny wore a white thong which covered very little. Wendy had a lacy cream pair. I'm not into thongs (though I keep one for hubby) and I wore beautiful French knickers.

Thus it was that four nearly naked ladies drank champagne, admired each other's bodies and undies and enjoyed good company.

Ronny told a couple of jokes. Jane roared laughing and her tits jiggled, causing us all to laugh even more.

Around 1pm we dressed again for lunch. Melbourne has gorgeous arcades filled with lovely shops and eating places. The weather was beautiful. I strolled hand in hand with Jane, Ronny with Wendy. No doubt some onlookers would have thought us butch. Who cared?

We chose a classy establishment. I ordered seafood (what else?) and it came superbly cooked. We had a glass of sauvignon blanc from New Zealand, perfectly chilled. The men were paying so who cared what the bill came to?

We needed our lunch to settle so went for a walk through the gardens, exhilarating in itself. This time I held hands with Ronny, Jane with Wendy. Once again we attracted some knowing looks. It was fun seeing people stare!

We took a cab back to the hotel. There was only one thing on our agenda: sex.

After a comfort stop we undressed together. The atmosphere was friendly but also sexually supercharged. Nothing was hurried. Everything was very sensual.

Coming to terms with what we were doing was nearly overwhelming. After this initial session we were able to enjoy a deeper appreciation of the joys that women can offer each other but, as we got used to the idea, we were tentative.

We needed a circuit breaker, as it were, to dispel our hesitancy. I finally kneeled on the bed and told the others to do the same.

'Now, let's watch ourselves get off', I declared, and began stroking my clit.

Jane came first. The rest of us, inspired by the beauty of her uninhibited show, came soon afterward.

Jane and I took the queen bed, Ronny and Wendy the king bed. After a while we were all on the bigger bed, taking turns with each other: kissing, caressing our breasts, using fingers and tongues on bums, clits and cunts. When things got too much we dozed for a while before getting back to business. I think we must all have hit double figures though no one was counting.

When I told hubby of the wonderment of our first episode he quoted lines from Yeats:

'All changed, changed utterly;

A terrible beauty is born'.

I think 'terrible' could be interpreted to mean 'awe inspiring' in our case.

Let me digress for a time.

There is still a taboo factor in woman to woman sex. Perhaps a naughty thing to do? More exciting for that reason!

We four all enjoy regular sex with our men but we found new boundaries, new experiences in having ourselves to ourselves.

It's almost trite to try to put these experiences into words but I'll try.

The softness of a woman's caress . . . the pure sensuality of her kiss (without whiskers!) . . . the manner in which hand, fingers and mouth tease tits, nipples, cunt and clit . . . !!!

Lying with tits pressed on tits . . . Shivers!!! Mouths exploring . . . nipple to nipple . . . the touch so soft that the sensations are almost imagined . . .

I'll go one further. There is something almost magical and sensual about kissing another woman after she's gone down on me. I love my tastes on her lips. I love tasting her and enjoying her cunt scents.

Are orgasms more intense with a woman than a man?

We Four discussed this on our train journey home. The answer we reached? 'It depends'. We have 'monster cums' with our men. We had similar cums with each other during our time in Melbourne.

The fact is, however, that women know how they love to be touched, where and when, and for how long. It can be almost autoerotic in the manner that women kiss and touch each other.

I say in passing that we have all resolved to let our men watch us enjoying sex with each other. We might even share our favours around our men.

'A terrible beauty is born'.

Back to the narrative. Jane's man had made a booking at a top Melbourne restaurant and had arranged to pay the bill.

We had a drink in a bar before dinner. We must still have what it takes because men present showed interest. We thought about going the tease but common sense prevailed. I gave Wendy a big kiss and Jane and Ronny followed suit. We must all have presented as gay. Sometimes—most times?—it's a good idea to get rid of a partly pissed male who is only bent on getting into your pants. One's female dignity has to be respected.

Dinner was wonderful, simply great food and wine in the Italian style. Our mood was mellow. Back at the hotel we just fell into bed. Jane and I were cuddled and asleep within minutes.

We had breakfast in another lovely little café. Hubby had been right in insisting that we have the extra day and night so as not to hurry things. We visited Victoria Markets.

We went window shopping but it proved more than that when we found a classy lingerie shop. We each bought two pairs. The owner was impressed by the sale and gave us a 10% discount, not easy to get in lingerie shops.

I bought two bottles of white wine which we took back to the hotel.

We took the wine easily as none of us wanted to miss out on the action due to alcohol-induced sleep. Sipping was the order of the day.

'Panty parade', ordered Ronny.

We each paraded our new ones. Classy items, as they should have been from their cost. We resolved to give our men this parade back home.

Ronny had brought along a penis toy, lube and a butt plug. We spent a couple of very interesting hours playing with them, using them on each other. I'm not a fan of toys—I don't own one—but I must admit that I enjoyed the sensations when my turn came around. And I was amazed at what I felt when it was my turn to use the toys on the others.

I took the toy out of Jane's bum for one of her cums and was astounded at her anal throbbing on my finger. Hubby has remarked on my 'bum cums' in like manner. He also loves having his lips and tongue feel the pulsations in my bum hole. Nature! Go the girls and all that!

We spent Sunday afternoon at the Monet exhibition. It was overpowering in its magnificence. Rest was essential after that and we caught a cab to the hotel and slept for an hour or so.

Refreshed, we sought out another good restaurant of the Vietnamese kind. Lovely food, fresh and flavoursome. Noisy, tables of Vietnamese people, fun.

We opened another bottle of white wine at the hotel but merely sipped on it, getting sleepier as we went along. I took the big bed with Wendy, Jane the other bed with Ronny. We had only brief cuddles.

On Monday morning we again had breakfast at a nearby café. The hotel charges $28 per person for breakfast. We got ours for $6 and the quality was much better. We then went for a long walk.

We had to be out of our room by 1 pm. That gave us just under three hours for further fun. We were all in the mood for it.

We started by another mutual masturbation, followed by a round of sixty-nines. Ronny wanted the toy up her bum and I did the job. We finished by taking turns in going down on each other. In a phrase, we were all fucked out. It was all I could do to muster the energy to take a shower.

We all were appreciative of our smooth slits, well worth the expense and the occasional discomfort. Hubby has long maintained that God or Darwin got it wrong by putting body hair on adult women. He adores the smoothness and the 'ring of fire' effect on the base of his cock when hair does not get in the way.

We all eventually went to sleep on the train journey home. Our men were there to drive us home. I confess I slept in the car as well.

Hubby cooked a lovely piece of fish for my dinner. I drank only half of my glass of wine before telling him he could have the rest.

My advice to women 'out there' who have thoughts about woman on woman sex?

Try it! You won't be disappointed. It opens up a new and wonderful realm of sexual experience: of subtle variations in body scent; of changes in breathing; of caresses stimulating new responses.

I'd make sure that your hubby or partner were onside with the venture. Some men have strong thoughts about their woman seeking pleasure with another woman . . . Male ego and all that!

Carnevale

A Sonnet Narrative

1

The train arrives in Venice, right on time,
A fantasy fulfilled, I'm really there!
Clear, sunny day, the Grand Canal sublime,
Fuss, noise and crowds and bustle everywhere.
A vaporetto first, to my hotel,
Green water sparkles, wakes and vessels dance;
In minutes I have yielded to her spell,
A captive to her charm and her romance.
High Moorish arches, palaces ornate,
White, cream and orange, apricot and pink;
My spirits in exhilarated state,
Intoxicated, yet compelled to drink.
A fascinating pageant on display,
I'm in a theatre, acting out the play.

2

Majestic vista of St Marco Square,
The heart of Venice, strikingly arrayed;

Vast throngs of happy people everywhere,
For Carnevale, the opening parade.
Emblazoned banners, trumpets, drums and pipes,
Spectacular, exciting to behold;
Puffed sleeves of silk in brightly coloured stripes,
Foot soldiers tall, imperious and bold.
Flag throwers, heralds, jugglers, acrobats,
Priest, noble, jester, harlequin and page;
Masks, jewelry, wigs, rosettes and feathered hats,
Rich costumes, splendour from another age.
In climax to this stunning, dazzling show
Balloons in thousands to the heavens go.

3

Through labyrinthine streets I wend my way,
Eventually the gallery I find;
A perfect start to this Venetian day,
Enchanting place to stimulate the mind.
Soft crunch of pebbles, stone walls, graceful trees,
Pure ambience of peace, tranquility;
New art in city spanning centuries,
A more delightful place there could not be.
Who is that woman on the garden seat?
She sits alone. Her style sets her apart;
My interest is aroused, we have to meet!
She's lovelier than any work of art.
No room for diffidence, no time to muse,
This opportunity I cannot lose.

4

A table in a restaurant nearby,
We chat away, conversing easily;

Her smile is sweet, a twinkle in her eye,
Our spirits are uplifted, blithe, carefree.
The gondoliers and workmen come and go,
Their banter jocular, their laughter loud;
The staff and owners they appear to know,
A friendly, cheerful, animated crowd.
Signora's pasta cooked with great finesse,
A shared dessert, a glass or two of red;
An hour we talk and yet I must confess
I can't remember anything we said.
'I'd like to see the Isle of Lace, would you?'
Without demur she says 'I'd love us to'.

5

Burano Island, sunbathed and serene,
Its houses yellow, blue, green, burgundy;
Domestic wash, intended to be seen,
Lace, boats, the shops and cafes touristy.
She's very beautiful, I tell her so,
She smiles and takes my hand, relaxed we stroll;
Her comely face has an alluring glow,
Contentment and excitement flood my soul.
She wants to buy herself a shirt, we find
A cotton one, embellished with fine lace;
Chic, feminine, her manner is refined,
She wears her clothes with elegance and grace.
Warmed by both sun and wine, mid-afternoon,
We take a ferry back through the lagoon.

6

Masks in their hundreds, lavishly on show,
From window, ceiling, walls intensely stare;

Fantastic, eerie, marvellous tableau,
Unseeing eyes gaze out from everywhere.
The mask, concealing true identity,
Conferring the advantage of disguise;
Conducive to pretence, duplicity,
Encouraging deception and surprise.
Of fantasy the heart, of guile the face,
The mask will tempt, entice and complicate;
Set man and woman on impassioned chase,
Illicit opportunities create.
Mask after mask we try, enjoy the fun,
And feel the tide of passion swell and run.

7

Musicians entertain the surging crowd,
Their hair is sequined, faces red and green;
The atmosphere is boisterous and loud,
Masks, hats and costumes liven up the scene.
We don our masks and join the revelry,
Exuberantly inch along our way;
Small kids are held aloft so they can see,
All ages laugh and chat, the mood is gay.
Bewitching girls for photographs present,
Rich gowns, dramatic headdress, masks of gold;
They're gorgeous, sumptuous, magnificent,
Bejewelled, aloof, exquisite to behold.
Impulsiveness and daring sweep through us,
In Venice, reckless, masked, anonymous!

8

Canal-side, at a restaurant we meet,
The water laps as gondolas glide by;

Vivacious, elegant, she looks a treat,
Her face and body thrilling to my eye.
Big crowds still swarm San Marco late at night,
A swinging jazz band sets a party mood;
The air is cold and clear, the stars gleam bright,
We join the dancing, energy renewed.
Dance turns to shuffle and she snuggles in,
Her head rests warmly, fondly on my chest;
Strong surges of desire well up within,
I lift my hand to cup her shapely breast.
We're caught in a euphoric, magic spell,
No words are said, we go to my hotel.

9

'You first'. She sits and watches me undress,
Puts tiny kisses on my cock erect;
Her fingers stroke my skin, a soft caress,
Her clothes slip off, her nudity's perfect.
'Now close your eyes'. I do as I am asked,
I feel her move across me, legs astride;
'Now open them'. My naked woman's masked!!!
Triumphantly she takes me deep inside.
Such sensuality I've never seen,
Her carnal zest exuberantly shown.
She takes me places I have never been,
The most amazing sex that I have known.
We drift into a sated lovers' sleep,
Our arms around each other, breathing deep.

10

Her air of intrigue, 'I have a surprise,
No need to dress up, just come as you are'.

I love the mischief glinting in her eyes,
'We'll meet at six o'clock, in Harry's Bar'.
"Four Seasons', just for you'. My mind is blown,
How generous of her to think of this!
Played in the church Vivaldi made his own,
The evening is perfection, simply bliss.
Musicians play with artistry and grace,
We sit enchanted, fingers intertwined;
True harmony of music and of place,
Our spirits celebrating, unconfined.
Entrancing concert, Venice, early spring,
Our lovemaking is tender, lingering.

11

The markets vibrant, cheery, feverish,
Noise, colours, smells of produce on the breeze;
Shrimps, garlic, peppers, mushrooms, lemons, fish,
Asparagus, beans, mussels, strawberries.
A fruit stall woman chats, a florist jokes,
A fish man flaunts theatrical routine;
A workman sings while trimming artichokes,
Exuberance in chaos is the scene.
Tomatoes lush and ripe, fresh from the vine,
Coarse crusty bread, cheese of celestial smell;
Sweet raspberries, light flavoursome red wine,
A feast for two, consumed in my hotel.
'A gentle stroll, perhaps?' She shakes her head,
'I'd rather spend the afternoon in bed'.

12

The gondola, romantically unique,
A golden sunset, perfect for our ride;

I've chosen one that's polished, stylish, sleek,
Our gondolier presents his craft with pride.
We settle, arm in arm, on leather seat,
Admiring carvings intricate, ornate;
Embroidered cushions, carpet under feet,
Gold seahorse statuettes, fine silver plate.
Through narrow side canals we make our way,
Slow-gliding, slipping soundlessly, serene;
The joy I'm feeling words could not convey,
Elated more than this I've never been.
Adventure and excitement, ecstasy,
Fair Venice weaves her magic artfully.

13

Slow morning walk through alleyway and square,
Church bells ring out to summon local folk;
The sound of children's laughter fills the air,
Old men in groups converse and smile and smoke.
Shafts of bright sunlight, sky of azure blue,
Pigeons call softly, seagulls stridently;
It's peaceful, calm, fulfillment flows anew,
We wander hand in hand, contentedly.
She senses that I have something in store,
Inquisitiveness sparkles in her eyes;
I knock upon a nameless wooden door,
'What's this?' 'It's time to spring my own surprise.
It's nearly time for lunch but first of all
We need to choose our costumes for the ball'.

14

Resplendent scarlet cape, long velvet gloves,
Red mask dramatic, feathered fan in hand;

This festive milieu she clearly loves,
I am the Doge, mask menacing but grand.
Soprano, jester, harp and violin,
Gold mirrors, candles, marble halls and floors;
Four hundred years intrigue these walls within,
Masked couples slip through ornamented doors.
Good food and wine enhance the revelry,
Tongues loosen, make liaisons, fingers stray;
A handsome suitor seeks her company,
A gesture of her fan sends him away.
Disguises, flirting, fantasy, romance,
High-spirited, until the dawn we dance.

15

Rialto Bridge, its beauty unsurpassed,
This lovely woman in my arms encased;
The hour is late but still the crowds go past,
Beneath her coat she's naked from the waist.
Her kiss reveals impatience of desire,
We find ourselves a darkened passageway;
She turns and takes me in, her sheath on fire,
Her nudity on blatant, proud display.
We're man and woman, venting primal lust,
No heed to where we are, our voices hoarse;
Instinctive, joyous, frenzied thrust on thrust,
We come as one, with monumental force.
We cling together in that shadowed place,
The tears are running freely down her face.

16

Departure day, she comes to my hotel,
I've booked a water taxi to the plane;

My heart is aching more than words can tell,
Not even Veuve Clicquot can dull the pain.
Eyes meet with knowing look, hands reassure,
We don't say much, our feelings are subdued;
I can't believe that we will meet no more,
The wait intensifies our sombre mood.
A fervent last embrace, it's time to go,
The universe is centred on this kiss;
I love this woman whom I've come to know!
I can't just walk away from her like this!
Anticipating what it is I'll ask,
She seals my lips, farewells me in her mask.

Chateau

A Sonnet Narrative

1

The limousine crunched up the tree-lined drive,
We tensed as the chauffeur stood to the door;
How thrilled we were to see our men arrive,
This escapade had been worth waiting for.
'They're perfect specimens! You have excelled!'
'I took my time. We three deserve the best'.
'To us!' Our mutual satisfaction swelled,
This weekend fantasy had long obsessed.
Maidservants took the men to be prepared,
Our orders comprehensive and precise;
No detail of their bodies to be spared,
Perfection to indulge our secret vice.
'We'll bathe and dress, then let the games commence!'
'A toast to the pursuit of decadence!'

2 The Head Maid

Our task was to prepare and groom the men,
Fine fellows of phenomenal physique;

Their body hair had been removed by then,
We shaved their faces silky-smooth and sleek.
A scented bath, each man washed carefully,
The scalp massaged, the long, dark hair shampooed;
A tepid shower to rinse them thoroughly,
Slow towelling of their bodies to conclude.
Our mistresses had chosen body scents,
And specified how they should be applied;
(A turn-on for us too, these gorgeous gents!)
Hair brushed devotedly, pulled back and tied.
A robe of silken softness, fine and black,
Slit to the waist in centre, front and back.

3

The grooming tempted us, for fun we spied,
Our peepholes gave an appetising view;
Broad shoulders, narrow waists, long legs we eyed,
Choice bodily delights we'd soon pursue.
Enthralled, I marvelled at their shapely thighs,
Supremely sculpted bottoms, bellies firm;
Soft penises gave promise of full size,
In time we would their staying power confirm.
A run of water down a manful back,
Engrossed, I watched its progress bit by bit;
Slow, tantalizing trickle to his crack,
I shivered at the thought of licking it.
Delectable male handsomeness on show,
Our bodies lively, randy minds aglow.

4

The three of us at table, laughter, wine,
At liberty our instincts to express;

The means by which we would the men assign
Had been devised. Which one would I possess?
Each man would wear a singular tattoo,
Imprinted on the upper, inner thigh;
The stallion, boar and Priapus we knew,
But did not know which symbol on which guy.
Three numbered papers, folded in a dish,
We drew in turns, deciding one, two, three;
The first then chose the motif of her wish,
The others followed suit excitedly.
That done, we moved into the drawing room,
'We're ready for the men now, I presume?'

5

Tall, statuesque, exciting to behold,
Magnificent, a feast for woman's eyes;
Proud, clit-engorging, confident and bold,
Each one a stunning, virile, sexy prize.
'First man, approach!' He came before our chairs,
Two of us drew his silky robe aside;
On soft and scented skin, bereft of hairs,
A rampant stallion, flaunting it with pride.
The Priapus was on the second man,
His massive penis pointing at the sky;
The boar required but superficial scan,
Impossibly erect on perfect thigh.
Consumed by our lascivious intent,
My sheath was wet, my nipples prominent.

6

Time then for introduction to our men,
In separate rooms acquaintance to pursue;

My eagerness was far beyond my ken,
Excitement, expectation, passion grew.
'Undress! Lie face down on the bed! Don't speak!'
I watched his male magnificence obey;
Divine, majestic body at its peak,
In high-heeled shoes and panties I would play.
I'd lick and kiss and stroke all over him,
Aroused by shapely shoulder, buttocks, back;
Flat abdomen, calf well-turned, waistline slim,
Hair now untied, cascading shiny black.
A banquet of nude masculinity,
Resplendently laid out in front of me.

7

My breasts and mouth and hands stroked bum and back,
To every sexual whim I could submit;
Taut nipples brushed enticing cheeks and crack,
Compelling surges stirred tumescent clit.
I turned him, he was marvellously long,
Voluptuary's penis, hard and thick;
Smooth-silken yet imperiously strong,
A cock to touch a woman to the quick,
Along, around, beneath I ran my tongue,
Kissed, licked and lapped and sucked its lovely length;
Mouth-watering the fruitful balls that hung,
Such contrast in their frailty and their strength!
Three times I sensed him just about to come,
To his indulgence I would not succumb.

8

'I've done enough. Your turn to pleasure me,
Take off my shoes and panties. Lay me down'.

Such frank behaviour, inhibition free!
In these licentious waves I'd surely drown!
His sensual ministrations were sublime,
Soft kisses, tiny licks, light finger-stroke;
My stallion and my satyr, in his prime,
My juices he continued to provoke.
I turned. Lips, tongue and fingers slow caressed,
Each touch a deeply satisfying thrill;
An age he took to kiss the swell of breast,
My sex he probed with patient, gentle skill.
Aroused, inflamed I sought his stiffened prize,
And guided him between impatient thighs.

9

He rocked his hips, slipped slowly into me,
The thought of this had turned me on for weeks!
Enfolding, holding him exultantly,
My hands spread on his smoothly muscled cheeks.
Sheer joy of being covered, opened, filled,
Impaled beneath that virile, handsome man!
A dream come true, a fantasy fulfilled,
Elatedly my mind and spirit ran!
I lifted to his thrustings, claiming him,
His balls bumped lustily on my backside;
Their juice profuse would fill me to the brim,
My woman's urge became a swelling tide.
So close . . . so close . . . then I could take no more,
I came as I had never come before.

10

We drifted into deep and sated sleep,
And woke to bird calls in the early light;

Complacently I felt his semen seep,
Our coupling a sensational delight.
His skin intoxicating, warm and sweet,
Aroused anew, I kissed his neck and chest;
We cuddled close, enjoyed the touch of feet,
He stroked my hip and buttock, cupped my breast.
I straddled him, my sleepiness dispelled,
And welcomed him into our liquid blend;
His penis, semi soft, soon rigid swelled,
Our passion even last night's would transcend.
Again my woman's sway I would affirm,
Rejoicing in my power to draw his sperm.

11

Broad, sunny terrace, crispy morning air,
Iced water trickled gently down our throats;
Stretched leisurely on soft reclining chair,
Well-rested, robed, we sat comparing notes.
The men had all passed their initial test,
Our instincts had flown unrestrainedly;
Intense virility we could attest,
A surfeit of raw sensuality.
Sweet oranges, black grapes, plump strawberries,
Warm croissant lightly spread with ginger jam;
Espresso coffee, rich and creamy cheese,
Coarse-textured bread, the thinnest slice of ham.
'Some time alone before we play again.
We'll meet by Aphrodite, say at ten'.

12

The water in the stream was cool and clear,
We swam and frolicked near a waterfall;

The strident sounds of peacocks we could hear,
Our Eden, that would heart and mind enthrall.
The men we sent to walk among the rocks,
We ogled them while resting on the grass;
So pleasurable watching bobbing cocks,
Butts well-proportioned, visages of class.
Beneath the waterfall we swam in pairs,
The water roared and splashed in grand cascade;
I reached between his legs and felt his wares,
With joyous, earthy randiness we played,
A game of hide and seek to get us dry,
Cavorting nude, at one with earth and sky.

13

Spread rugs, a gentle breeze, secluded glade,
Our swim had given energy afresh;
Chilled chablis, lobster, peaches, dappled shade,
Our thoughts returned to matters of the flesh.
Magnificently hard, our men reclined,
We mounted them to exercise control;
Our bodies hot, our spirits unconfined,
Enraptured ride on lust-inspiring pole.
While fucking mine I watched the other two,
And quivered as they took those big cocks in;
A riveting, exhilarating view,
A thrilling blend of decadence and sin.
In time rang out all six climactic cries,
We capered off, fresh semen on our thighs.

14

We lazed and dozed until late afternoon,
Then met in cloistered garden for champagne;

The sky was clear, that night would be full moon,
Our conversation in light-hearted vein.
'Wow, yours was big! How ever did it fit?'
'You have the most fantastic arse and tits!'
'I had to take him slowly, I'll admit'.
'I came so hard I nearly lost my wits!'
A second bottle, vintage Veuve Clicquot,
Hilarious, salacious repartee;
'I've got a lovely wet patch down below!'
The others laughed in concert: 'So have we!'
Close friends in bawdy conversation frank,
'To Womanhood!' The toast we gladly drank.

15

Sweet-scented bubble bath, red candles lit,
Vivaldi mandolin in muted tone;
A maid slow-brushed my skin with massage mitt,
Then rinsed my hair and left me on my own.
So peaceful and relaxing lying there!
Consuming all my thoughts the day's delights;
Warm sun, cool stream, invigorating air,
Arousing, heady, stimulating sights.
I closed my eyes, could feel him still inside,
Hard, woman-gratifying, long and thick;
A sweaty, unrestrained, triumphal ride,
Hot pulsing flow, my pussy semen-slick.
The maid returned, towelled dry my steaming flesh,
My mind and body craved adventures fresh.

16

Skin creamy-smooth, gown figure-hugging, black,
My breasts its neckline tokenly concealed;

Diaphanous, slit to the thigh, no back,
Seductiveness of nakedness revealed.
This night in mind a gown we'd each designed,
'One garment only' wickedness decreed;
Conducive to a daring state of mind,
Facilitating every carnal need.
Our eyes lit up, we 'Oohed' in unison,
Curved shapeliness alluringly displayed;
Of inhibition, hang-up there'd be none,
Libido we would blatantly parade.
A glass of chilled sauternes, its colour straw,
This was a night we'd long been waiting for.

17

Rich curtains, drawn, in red and gold brocade,
Soft glow from candelabra, chandelier;
From ornate vases, urns, blooms in cascade,
Quartet by Mozart, pleasing to the ear.
Three places set with silver cutlery,
Rare plates and cups of elegant design;
Fine glasses made by hand, exquisitely,
A gourmet menu and the best of wine.
Black leather shoes, black trousers, shirts pure white,
Our men were appetisingly attired;
A musky after-shave, its scent but slight,
Yet quick to get imagination fired.
Their service excellent, then as foretaste,
They served our cognac naked to the waist.

18

Long gallery, gilt mirrors, candle light,
Scenes pastoral, stern portraits lined the walls;

Grim ancients in whose minds we'd reignite
Liaisons secret, lavish costume balls.
I pressed into my lover's manly chest,
His muscle-rippling back my arms around;
Exulting in the pressure on my breast,
His knee pushed forward, pressing on my mound.
Slow, steamy dance, lust dominating thought,
Desire for him an overwhelming urge;
I licked his skin, my mouth his nipples sought,
And felt a tidal wave of passion surge.
Lips locked, tongues met with urgency, hands strayed,
Curvaceous bottoms mirrored as they swayed.

19

Snug drawing room, carved panels, tapestries,
Ornately woven rugs on polished floor;
At atmosphere conducive to the tease,
A place to act the strumpet, play the whore.
I shed my gown, on silk chaise longue reclined,
One foot a-floor, one leg upon its roll;
Libidinous and wanton state of mind,
At first touch of his mouth I lost control.
He licked and lapped and sucked my willing lips,
Then thrust his tongue with raw intensity;
I pushed against his face with lifting hips,
My randy clit bestirred convulsively.
My blinding, noisy climax all amazed,
I'd never come before while others gazed.

20

Bedchamber softly lit, four poster bed,
The kind of room where sexual secrets dwell;

Tall canopy of gold and silken thread,
On satin sheets we laid a nude Michelle.
And held her down, one to each arm, each leg,
Impressively erect her lover knelt;
He stayed his entry, teased her, made her beg,
Then took her, to his balls. It made me melt.
I held an ankle, so could watch in awe
The flexing of his buttocks as he thrust;
He'd hold, she'd toss her head, entreating more,
He'd lunge with vigour, answering her lust.
She moaned in satisfaction of her need,
His cheeks in spasm as she claimed his seed.

21

Exquisite garden, off the drawing room,
White gravel path, superbly sculpted trees;
Dew-misted lawn, bright moon, sweet scent of bloom,
Nicole presenting, svelte on hands and knees.
Her lover kneeled, delectably full stand,
His cockhead eased apart her plumpen lips;
I shivered as I sensed her sheath expand,
Tensed when he gripped her firmly by the hips.
Petite Nicole, ensheathing massive male,
Rejoicing in her femaleness, eyes closed;
Her body seemed diminutive and frail,
Yet total dominance her will imposed.
She fucked him jubilantly, fervently,
And came in sweeping waves of ecstasy.

22

Relaxing spa, all six, all briefly spent,
Warm water streaming soothingly on skin;

Mere pause in our lascivious intent,
Mere respite in our appetite for sin.
Our mood subdued, our memories enthralled
By images of bodies having sex;
Audacious, lewd, exciting sights recalled,
My mind obsessed by watching buttocks flex.
Our lovers dried and robed us tenderly,
We left them for a while to sip champagne;
The time had come to share around the three,
Our pleasure to pursue in new domain.
Enthusiasm we could not disguise,
Their cocks had rested, now again must rise.

23

Dim drawing room, the maids had cleared the floor,
Deep, downy bedding laid out in a square;
We took a different partner from before,
The favours of the others we'd now share.
I pressed into a man, enjoyed his kiss,
His cock was hard and hot against my flesh;
I straddled him, ensnared his shaft with bliss,
He stretched and filled me, rapture flamed afresh.
I rode that gorgeous, stiffened staff sublime,
And took his length until he touched my top;
A wondrous rod of manhood in its prime,
Magnificent! I didn't want to stop.
And yet a time to change we had agreed,
Dismounting him, I found another steed.

24

Nicole held her man's penis at full stand,
Michelle, splay-legged, lay upon her front;

Nicole uncompromising with her hand,
Michelle's man thrusting deep into her cunt.
Promiscuous adventure, free for all,
I sought the nearest sac of balls and licked;
I watched Nicole across the bedding crawl,
The biggest of the penises she'd picked.
An eager tongue my anus ran around,
I jutted out my backside, loving it;
My tumid clit a questing finger sought,
A steely cockhead slipped into my slit.
Unfettered, brazen sexuality,
A joyful pageant of carnality.

25

Unbridled, unrepressed debauchery,
Tits, bums and mouths and balls and cocks and cunts;
The sights and sounds of sexual revelry,
Loud sighs and cries and moans and groans and grunts.
Intuitively combinations changed,
Nude limbs untwined then intertwined anew;
Bare bodies disentangled, rearranged,
Abandoned, wild, unshackled by taboo.
Two men took turns to take me from behind,
The first held back, the second of them came;
Voluptuous in body, spirit, mind,
Free-spirited, no modesty or shame.
A while I rested from this scene debased,
Returned, refreshed, another cock encased.

26

Fulfilled, contented, sated, sticky-thighed,
We took a drink, the men we sent away;

How pleased we were! Our smiles we couldn't hide,
Exuberantly libertine foray!
Nicole, slim legs outspread, lay on her back,
I kneeled and sucked her nipple lovingly;
Her fingers stroked my thighs and cheeks and crack,
Michelle used mouth and hands so tenderly.
The two of us long pleasured thus our friend,
On journey unbelievable she went;
Trust, understanding, lust in lovely blend,
Her coming was a beautiful event.
I held her hand until her soul returned,
Through casement window dawn could be discerned.

27

Michelle lay sleepily, at peace within,
She smiled at me and murmured a request;
I sensuously rubbed her flawless skin,
Her shapely body sensually caressed.
Strokes velvety, for both a welcome balm,
The perfect way to end the night, unwind;
Replete, relaxed she purred in blissful calm,
Her pleasure metaphysical, refined.
Nicole my forehead sensitively stroked,
Then eyelids, temple, cheeks and line of jaw;
On nipples, breasts such joy her touch evoked,
Slow belly rub, palm cupped around my core.
Soft pressing on my clit, release profound,
Embracing me, she slowly brought me round.

28

'Oh god, I need a coffee, short and black!'
Of all weekend this time would be the worst;

'Of course, madame'. Two pillows for my back,
Cool water to relieve my raging thirst.
My headache less severe than might have been,
Dulled down by morning-after lethargy;
Save from my well-used cunt a twinge obscene,
What you'd expect from having sex with three.
A scented bath, a flute of Veuve Clicquot,
The maid with sympathetic, gentle touch;
The water warmly soothing down below,
I'd had my fill of rampant cocks and such.
We pecked at lunch, subdued yet keen to find
Adventure of more cultured, courtly kind.

29

Bright sunny garden, brushes, pots of paint,
Men into works of art to be transformed;
Artistic licence loosed without restraint,
Great deeds of living art to be performed.
Our theme from mother nature: vivid flowers,
Our canvas: legs and belly, butt and back;
A searching test of our artistic powers,
I giggled as I strove to paint his sac!
Excitement and enthusiasm reigned,
From time to time we'd rest, our men compare;
Aesthetic talent, stunningly unchained,
Such aptitude, such genius, such flair!
Three gems of human creativity,
Such classy art works one would rarely see.

30

Mid-afternoon, warm sun, back in the glade,
Contentedly we lounged and sipped champagne;

The music of Debussy, sweetly played,
Our works of art with dance would entertain.
Bare graceful bodies moved majestically,
We gazed in admiration and in awe;
Inspiring show of human symmetry,
Lithe harmony of movement to adore.
Then glowing, sweaty limbs cooled in the stream,
Dismay, frustration in our faces showed;
As paint washed off we sensed a fading dream,
Ah, could we not prolong this episode?
Their lovely forms we followed through the trees,
Breathtaking beauty fanned by gentle breeze.

31

'We did it, friends!' A final glass of wine,
Our mood reflective, sober, wistful, sad;
Our sentiments too complex to define,
What an amazing interlude we'd had!
We left as we'd arrived, each on her own,
Reluctantly we hugged and said farewell;
It seemed so short a time, the hours had flown,
On cherished moments each of us would dwell.
I drove off first, with hurried kiss goodbye,
Emotions mixed, tears flowed abundantly;
Our fantasies and passions had run high,
We'd lived for pleasure, self-indulgently.
Within my sheath a pleasant woman's-ache,
We'd dared of life's excesses to partake.